Spheres of Deception

by

Terry Edwards

'Intelligence isn't always intelligent'

AuthorHouse™ UK Ltd.
500 Avebury Boulevard
Central Milton Keynes, MK9 2BE
www.authorhouse.co.uk
Phone: 08001974150

The main characters and events in this book are fictitious. Any similarity to real persons, living or dead, is coincidental and not intended by the author.

First published by AuthorHouse 9/6/2011

ISBN: 978-1-4567-7601-5 (sc)
ISBN: 978-1-4567-7602-2 (e)

Front cover image is from "dreamstime" http://www.dreamstime.com/

This book is printed on acid-free paper.

A fast-moving and scary 'security apparatus' psychological thriller, impacting appallingly on the lives of Phil and Ruth, Spheres of Deception is Terry Edwards' first novel.

Particular thanks go to my good friend Dave Collier without whom the discovery of this image and the subsequent successful development of the front cover would almost certainly never had happened.

Dedication: to my wife Patricia without whom this novel—all of my work for that matter—could not possibly have been completed. *The need for the love and support of a lovely wife can never be overestimated.*

Chapter 1 Banged-Up

"Bang, clang, clunk". Here it is again—doors and gates several yards away being opened, closed, re-locked, keys rattling, and so on. These sound-effects are soon followed by that familiar sound of ever-louder footsteps and Phil's heart beats rather faster than usual once again. At least one prison officer is on his way down the corridor that leads to Phil's cell. Within a few seconds there's the click sound of the small, outside peer-through flap on Phil's door and simultaneously a pair of eyes are staring at him through the slot. The look in those eyes already betrays the guy's thoughts. Firstly, "… is he still alive and even slightly active? Secondly does he need anything—apart from immediate and unconditional release, that is?"

Basic requirements include: food which is most often inedible, water which is just about palatable, replenishment of soap, emptying and cleaning the toilet and (*very* occasionally) changing the bed linen. The officer enters Phil's cell and places a bowl of what they have the insult to call "broccoli soup" together with some bread that already shows traces of a bluish mould. Water is already available from the tap which is reinforced and fixed very solidly to the foundations using substantial industrial welding equipment by the look of it. And the water is just cloudy enough to raise suspicions as to its safe drink-ability. This is Pentonville Prison in London.

On at least one occasion in the recent past the food clearly included something totally vile. Something which would make even the most hardened criminal retch. There it was, right there on the plate, just off centre and slowly drooping off the miserable-looking cabbage. And it was unmistakably—human spit. This dreadful addition to his "meal" embodied a green streak and surely must have been deliberately done either by a "cook" or even by this officer. This would be their idea of either hoping to wind him up or maybe just to let him know how they hate him and indeed basically hate all prisoners. "You are the scum of the earth" one can almost hear them say.

These people tend to forget two things: firstly whatever they have done—however terrible—each prisoner is actually a human being with feelings; secondly a significant minority of prisoners everywhere in the world are in fact innocent of any crime. In Phil's instance both features are true: he is indeed a human being with feelings and as it happens he is indeed innocent of the "crime" of which he was accused and "proven guilty".

Earlier Phil had told a visitor: "So far I have referred to 'my' cell and this is now the case in that I have a cell to myself which is a big improvement from the first six months here when I shared a cell with a total weirdo. This guy could never stop talking about himself, would never enter into a proper conversation and frequently engaged in multiple-fart-mode—most often around three in the morning!"

Naturally each cell is fairly small and only includes the most basic equipment and fittings. Apart from the wash-basin and toilet there is a rudimentary bed plus a steel table and chair all of which are firmly reinforced and fixed very solidly to the foundations just like the taps over the sink and the wash-basin. The reason is obviously that the prison authorities (and probably the officers) would prefer prisoners not to be wrecking the place by ripping-up cell fittings and also possibly employing these as weapons. A little steel-barred window is set high up on the external wall and this lets in a miniscule amount of sunlight on the brightest day.

It's Wednesday afternoon and now the "Bang, clang, clunk" routine heralds an important although regular announcement:

"All prisoners on this row and yes that's including you R367. OK, so its visitors' time and amazingly someone's here to see you of all people. They must be totally mad as hatters. Make sure you're ready in ten minutes and I'll be back to escort you to the visiting area."

"All right, thanks."—Phil Kerridge feels like totally ignoring the wretched and sarcastic "boss" but his subconscious tells him to go steady and be grudgingly polite.

Phil's sister Veronica has once again turned up to meet with her brother and is being "processed" by the prison visitors reception people. Isn't that word "processed" just wonderful? Sounds something like corned beef or even a computer processor. This is yet another example of the dehumanisation that characterises these establishments. The first bit is easy—just completing a basic form to confirm one's identity. But the next phases are more stringent and somewhat scary. These days they want one's finger prints from both right *and* left hands which is generally double the requirement in US Immigration. There's an eye (iris) scan the result of which is checked against a database with your iris image, followed by the depositing of practically all your personal possessions into lockers and finally a march-through and stand-still during which a sniffer dog checks you out for possible narcotics or even traces of such. By the way, prisons are certainly not the only places these days where you must have your iris scanned. This even happens to "ordinary" people on passing through immigration in, for example, American airports.

Do you look *that* much like Osama Bin Laden?

All the while you naturally observe the other visitors but it is very difficult to strike up a conversation because tensions are high and after all this is an exceptionally difficult environment for every visitor. Some people have travelled long distances to get here, up to several hundred miles. Some are clearly cultured folk (some even with university degrees, etc.) but there is always a hard core for whom this type of thing has been effectively a life habit for many years. Much bad language is around and this noticeably upsets the more sensitive people although nothing is said which might escalate the situation.

At the end of all that you just sit for many minutes and wait for the visitor-duty officers to come and let you into the visiting area. By the way, this all eats seriously into your time for the much-treasured visit and so everyone becomes increasingly irritable over all this bureaucratic fuss. After this it's a walk through the outer yard with its two layers of rolled razor wire around 20 feet topping-out the dreary and impenetrable walls.

At long last Veronica is now in the visitors' area and she is directed to a table with two chairs which is where this rendezvous will take place. Just like everything in the cells each steel chair plus the steel tables is rigidly fixed to the concrete floor using all-welded units and strong foundation bolts. It is a very austere environment indeed. To top all this out there's a guarding position along the centre of the main wall with two or three rather threatening looking officers sitting at a desk. And once prisoners start coming in at least one extra officer marches up and down the aisles to check the status of every meeting. Just about the only item in the whole room reminiscent of the fact there's a "normal" world outside is the refreshments bar. Indeed the only money you as a visitor are allowed to bring into this area is enough to buy some drinks and snacks for you and Prisoner R367.

You could cut the atmosphere in this place with a blunt knife.

The two hug together and exchange kisses. Veronica: "Hello Phil. How have you been coping since we were last together?" "Not too bad", says Phil almost untruthfully - he'd really like to tell her he felt pretty dreadful most of the time in here.

"Are you eating all right and managing to sleep reasonably?" asks Veronica. Phil avoids telling his sister about the vile food, the spit incident and so on. He just decides to stick with what are really minor platitudes—at least for this visit.

After as much intimate family conversation as can possibly take place in such an oppressive environment the officers are always keen to announce (many, many minutes before the actual deadline) that "time is up"—all visitors must now leave the area and all prisoners are to return to their cells.

Phil and Veronica exchange what must be their final hugs and kisses until next week.

It's amazing how much easier it is getting clear of this place than it ever was coming in but the leaving procedure is strangely slow because of the dead weights of all those heavy hearts. Another sad journey home commences. For some this is hundreds of miles whereas others live only a few minutes' away. Either way Veronica is returning to a building she still termed "home" although every time she returns Phil's situation preys on her mind except when she is very busy. In common with all the other visitors Veronica is "free" whereas her dearly loved brother remains incarcerated. Such a situation is bad enough when a person is imprisoned for a definite and properly proven crime. It is at least ten times worse when they are without a shadow of a doubt in fact totally innocent of any crime.....

One interesting thing Veronica has discovered is that the Americans tend to call prison officers "bosses" whereas in the UK the more usual and indeed more colourful term is "screws". Common belief has it that the term "screw" in this context derives from the fact that in much earlier times prison officers were responsible for implementing screw-systems to apply torture to prisoners. The tighter the screws were made—the more likely it would be for most prisoners to scream out their supposed guilt although probably in many instances they would, like Phil Kerridge, be entirely innocent of any crime.

The Intelligence People

In today's world, please distinguish between "intelligent people" and the "intelligence people". Intelligent people usually perform well at complex tasks whereas members of the intelligence services often fail at the simplest of tasks. Even teams of "professionals" operating in the intelligence services very often make elementary errors of judgement when it comes to the vital international research they are paid to conduct. Intelligence services include: the CIA and NSA in the USA; the

KGB in Russia; GCHQ, MI5 and MI6 in Britain—and the famous Mossad in Israel.

Many months back Phil had summarised on a whiteboard what the acronyms CIA, GCHQ and NSA stand for and where each is located:

- CIA = Central Intelligence Agency (headquarters: U.S.A.);
- GCHQ = Government Communications HeadQuarters (located in Cheltenham, England);
- NSA = National Security Agency (headquarters: Fort George Meade, Maryland, U.S.A.).

Phil has also made it abundantly clear that these three agencies, taken together with Israel's Mossad, were most definitely the ones that were for some reason so highly interested in him and his wife, Ruth.

It is all too easy for an individual or even a family to become known to the intelligence services and for these services to subsequently determine, albeit erroneously, that these individuals or families are most likely guilty of the most terrible crimes against whole states. Both Phil and Ruth had somehow fallen foul of the CIA, the NSA, GCHQ and Mossad and amazingly they had achieved this dubious distinction independently!

Back a few years the couple had experienced first-hand just what modern "policing" and so-called "justice" can amount to in certain circumstances in modern Britain. From independent information received it is practically certain that what many used to admire as the marvellous British justice system was in actual fact far from being particularly good even many years ago and probably right back through Victorian times. Clear examples exist of how the "truth" could be twisted to suit the sensitivities of dignitaries or for people who offered back-handers i.e. bribes. So it should hardly be surprising to find appalling miscarriages of justice fundamentally caused by greedy, often unprofessional, arrogant and ambitious 21st century "professionals".

Two examples of cases brought under the fashionable guise of "sexual misconduct" came to Phil and Ruth's direct attention. In one instance a guy had become briefly attracted to a lady who turned out to be classed as a "slow learner". Events soon proved she was not that much of a slow learner and indeed she had several children by other men. However, the absolutely key factor is that she was under the "care" of one of Britain's well-intentioned Social Services groups. In Britain the government-operated Social Services are significantly under-manned but in spite of this most perform a good job. When they don't perform—and quite often they definitely do not—serious dangers lurk that will trip-up the unfortunate victim. And by "victim" here we mean the wrongly-accused perpetrator and not the lady in question.

Anyway, a mockery of a trial ensued and the poor victim was committed to prison for around one year. In fact no rape whatsoever had taken place but the "system" couldn't bring itself to imprison someone for sexual immorality!

The second "sexual misconduct" case was even more serious an injustice because although individuals within a group of schoolgirls claimed the guy had sexually molested them, absolutely *no* material evidence was presented. It all began with a series of totally naïve events in which the accused, very unwisely, was alone with several of the girls for extended periods of time—for entirely innocent reasons. The girls concerned approached the police—clearly, as it turned out, to see whether they could stir up trouble and make some money out of it into the bargain. All it wanted was just the one female police officer, highly (even bitterly) motivated and ambitious within her job to get onto this case and wring every possible innuendo out of all twists and turns. Of course it just could have been a male police officer but as it happens in this case the officer was female and that mattered because naturally a female officer would be biased (even if slightly) in favour of the girls.

Again the case came to Crown Court "trial" which can only possibly be placed in quotes because this was decidedly a travesty of what should have been genuine justice and not really a proper trial at all. Close friends of Phil and Ruth well remember the one full day they spent there in the visitors' gallery and unforgettably how the "Judge" showed his total lack of professionalism by wishing one of the girls a happy birthday since it was apparently her birthday the following week.

It was transparently clear to all those who attended the "trial" right the way through that on balance and in a fair society a pronouncement of not-guilty should logically have been made. Yet, amazingly at the end of this highly stressful period the poor guy was pronounced "guilty" and a three-year prison sentence was handed down.....

And prison life is generally worse for people who have been convicted of sexual misconduct of any form which means these poor guys received a double-dose of inappropriate mistreatment (and there surely must be more such travesties worldwide).

Meanwhile the reality of Phil's situation now meant he was becoming deeply depressed which was made worse by his constant realisation that Ruth was also suffering in a similar manner – except she was located around four hours' flight time due southeast.

Chapter 2 A Sense of Security

"Oh, no - not this Kerridge chap again. He's such an awful nuisance and really I reckon he's just a complete waste of time."

Nigel Penley was in a meeting with two of his senior security advisors at the UK's Government Communications Headquarters, or 'GCHQ', based in Cheltenham, England. They had reached the third item on their agenda that morning: Case Number 169203. This was Philip Kerridge's file updated with terse descriptions of the latest developments. Kerridge had been tracked reasonably closely for the past ten years and once again his activities were giving concern to the security authorities.

A somewhat over-zealous middle-aged chap, Nigel Penley is the senior international security officer at GCHQ. Quite a tall man, with dull bluish eyes, he has a tendency to walk around rapidly in his light grey "fifties-look" three-piece suit regardless of the urgency of the moment. He is notable for having a particularly cold and humourless manner.

Penley ran his hands through his mop of thick heavily greased hair, unconsciously making his hands greasy in the process, and glumly stated: "OK, I suppose we'll have to organise for this case to be accelerated and set to 'Orange Alert'. Let's put this in motion and make sure that all the relevant agencies are informed."

One of Penley's advisors is Arnold (Arnie) Maitbury. Arnie is an American based at a facility known as Charteridge (located in central England) and he has highly "interesting" information on Philip Kerridge - gleaned from both national and international intelligence.

As the world's biggest spy base Charteridge is easy to find - but much more difficult to enter without possession of the relevant top-level security pass. It is in the heart of the English countryside and only about twenty minutes east of Majorfield town - just off the main highway. There's a well-marked crossroads located just as the highway is beginning to slope down a hill. To the right the sign blandly reads: "RAF Charteridge". The British Royal Air Force may indeed effectively "own" that land, or a part of it, and may also have an historical claim to operations there. However, the real purpose of this base today is widespread international security operations.

The National Security Agency (NSA), headquartered in Maryland, North America, is firmly in charge of current activities at Charteridge and it is certainly misleading to call it "RAF Charteridge". Keeping the name "RAF Charteridge" provides an effective cloak - sounds much better than "NSA Charteridge".

According to Arnie Maitbury's information, Kerridge was planning to leave his present employment and actually have the temerity to attempt going it alone! Potentially even worse is the fact that he has recently formed a relationship with a lady named Ruth Smith on whom a substantial Mossad file already exists. Mossad retains all the details on Ruth's visit to Itari in the Golan, her meeting with her friend Nanyana, her overstay there and the fact that the Israeli military police came to "rescue" her. As far as Mossad was concerned Ruth Smith was a potential security risk.

Over the several decades of its existence, Mossad has without a doubt been a pillar of strength to the nation of Israel during its many conflicts since 1948. Surrounded as the country is by hostile neighbours, ranging from Libya to Iraq and saddled with the intensely difficult Palestinian situation, Israel remains the focal point of the Middle East. The country has also been at war with Egypt, the Lebanon and Syria during the 1960s and 1970s. Of course another tremendously important thorn in Israel's side is Yasser Arafat, the PLO, Hamas - and Islamic Jihad. On balance the "peace process" means that there is a need for even more careful security checking because enemies may well be inclined to take advantage of the apparent improvement in the political situation.

Given the current Iranian hard-line concerning Israel and "the West" more generally, the fact that Hamas now rule Palestine and the failed military incursion by Israel into the Lebanon (summer 2006) the environment in the Middle East is practically white-hot. And Mossad will be busier than ever.

Practically all Mossad activities are of a covert complexion and a wealth of books and other sources of information exist on this intelligence organisation. Probably most of the Israeli Intelligence Service's operations are successful, but this is certainly not always the case. For example there was the high profile bungled attempt to assassinate Yasser Arafat and his "henchmen" (as they were thought of then) when they were staying in Tripoli many years ago. Like most failures of prominent people and organisations this one is now well documented.

"We have some most disconcerting news from our counterparts in England regarding subject number NG51783 that relates to one Ruth Smith. Our records tell us that this subject came onto our files for the first time in 1985…..".

Morti, full name Mortimer Manahu, began discussing developments with his colleague Victor Peres. The location is Mossad HQ in Tel-Aviv. Mortimer Manahu is a dapper Jew who habitually wears a fashionable neat check sports jacket covering a short-sleeved white shirt tucked into his well-pressed trousers. He is quite a tall, thin man, weighing-in at around 11 stone (70 kilos), balding and easily exuding exterior charm. Generally of calm and serious disposition, in many respects he represents the traditional "iron fist in a velvet glove". In contrast the fair-haired and burly Victor Peres is middle-aged yet lively and quite excitable.

Morti and Victor are both experienced Mossad

officers and they rapidly decided what should be done at this stage.

Morti: "We clearly have to re-open the file on Smith and then monitor the movements of both her and Kerridge - singly and together. We must also of course maintain regular contact with GCHQ in England, exchanging updated information on their activities and movements."

"Do you think we need to start a new file on Kerridge?" asked Victor.

"No. Smith is our main problem and our principal target so we'll make do fine with extending our existing file on her. We can add a caption to the effect that from now onwards she is often in the company of Philip Kerridge."

Victor commented: "Of course our near-continuous dialogue with GCHQ in England will automatically mean that all Western security agencies, including the NSA in the States, will be kept regularly informed on all matters relating to this case."

~*~

"Just look at this one." Victor Peres reacted excitedly to the security briefing message on his screen. He had made his daily "click site" visit to the Ruth Smith file and was nothing short of astonished at the news with which he was presented.

"You'll *never* believe this - not in a million years. Remember that Ruth Smith? The 'Nazareth-nurse' girl who made the mistake of overstaying her Golan welcome a few years back? Well, uh, just come over and take a look at this."

Daniel Steinman, another colleague of Peres, was in the office and he strutted across the room to see what the fuss was all about.

Steinman is over six feet (a touch under two metres) tall, quietly spoken and sporting a thick mop of silver-grey wavy hair. One very noticeable thing about him is his strange staring manner. He looks at everyone he meets in a way that suggests he is looking *deep into their very souls.* Many years later Phil Kerridge would have an experience, leaving him with vivid memories of Daniel Steinman.

It couldn't be clearer, in plain text after downloading and decoding:

"The Kerridge couple (Ruth Smith was now Ruth Kerridge by marriage) are in the advanced stages of planning their honeymoon *in Israel* this September."

"They must be planning something else too. It's too much of a coincidence that they have chosen our country for their honeymoon. What with her record here and the effect of her husband with his background teaching the British Army etc.." Steinman was quite annoyed about the whole scenario. After all, things had been relatively quiet in Mossad for many years and now these wretched English people were already getting in the way of regular state-funded swimming, tennis, and other activities vital to State security (?) Now they were all obliged to do something towards security operations.

"Obviously we must intensify our surveillance of these two 'wretched people'. Let's get Morti in on this one."

Both Daniel and Victor had ideas for Morti. Victor was the first to broach the subject and he suggested something "interesting" for Morti to consider.

"Now, Morti, we know that a place called Alexander's Castle is on their itinerary and that overlooks the city walls of Jerusalem. It's easily accessible - look, here it is."

All three pored over a local map of the city and this clearly indicated Alexander's Castle, including all access routes.

"All your experience, also the fact that you're approximately the same age group as these Kerridges, makes you practically ideal in terms of a set-up to 'gently' interview them at a pre-determined time at the Castle."

In the end Morti had to concede that he should probably perform this task and he was duly booked into Alexander's Castle over a few days to cover the stay of the couple.

Meanwhile a highly significant middle-eastern country known as Iraq, ruled by a "well loved" guy named Saddam Hussein, was becoming increasingly hostile towards all western powers - including Israel.

Iraq's medium range Scud missiles were being

swivelled round to target both Israel and Saudi Arabia.

"These guys have changed their plans, no doubt." Victor was convinced that the Kerridges would obviously re-arrange their plans to avoid Israel and enjoy their honeymoon elsewhere.

"That's your little vacation in Jerusalem down the pan, Morti."

"I don't think so. Just take a glance at this confirmatory information coming in." Morti was looking especially serious, even by his standards, he was calm to the point of gloom.

The screen full of information clearly stated: "Case NG51783:

Kerridges remain on track for Israel, full itinerary follows:...."

The detailed itinerary included their initial stay in Tiberias, their phone calls to Ruth's friends in Nazareth (now a strongly Arab town), the planned stay at Alexander's Castle in Jerusalem, a visit to Jericho, then down to Eilat, etc.

"Sorry guys. This couple are very determined indeed and they must be to remain on track for this 'honeymoon' whilst all the time the Middle East security situation steadily deteriorates. In fact either they plan something totally audacious or else they must be truly mad."

Now convinced that a serious breach of security could well be imminent, the Mossad team of three, Morti, Victor and Daniel, met to decide precisely how they would track the Kerridges. The process must continue all the way from the El Al check-in desk at London's Heathrow Airport, right through until they "satisfactorily" left Israel.

Well, this is what they were hoping would happen.

Victor contacted El Al at Ben Gurion Airport and made it abundantly plain that their opposite numbers in London must be briefed on the plan. The Kerridges had to be scrutinised in depth and given a much more intensive search and interview than usual in the Heathrow security area. The team also decided that their return air tickets as well as their car hire voucher should be confiscated from them in-flight. This was primarily to see what their reactions would be.

All the well-known standard procedures were of course carried out. The couple would be bugged electronically every step of the way and distant physical surveillance would be added to this. Since the Kerridges had planned in detail ahead this was a relatively easy process and each stop-over could readily have radio bugs planted.

The car situation was especially critical and Mossad would wait until the *specific vehicle* was definitely selected. Then they could plant their first bug well hidden inside the radio aerial base in the car's ceiling. Later on an opportunity would be taken to plant a secondary listening device embedded within the vehicle's dashboard.

This would provide a back-up in case the aerial-bug failed.

"Look you guys." (Something excited Victor about this scenario.)

"Kerridge is an electronics man with a special interest in radio communications. He really could just 'suss' what's going on here and end up de-bugging our bugs. Let's back all this electronic stuff up with some cunning physical intervention as well."

"What do you mean, Victor? How on earth can we get a Mossad officer near them without raising their suspicions?" Morti was at least as concerned as Daniel about this prospect.

"Right. Well I've given it some thought and my suggestion is for you, Morti, to do two specific things in connection with your Jerusalem interview. The first is for you to insist they proceed along specific routes on leaving the city. They plan travelling south to Eilat, which is fine, but we don't want them going anywhere near Jericho on their present plan do we? As we all know Jericho is full of Arabs and we can't control who they might be aiming to meet there or for that matter just encounter anyway.

Also, having established their routes, my further suggestion is that we should line up at least two individuals who can thumb lifts at just the right times for our Kerridges. Brits generally like giving people lifts and there's a good chance they will take the bait on at least one or, if we're lucky, both occasions."

Daniel was the first to react to Victor's idea: "OK, let's do it.

Who shall we approach for the 'hitch-hiking' plants?"

"I think they should be greatly contrasting so as to increase the probability of our Kerridges taking the bait at least once. For example there's David Olgar who works in software scanning systems maintenance. A great thing about David is that he is also an accomplished amateur actor and this could of course be useful."

David Olgar is a wily and burly Jew who can come across as somewhat mentally thick. He is in fact highly intelligent, having a PhD degree from Tel-Aviv University's computer science faculty.

David is always well-tanned and has black curly hair.

"How about this? Olgar, given a few days of unshaven stubble and greasy clothing, would make out as a typical garage mechanic."

The others laughed at Morti's suggestion. "It could easily be arranged for him to come rushing out from a lay-by en route Dead Sea - thumbing desperately just before the Kerridge's car is about to pass."

Victor: "Let's have Olgar with a large vehicle tyre over his shoulder to add extra effect…"

Victor spoke with David Olgar who readily agreed to all this. He was actually very enthusiastic because he never liked the English much anyway. He added yet another suggestion, one that would provide extra "street cred" as well as making life easier for him.

Throughout the journey he would nod negatively at any questions such as: "..do you speak any English".

Thus the stage was set for "phase one thumbing line-up".

"What can we do about the second intervention? You said this should be in stark contrast to our garage mechanic." Morti initiated the final part of their deliberations to complete this plan.

"I've just had an idea about this." It was Daniel Steinman's turn:

"Victor, we all know that you have a highly attractive daughter, your Esther, and I really think that we should approach her for a role in this little venture."

"Oh - no!" Victor broke in with noticeable emotion in his voice.

"Don't let's involve Esther in anything to do with questionable activities on our 'shady' behalves. She's hardly an innocent but she's my girl and her daddy certainly won't ever have her used.

- What did you have in mind anyway?"

Now Victor Pere's daughter Esther is quite gorgeous. An attractive sultry Jewess, she would easily turn the head of any guy. Not only does this girl possess classic features, long hair and a near-perfect figure, she is currently studying politics at Béér Sheva University.

As it happened she was naturally somewhat resistant to the idea of posing as an "innocent" hitchhiker on the road from Eilat to (ultimately) Béér Sheva and it took a little more persuasion to encourage her. She finally agreed to accept a down payment of 5,000 Shekels in cash, freshly withdrawn from Mossad's main account Tel-Aviv, and she would be suitably seductively dressed-down for the occasion.

After several further loud protestations her dad (Victor) regretfully agreed.

Thus the stage was now also set for "phase two thumbing lineup".

Back at GCHQ in England, Nigel Penley is informed about all the main developments that were now planned for the Israel scenario. He's not told about the "thumbing lifts" exercises but he is satisfied that his case 169203 will be pursued effectively whilst the Kerridges are in Israel. Other frequent investigations will be followed through when these two nuisances have returned to the UK.

Chapter 3 On the Fly

"Thanks a lot, Pete, to you and Megan for looking after us so *very* well this past couple of days and for being the best cabbie in the world - given the way you've found such an efficient route around Uxbridge and West Drayton and got us safely to the airport."

The staging post for their honeymoon in Israel, Ruth and Philip Kerridge now found themselves at the El Al check-in at London's sprawling Heathrow Airport. In fact this is generally reckoned to be the world's busiest airport, on account of its strategic location linking Europe, America and both the Middle and Far East regions - as well as the southern hemisphere. Having been dropped off by their good friend Pete, Ruth and Phil are now shoulder to shoulder in a long line of people checking in. You could hear the familiar hum of background noise from prospective passengers preoccupied with cases and documents and the baggage check-in procedure. Allowing themselves a few moments to observe what was going on around them, the couple wondered what nationality was *not* to be represented here. Could one see any Burmese, for example? (How would you tell by just looking whether someone was Burmese rather than, say, Indonesian anyway?) It was notably busy at Heathrow that afternoon.

Now decidedly middle-aged, Ruth and Phil had met for the first time in 1989 via Ruth's "lonely hearts" entry in the local paper. This followed swiftly on the heels of a period of tremendous uncertainty for Phil that included his near-death. It also sprang from a long time of loneliness after many years overseas for Ruth, who at the time was a highly eligible spinster. Two people literally made for each other, their ages were clearly ideal (Phil being two years' older than Ruth) with just the right types of complementary differences and yet extraordinarily so many important things in common. Physically they are also right for each other. Ruth's distinct assets include a lovely laid-back character topped with beautiful grey-blue laughing eyes and her wavy fair hair. In contrast Phil is a dark, swarthy and rather brooding character with brown eyes and a receding hairline. He is an academic and industrial "whizz" in radio electronics whilst Ruth is a qualified nurse with a wealth of knowledge and experience. They were to share many experiences around the world after they married in 1990.

Pete and Megan Warren are old friends of Phil's. The grey-haired (thinning) Pete was a contemporary student with Phil when both attended lectures in electronics at the University of London way back in the 1960s. Pete Warren has a well-developed sense of humour and enjoys being with his friends - especially when helping them out. Dark-haired Megan is Pete's beautiful wife and these two had now been married for around 30 years. They live in the Western outskirts of London, not far from Heathrow.

Whilst standing in line at the Heathrow check-in Ruth and Phil double checked that they had all the necessary documents required by the check-in lady i.e. tickets and passports. At last it is their turn to place their cases on the weighing belt and to hand over passports and tickets for inspection. Phil's documents are checked first and deemed to be in order. Now Ruth's documents are being checked.... And it is immediately noticed that Ruth's passport is still bearing her maiden name and there is the clear disparity between her ticket and her passport. Something of a 'domestic' ensued.

"Ruth, how could you possibly have missed this?"

There in the airport departures area Philip began to throw a wobbly, much to Ruth's embarrassment. He (not a little hot under the collar) said "Well, let's calm down, think and then do what we can to retrieve the situation. After all this is an innocent mistake, easily made, and we do have valid tickets as you can see."

Ruth realised that there was nothing for it but to set about proving their identities, including the fact that she was now married to Phil and so naturally had the same surname. In all probability they were not the first to have made this mistake and a senior member of the El Al staff was taking all their documents away into a back office.

Both Ruth and Phil imagined that he made a phone call or two to check everything out.

At last these problems had been cleared and the couple felt a considerable sense of relief because their main baggage was on the conveyor and they could leave check-in with their boarding passes.

However, as it turned out this was only the beginning of a rather intriguing sequence of events.

Now all they had immediately ahead of them was the inevitable chore of the standard security system where, as at all international airports in the world, you and your hand luggage and valuables are put through X-ray inspection, etc. This all seemed to proceed normally until they reached the other side of this system where they were suddenly faced with their second surprise of the day - only this time everyone, all the passengers, were involved. What they now had to endure was the passenger security interview.

"What is your name and occupation?"

"Did you pack all your cases yourself?"

"Have they all been within your sight at all times since packing?"

"Has anyone offered to pass anything to you whilst you've been at this airport, or before, whilst you were preparing for the flight?"

"What is the main reason for your journey to Israel?"

and: "Why did you choose to fly El Al?"

"You do understand why we have to ask you these questions, don't you?" the interrogator was asking them politely.

"Yes indeed," they replied, trying to appear sensible and wise:

"We want a safe flight and we certainly desire to live at least a little longer!"

Naturally they considered that they did fully understand the reasons behind such questioning. You would have to be extremely ignorant and naïve not to appreciate the sensitivity of the Israelis, given their appalling on-going experiences of terrorism on an horrific scale. Practically every few months something untoward occurs and certainly not a year goes by without political atrocities being wrought upon this nation. The most frequent manifestations of such terrorism are Islamic and are ironically termed "suicide martyr-bombers" within the country but there is also the potential threat of a terrorist-induced air disaster or hostage-taking. As far as this couple are concerned "enduring" this questioning and general security checking is well worth it and generally welcomed if it decreases the likelihood of terrorist attacks.

However, they couldn't help but notice that their interview was already taking substantially longer than anyone else's. What's more their main cases, the ones they checked in earlier, were now in front of them again and Ruth and Phil were being requested to open those cases. Obviously they complied with this request without complaining (although by this time they possibly could have been excused had they complained) and the staff ponderously checked through their stuff, which to say the least was pretty embarrassing.

Later, much later, they discussed this entire event and it slowly dawned on them just why they were so closely interrogated. You see, well, what a couple they made from the Israeli security viewpoint.

~*~

Before they even knew each other, through the mid-1980s for a period of just under three years Ruth was occupied with a nursing position in a mainly Arabic populated area in Israel. She reflects on that experience, working there as a single woman and nursing largely Arabs, as amounting to a mini-lifetime because it included most of the key ingredients of an entire life. Grief, happiness, pain, pleasure and sorrow – all these emotions were heightened at different times during this period. Those few years, Ruth says, matured the naïve girl (via a few mistakes) making her into hopefully a wiser woman.

Never before had she met the challenge of keeping the cockroaches at bay, and the mosquitoes deflected as far as possible from the "sweetness" of her blood. In fact this was Ruth's first experience of demanding, sub-tropical, living.

It was during this "naïve" phase that Ruth had her first experience of Israeli security as a result of a visit for a few days to friends living in the small hamlet of Arab families, known as Itari, located in the disputed Golan Heights region. At the time the Israelis occupied this region. All movements into and out of the area were monitored by the Israeli army and you needed a special official authorisation pass, issued by the police, before even contemplating possible entry.

In the Golan none of the streets were asphalt-surfaced and there were absolutely no street lights anywhere. Instead of proper roads there were just dirt tracks and any ideas about "mains services" had to be entirely forgotten. Water was purchased from deep wells, candles provided light, oil and wood-burning stoves supplied heat and cooking.

Ruth's friend was a short, rotund and heavily pregnant lady named Nanyana. She only had Arabic and spoke not a word of English. All communication was a mixture of sign language and the smattering of Arabic that Ruth had recently learnt. The place exuded an atmosphere of distinct poverty - like everywhere else amongst the Arabs here.

Having been checked in by the Israeli police Ruth was driven to the home of her friend, spending a couple of days there. Eventually, when day was about to break, Israeli military police came to see if she was safe. She was separated from her hosts and questioned although the police said this was to check that she was all right and was not being held against her will. "Have you seen anything related to drugs?" the soldier asked. "No. Why, is there a problem here?" Ruth responded.

The military had noticed a sterile syringe still sealed in its wrapper on the mantelpiece: "What was that for?"

Ruth told them that her friend was pregnant, needing vitamin support and that this treatment was being provided by intramuscular injections. As she (Ruth) was a qualified nurse she was asked if she would be prepared to give the required injection to her friend. As it turned out, probably mercifully, Ruth's services were not needed because her friend's physician had earlier administered the injection.

Now this entire event was wholly innocent and indeed she was treated well and that also applied, it seems, to her Arab friends. It is practically certain however that this event would have been thoroughly logged in detail with the authorities.

So, in this respect, Ruth had and still has an understandable "security record" with the Israeli Mossad intelligence agency.

Perhaps Ruth's "security record" would be enough in itself to result in their unusually lengthy interrogation at Heathrow but, you may have guessed by now, with his background Philip is also a potentially interesting individual from this security angle. He had never been to Israel or anywhere else in the Middle East before, but just his background in the UK makes for an intriguing situation, especially when you consider this couple ***together.***

Up to 1986 this guy was "safely and cheerfully" teaching British military staff electronics and telecommunications. His job was with the UK defence authorities for whom he occasionally travelled abroad and he had been issued with a passport that was specifically authorised by those authorities. This fact was clearly stamped on the document.

Now, although he had left that job, five years before this Israel trip, to take up private consultancy, the very same passport remained valid and current. And yet he was now a sole-trading private consultant in electronics and telecoms.

Here you have it: a couple where the wife has this security record with the Israelis and her husband has a suspicious background after leaving a "safe" job teaching electronics to military staff and now independently consulting in the same sensitive field. And yet, quite seriously, this overall situation had never occurred to this couple before. When you are in love you just don't think about these things.....

"What would you like to drink, madam? And you, sir?"

They were now an hour or so into the flight and dinner was imminent. Ruth asked for a glass of dry white wine and Phil had an even drier red. In-flight food is frequently the subject of derision in many conversations but this is often surely unfair.

"Gosh, such nice tender lamb and also everything else about this dish is superb", said Phil flatteringly.

"Yes, it looks good and my cheese special is great too," responded Ruth.

When you think for a moment about the airline environment isn't it amazing that passengers expect an extraordinary level of service under the conditions? After all, here you are cruising along way above the clouds and travelling at around three-quarters the speed of sound. Although these remarkable aircraft are sometimes called "hotels in the sky" when you think about it where's the dining room, or the reception area, let alone the swimming pool. In reality you are shooting along in what is little more than a fancy metal tube and demanding top-quality food and drinks that must be pre-packed.

Considering all this we should all thoroughly congratulate each airline that serves even half-decent meals and, in spite of all the complaints, that certainly applies to most airlines. Admittedly, severe economic constraints have forced many airlines in the 21st century to become much more sparsely appointed with increasingly little if any on-board services except on long-haul and this is completely understandable.

"Please excuse me for troubling you sir, and also you, madam,".

By now the El Al craft is only about one hour from the expected time of arrival at the Ben Gurion Airport in Tel Aviv.

"This is just a routine check, but may we take a further look at your air tickets and your car hire voucher please, don't worry we shall let you have them back before leaving the aircraft."

They *did* worry, at least a bit (especially since these were their return air tickets), but these are the drowsy early hours of Sunday morning and they are far too tired for it to dawn on them that this seemed rather irregular.

Another three-quarters of an hour elapsed and the standard procedures began in preparation for landing: signs requiring seat belts flashed on, seat backs had to be raised into the upright position etc. A cabin crew announcement reinforced the fact that this was the final phase of the flight and she told them, whilst a colleague walked the aisle checking, that they would be landing at Ben Gurion in about twenty minutes. Ears popped, tummies heaved and their aircraft gradually descended through the early morning haze of Tel Aviv. This is the land which has such a glorious history and which will indeed continue to play such a vital role in the future of the human race.

"What a beautiful landing." For Phil this is a "fragrant moment" and they both looked forward immensely to the wonderful time planned ahead. Ever since her first sojourn in Israel Ruth had always been impressed with that sight of the tall pine trees set against the silver-blue sky. The early morning atmosphere is balmy - already warm - and the day would steadily heat-up. At last they would be entirely putting their Heathrow airport hassles behind them and a truly marvellous honeymoon/holiday lay in front of them. Or so they thought.....

~*~

Now they had made it without difficulty through baggage reclaim, passport control and the customs exit point. They could collect their car for this ultimate of all getaways. But, whoops, perhaps just two minor problems?

"Ruth, darling, did the El Al cabin staff return our documents to you? I'm guessing you have them with you somewhere, don't you?"

Well, Ruth hunted and hunted everywhere but, would you believe it, those airline staff had failed to return, failed in their promise to give back, either their air tickets *or* their car hire voucher.

"This is absolutely the final straw, isn't it?"

Phil returned immediately to the main arrivals area, enquiring as to what had happened to their tickets. Officials claimed that a search was made of the craft and staff had been questioned to no avail.

Apparently no one would own up to knowing anything about this incident......

It was around 5:30 *a.m.* on Sunday at Ben Gurion Airport and all the forlorn two can possibly do was wait three solid hours until the Avis car hire office opens up and, once again, hope they can somehow get the car that must be awaiting them. As far as the return air tickets were concerned they were told to go to the main El Al office in Haifa at the next working day opportunity. This resulted in a tremendous sense of exasperation.

By around breakfast time the helpful Avis car hire people had sorted everything out and they had their car which represented yet another testament to this age of computerisation. After much stress and frustration they began to navigate north of Tel Aviv towards Nazareth and eventually (they hoped) across the hills to Tiberias where they were to stay for their first few nights. The small Fiat Uno car performed excellently and included the blessing of air conditioning that was such a boon in the hot weather of early September. They had two maps with them, the "standard" Avis one with the car and also a more detailed map brought over from England, and so they considered themselves well supplied for local navigation.

Ruth and Phil drove north out of Tel Aviv but it wasn't long before they found out that road signs, numbers and language were often in conflict. They frequently gave directions in Hebrew alone and sometimes in both Hebrew and Arabic. Now neither of them knew any Hebrew and Ruth's smattering of Arabic wasn't enough to discern more than the occasional town name. Neither of their two maps was much help in this respect and into the bargain the road numbers failed to match anything they could see on these maps!

They had to fall back on a crude mixture of logic and common sense.

"Provided we continue more or less northwards

and then turn right towards Nazareth then we must be travelling roughly in the correct direction", Phil argued.

Now the land of Israel is only about the size of Wales (UK) or, say, Belize in Central America. So it would seem only reasonable to assume that one could hardly go wrong in directions around this small country - but...

Somewhere up this road towards Netanya, many miles north of Tel Aviv, they followed two vehicles for quite a lengthy stretch of the highway. In front of them was a small truck and this blocked their immediate view, they hadn't noticed there had been a change of road and continued behind the truck eventually going through a narrow gateway (odd, they thought) and: straight into what turned out to be - the Israeli Police Academy...

This area was limited and all they could do at first was to continue on until there was room to make a U-turn. Their very first opportunity for this manoeuvre was right alongside the swimming pool and the crowds of people there seemed either too bemused or so completely unbelieving that there was no sign of consternation.

This is more than could be said for the three police guards on duty. Phil and Ruth now approached the same gate they had just driven through following the truck. Instinctively, guns were initially readied but the guards soon realised what was going on and frankly at this point everyone was enjoying a good laugh. No doubt about it, everyone involved was tremendously relieved—although no doubt the guards would have been in serious trouble with the Academy Commandant later on.

This all brings back memories of the famous song: "I get by with a little help from ma' friends, etc., etc." With some helpful directions, courtesy of the Israeli Police Academy guards, they were now set on the remaining portion of the route to Netanya and on towards Haifa further on up the Mediterranean coast of the country.

The white beach at Netanya had been freshly raked early that morning, the sand was hot and had that crunchy consistency, multicoloured sunshades were variously scattered on the beach and a swim in the inviting blue sea could not be resisted. After this they found a well-designed, attractive and (what else?) air-conditioned restaurant where they enjoyed breakfast. More recently it is so hard to imagine the utter horror of the terrorist bomb that was detonated at a café in that very city.

One is inclined strongly to hope that "violence will never achieve anything good" but doubtless for example the Provisional IRA in Ireland would disagree.....

A kind of exhausted anticipation practically overcame them now. They were both wearing the same clothes in which they had travelled from England and, although interiors were air conditioned, the heat was becoming a problem whenever they needed to be out of doors - in fact practically everywhere!

The remaining section of the journey was

amazingly easy. They found the "right hand turn" to Nazareth without difficulty and reached Tiberias by mid afternoon. Their resting place was a hospice located right beside the beautiful and famous Sea of Galilee. Not so many folk know that it is really a freshwater lake, known as Lake Kinneret locally. The very place where Ruth had, on so many occasions in the past, sat and soaked-up the peaceful atmosphere, remembering, as she was taught at Sunday school, how Jesus of Nazareth also sailed and rested after busy days dealing with the crowds. They enjoyed the surroundings, explored a little, had a substantial dinner and then settled in for a warm and humid night, with large colonial-looking fans their only means of keeping cool.

Phil expressed some surprise and disappointment to discover that modern Tiberias is as highly commercialised as practically any other tourist-attracting city on earth. This should of course be expected but the very beautiful history of this special place made the usual "burger joints" and bars and similar seem appallingly out of place to him.

After all Jesus of Nazareth, the greatest human being of all time and the only perfect man, actually walked and ministered here. Nowadays, like most places in the region, the city has its mosques, synagogues and various other places of worship. Also, rather sadly, "St. Peter's fish" are advertised everywhere.

Whilst the weather was very warm everywhere

in the Galilee region, down at the Sea of Galilee itself, which is several hundred feet below "standard" sea level, the climate is stiflingly hot in early September. Their en-suite room at the hospice was *not* air conditioned, being gently cooled with the aid of electric fans. There was a large ceiling fan with two speeds, one slow and the other so high that the ceiling looked precarious, and a tabletop sideways-nodding fan unit without which Ruth just couldn't sleep.

Occasionally, they set the ceiling fan to high speed and this caused it to vibrate violently. The couple hoped the vibrations would not be sufficient to bring the ceiling itself down. There were also other manifestations of good vibrations (!)

Although the ambient temperature in the room fell slightly overnight, passions went in the opposite direction. Remember, these two are on honeymoon. Later, being exhausted, sleep came easily....

With their backgrounds, religious studies at main school and also Sunday school as children, they were well aware that this entire region is of immense significance to us all. Galilee, the region sporting numerous famous place names such as: Capernaum, the Mount of the Beatitudes, where Jesus preached his famous Sermon on the Mount, and the Kibbutzim of Ein Gev and Ginosar. There is also Tabgha, where the miracle of the loaves and fishes took place, and Cana of Galilee where the miracle of turning the water into wine was conducted.

Now they could visit all of these and many more places equally famous in name and for their significance in history. Without a doubt the most entrancing occasion was the few hours spent at the Mount of the Beatitudes. The nun in charge kindly let them in just after a coach party had left and apparently this is most unusual because visiting times are quite strictly observed. Ruth and Phil must have honest-looking faces, although maybe Mossad and GCHQ would not agree on this point... Sitting under some trees and with Capernaum facing them in the valley, nuts gently dropped from the trees and made a little clicking sound as they hit the ground. This, it seemed, must be one of the closest places to paradise on the planet.

During this portion of the trip they visited friends living in Nazareth, who were new to Phil but originally Ruth's friends when she was on that two-year sojourn in Israel. Bishara Nadir, an Arab, had been married to Ella (a Romanian by birth) for many years now and they had a family of several children. They were a bright, professional couple and the mix of natural languages was clearly paying off for their children several of whom had now become fluent in at least three tongues: Arabic, Romanian and Hebrew. English was also steadily coming along. What a fascinating and colourful family they made and Phil enjoyed playing with the kids.

As usual, unfortunately life could not be enjoyed as a constant "bowl of cherries" and there was still unfinished business to be completed. Since the city of Haifa was not too far west of Nazareth, Phil and Ruth needed to visit Haifa to sort out their missing air tickets.

This visit proved once again to be a source of grief, but the fact that it meant familiarising themselves with Haifa made up for the problems because this is such an interesting city. Like many cities today, Haifa is a mixture of the wonderfully ancient and the utilitarian modern. They delighted in and wondered at the ancient aspects of this intriguing city and they made some use of the modern shopping mall. This city was the first to become re-controlled by Jews following the end of the British mandate in 1947.

The only positive thing to come from their visit to the El Al office in Haifa was official confirmation that they had indeed been issued with the return air tickets, back in England - big deal.

"Yes, we have confirmation that you were issued with return tickets. Now you should take more care of such valuables, you know. But we are afraid that we cannot in fact re-issue tickets from this office. This must be done at the El Al offices in Tel Aviv Airport. Oh, by the way, this will cost you 165 Shekels!"

They could hardly believe their ears. After all this, including the manner in which their tickets had "disappeared", and now they were asking us to visit their Tel Aviv Airport offices just to obtain reissued copies. And what's more El Al was going to "fleece" the couple the equivalent of around £50 (about US$80).

"No doubt in my mind, Ruth, there's been something very questionable going on as far as our 'security' is concerned ever since Heathrow at least." stated Phil glumly.

Ruth agreed and added: "Yes, it probably began before we even started out for Heathrow. It seems that they, I mean the 'security authorities', are deliberately putting obstacles in our paths and making life generally difficult."

Since their plan included them going to Jerusalem later that week anyway it would be relatively easy for them to call in at the airport en route. So now they left Haifa northbound, aiming to eventually reach the far northeast border.

The historic town of Akko (or "Acre") is only a few miles north of the city of Haifa and, rather like that city, it has both old and also relatively new sectors. Akko's population numbers around 38,000 today and both its fishing port and its Crusader landmarks, like the Khan El-Umdan and the Turkish clock tower for examples, are most attractive. The people of Akko are mainly Arabic and the town has a distinctly middle-Eastern atmosphere with many buildings exhibiting a Turkish appearance, as well as *that* clock tower. The city square is beautiful, with a walkway beneath ornate arches taking up most of the perimetre. You are likely to find horse-drawn transport in front of you at almost any time and youngsters play by jumping off the rocky outcrops and into the sea.

Travelling north of Akko with the sparkling sea to the left, they encountered the next main town that is Nahariyya. The population is about half that of Akko but the main contrasts are the fact that most people are Jewish, the atmosphere is now much more westernised and there is a significant amount of modern industry in Nahariyya.

Continuing north, passing the coastal Kibbutzim, one rapidly approaches the border with the Lebanon and at this northwesternmost point the border location is called Rosh HaNiqra. This small town is located on the top of cliffs that are hundreds of metres above the sea with a steep drop and a little restaurant extremely close to the edge. A terrific panorama opens up as one looks out to sea here – to the Kibbutzim in the south, out across the Mediterranean and north to the coastal waters of the Lebanon. At this time of day, in the middle of a sunny afternoon, the sun causes a fascinating scintillation of light off the millpond-flat water. There is a cable car by means of which you can travel down the cliffs to a system of caves at the bottom.

"Phil, look, this is one of the tense border positions with the Lebanon."

Ruth had been here before and also to another border location at Metulla further inland, having a buffer zone about a kilometre wide.

Guided tours are frequent to every border point. The military presence is strong with armed guards on the alert all over the place and a big, clear sign states categorically: "NO PHOTOGRAPHS".

You can just about take the risk of camera shots but this must be extremely cagey. The minimum requirement would be to set the camera up well away from the border and point it in any other direction you like. Then it's quietly but rapidly turn round and shoot - always rather hoping that it's not you who gets shot first!

A naval frigate could also be seen patrolling the local waters some 300 metres from shore. A constant vigil has to be maintained in this area because of the frequent incursions from the sea mainly by terrorists based in the Lebanon.

It is now time to leave this northern coastal region of Israel and return to Tiberias via Nazareth. This is the famous town in which Jesus lived as a boy. It is where he learned carpentry from his earthly father Joseph before beginning his public ministry. Still today there is much carpentry in Nazareth and there is a street that gives the impression of having nothing but joiners' shops. Upper Nazareth is home mainly to the Jewish population whereas Old Nazareth is populated largely by Arabs.

"Everything in the car, darling?" They performed the ritual last check around of cupboards, beds and bathroom before leaving Tiberias and then they were off to Jerusalem with an all too brief stop at Caesarea and then Ben Gurion Airport again. Caesarea was once the Roman capital of Judea and its ruins are amongst the finest in Israel. It was a fortress town and includes a Crusader city.

The stop at the airport, to finally collect their

reprinted return air tickets and divest themselves of 165 Shekels, had indeed to be brief and they then took the 38 miles along the major highway towards:

Jerusalem.

Chapter 4 Western Wall

After driving across the mainly flat terrain for most of the 50 miles from Tel Aviv they are at the foot of the long and quite steep incline for the final phase of the journey, up the hill to Jerusalem. - And nothing, absolutely nothing, could have prepared the Kerridges for the sight that opened up in front of them. Admittedly Ruth and Phil had the benefits of time of day and weather. It was late afternoon on a fine clear day as they suddenly turned into the city. Then the marvellous view was immediately in front of them and it was all the more incredible for that.

The near-horizontal late afternoon sunshine impinged on to those majestic, indeed magnificent, high walls that now took on a golden hue. They clearly also incorporate some magically historic architecture with beautiful towers of many distinctive forms. It is difficult if not impossible to describe in words the effect this is having on both of these people as they entered the most sacred and precious city on earth. Again, Ruth had been here before but the whole experience is entirely new to Phil. There is no way they could simply continue on as though this were just any road and neglect the beautiful scenes around them. They stopped the car, annoying some other drivers as they pulled over to absorb this environment as though it was the best milk and honey.

The sight compelled a time of contemplation, but now they had to turn their attention to finding the guesthouse they had carefully chosen. This is Alexander's Castle and it is located just outside the city walls. This type of location is especially important in a city like Jerusalem since the compactness renders the use of a car locally questionable and essentially useless within the walls of the old city. Also the Castle is built on a ridge with tremendous views across to the city walls, which is a special bonus in their case because the camera is put to work immediately.

"Just look, we've got a balcony with virtually panoramic views across to those wonderful sights." Phil is understandably excited.

"Ruth, please pass me the long lens. That's it, it's the longest one in the bag."

This lens is now well positioned on the tripod with the camera attached to the appropriate end. Such a system is also a form of telescope and the views were indeed excellent. Much photographic panning took place for many different colour exposures had to be completed, capturing various scenes. For preference Phil used his conventional Pentax "Spotmatic" rather than a digital camera. As the sun began to set in the western sky so the floodlighting took over and this was giving the walls yet another, more brilliant, texture - yet another mystique.

Here for several days, with the fine weather

continuing and with so much to pack in, the two made their way out for dinner locally.

They finally get to bed extremely tired, ready for a good night's sleep but also keen to get deeper into the exciting time expected ahead.

You could spend many, many days (indeed weeks or even months) in Jerusalem and still want more time to do further things, experience more of the history, indeed of the people. Many places are just so deeply moving and beautiful that one would consider repeat visits and without a doubt many visitors return again and again to locations they have visited many times before. Ruth and Phil were covering most of the notable and interesting locations.

One evening they re-visit the Western Wall (often known as the Wailing Wall). This ancient stone construction must be about 50 metres high and perhaps 200 metres long facing west. It is of deep significance to the Orthodox Jews who pray in front of it and insert prayer notes into crevices, joining-in with the prayer notes already in place.

The praying takes the physical form of intense bodily nodding. Some say it is a reminder of the time when God was going to deliver them from captivity in Egypt, they were told to be ready to move out at short notice. The term "Wailing" originates from the fact that the Jews still mourn the loss of their Second Temple that used to be on this site until its destruction in 70 AD.

To the right of the Western Wall there is the Temple Mount, the Islamic El Aqsa Mosque and the Dome of the Rock. The proximity of two opposing faiths, with Jewish adherence on the one hand and Arab (Islamic) adherence on the other, means that this small region is highly charged in both political and religious terms. It is in many respects like a tinder box and almost anything can spark trouble at any time. So, as in many locations in Israel, security is of paramount importance and army personnel are omnipresent. By the early years of the 21st century the Middle East environment had become one of war between the Israelis and the Palestinians and much of the Israeli army is actively engaged in the West Bank and Gaza. Phil and Ruth's visit preceded that time of emergency and indeed the even more frightening prospect of war between Israel (plus other Western nations?) and Iran.

The Holy Bible clearly indicates that one day, coming ever-sooner, a guy named the "Antichrist" will appear on Temple Mount and will be successful in declaring himself world leader. Together with a growing band of people Phil and Ruth believe this guy is already around right now and is in fact a prominent Jordanian Prince.

Their main reason for returning to the Western Wall at night was once again photographic and so there was Phil setting up his tripod, long lens and camera. This is quite in order at the Western Wall because cameras are allowed on any day except on the Sabbath. However, not many people bring tripods and the other trappings associated with serious photography, so doubtless they were being watched. One most rewarding result of this "mission" was a fine time exposure showing the moon above the Wall.

A little later on they have completed all the photographic exercises, so the camera plus attachments are stowed ready for walking back to Alexander's Castle, then: "Crackle, …..crackle,.." army personnel mobile radios are suddenly highly active and voices become raised.

Groups of army staff run round them and make towards a small archway at one end of the Wall, rushing through. Shortly afterwards there is the sound of gunshots and then it becomes much quieter. They continue on as calmly as possible, the gate guards give Phil's equipment (particularly the tripod) a meticulous inspection, and the couple quietly leave the outer walls of the old city.

It was getting cooler in the late evening now and there was a fairly lengthy walk back to Alexander's. As they rounded the far portion of the wall their eyes began itching and they could detect a breeze blowing from the precise region within the walls from which they earlier heard the gunshots. They conclude that they had just experienced their first small dose of tear gas, and therefore their first fairly close encounter with possibly only a scuffle, or maybe a more sinister Arab-Jew confrontation.

Needless to say it was a special pleasure to reach the relative safety of the guesthouse. From their balcony looking back over the valley to the city they saw a sight they could not ignore, out came the camera again and they were taking more pictures of those memorable floodlit walls. Although they could have stayed right there it was necessary to get ready and find a place to eat. Dinner had been very enjoyable and they returned, talking incessantly about what they had seen so far, tired and ready for a good night's sleep.

In Israel one is frequently reminded of the military presence and Western Wall activity is one manifestation of this. The next evening they decided to drive along the road, at the foot of the Mount of Olives and continue on in the firm and confident belief that Alexander's Castle was getting ever closer.

"Ruth, this just doesn't look right somehow." Soon the surroundings change dramatically. Instead of the familiar lights of vehicles and city buildings on both sides of the streets houses and shops are now in darkness and the absence of cars and civilian trucks seems somehow awesomely significant.

"No, Phil, where are we - what's gone wrong?"

"I think we could be in a part of East Jerusalem and in any event this is clearly not a good place to find ourselves in at night."

Nervousness is understandable in this situation and this state becomes especially acute when a heavily armoured vehicle (and the only vehicle apart from theirs) rapidly wound its way round a corner travelling in the opposite direction to them.

"Let's try to trace our way back in the direction we came in, and then attempt again to get on to the correct route." Phil made a U-turn and eventually drove out of the seemingly inhospitable area. Within half-an-hour the Castle was reached and another little adventure was over. How many more of these 'minor excursions' were waiting for them, they wondered?

"Why can't we be more like 'regular tourists' who, presumably, hardly ever get into such scrapes? What's more we're supposed to be on honeymoon here!" Ruth mused.

"Well, at least it's all highly educational in addition to being exciting." Phil is determined to sound positively upbeat about it all.

It is their last night in Jerusalem andlast nights" are traditionally special in a good sense, unless you've had a rotten time, and in spite of the various incidents they greatly enjoyed this famous and beautiful city. In the time-honoured way they therefore make for an excellent recommended restaurant and enjoyed another gorgeous dinner. On their return to Alexander's they settled down for a peaceful night, the last occasion on which they planned sleeping in Jerusalem on this trip at least.

The various comings and goings around any hotel are just accepted and most people are quite unaware of the identities of their fellow guests, unless they happen to meet and talk either late evening or at breakfast. There again the opportunities at breakfast can generally be regarded as limited to say the least since guests are usually still drowsy from the previous night, or in a bit of a rush to get on with their day, or something of both these factors. As honeymooners/holiday makers they are certainly completely in ignorance as to who else might be staying at Alexander's and in any event this is their day of departure, when they plan to make the journey south into other exciting regions of Israel.

"See you presently, darling, I've got a few things to pack before eventually coming down to breakfast and if I don't do them now there's a real chance they could get forgotten." Phil proceeds to complete the packing of various extra items that include, with special care, his camera and its accessories. Then he leaves the room, locking the door behind him, and enters the communal landing......

"Good morning, how are you this morning?" The greeting has come completely "out of the blue" from a stranger who manages to exit from the room next door to theirs at precisely the same time as Phil begins his walk across the landing.

"Fine, just fine – how are you?" Phil's response is a little diffident for two reasons: firstly this is their leaving day, and that often makes conversation difficult with a stranger, and secondly:

Who is this guy anyway?

The rather persistent stranger walks with Phil into the dining room:

"Mind if I join you for breakfast?" Ruth and Phil have already selected their table, indeed Ruth is quite advanced with her meal having been down for several minutes. Without further ado and with no courteous opportunity for either of them to refuse him their "stranger" just insists on sitting with them. This guy effectively made it virtually impossible for them to rapidly think up some excuse strongly suggesting they wanted the breakfast time to themselves.

Their sudden "friend" is a fairly thin and balding man, wearing a neat check sports jacket that covers a short-sleeved white shirt tucked into his carefully pressed trousers.

"On holiday?" he asks, "where are you from?"

A usual sort of opening gambit to express friendliness, they reckon.

It isn't long before they begin to feel that there's something a bit odd about their "friends" conversation. It soon has all the makings of an interrogation. They discover that he's a Jew who lives in Jerusalem and apparently has a family also living in the city. "How come you, a Jew, living locally is staying here in a Christian guest house staffed largely by Arabs?" Ruth asks.

"Oh I often come here because I use it as a sort of retreat to get some peace."

Does this make sense, they are thinking, a *Jew* who lives in Jerusalem anyway deciding to stay even occasionally at a *Christian* castle-style guesthouse?

Ruth and Phil begin to think there's something unnerving about this man's attachment to them. Noticeably, he concentrates his questioning on Ruth and for some considerable time Phil is not allowed any space.

"Have you been to Israel before?" he asks.

"Oh yes I lived here for nearly three years."

"Really, where were you living?"

"I worked in a hospital in Nazareth for two years, following which I lived as a tourist for a while."

"Did you make many friends?"

"Oh yes."

He is taking an unhealthy interest in who Ruth's friends are and where they live etc. She begins to feel a sense of unease with his line of questioning since there is something disingenuous about it. This feeling intensifies as he brushes aside any interjections from Phil.

In any case he (their sudden "friend") continues to show an unwelcome interest in their activities, including where they have been, who they have met and what their plans are for the coming days. He is also particularly interested in the remaining route they are planning for the south of Israel.....

Now, why oh why should he be interested at all in this? Why indeed is he questioning Ruth so intensively? A brief lull in the conversation takes place whilst this "friend" goes to get some more food. Whilst he's doing this Phil and Ruth just look at each other in sheer disbelief that this is happening. The couple's "new friend" then returns to the table and Phil starts with: "By the way, you might be interested to know what I do for a living. In fact I conduct private consultancy in electronics, much of it military related..." (Anyone would think he's getting not a little jealous of this man taking such an interest in his new wife).

Whilst it must be admitted that Phil *is* deliberately trying to wind the guy up with all these deliberate references, having 'smelled a rat' as it were, at this point Phil finds himself rudely interrupted in mid-sentence as, dismissively, their "friend" turns back to Ruth:

"What are your plans now? Where do you intend travelling during the remainder of your vacation?"

They both chipped in by telling him how they planned visiting Jericho initially but their "friend" interrupted vigorously with:

"Don't go there. They… (Phil and Ruth made a rough guess as to who the 'they' are) will stone your car. Look, be sensible, it's really dangerous."

The put-off regarding Jericho is almost paranoid, but Phil is left wondering which is the most dangerous: trying to live with this intense "security" – or "joining the Arabs in Jericho"….

They continue, trying to keep their conversation generally broad about their travel plans for the remaining journeys as he proceeds to exhibit the nerve to recommend routes for them. Now, *they* could be the paranoid ones of course, but it was the way in that all this was happening. It's the social ambience surrounding this event that made all of it seem highly suspicious.

Ruth and Phil have discussed this aspect many times since the event and have never come to a definite conclusion, but they always ended up considering it smacked of Israeli security. Maybe and in fact very likely: Mossad. This could *not* have been just an innocent and coincidental meeting.

Eventually Phil is "allowed" to tell their "friend" about his line of business and he appears interested in this also, although it clearly ranks a lowly second compared with Ruth's background and friends.

The guy tells them that his brother worked in quite a senior position at a semiconductor microchip factory in Mevasseret Zion. Although the corporation operating this factory is the best known microchip manufacturer ("inside" computers), and much information is available to Phil, despite considerable efforts from England it never proved possible to track this guy's brother down. Much Internet surfing led nowhere in this respect.

"Goodbye. It's great to have met and chatted with you…."

What hypocrites we can all be when it's a matter of seeming "courteous". What is passing through both Ruth's and Phil's minds is more like: "Glad to see the back of you. You irritating and strange mystery man." Who does he think he is anyway?

By now much more of the morning had already passed than they would have liked, because of a breakfast conversation they would rather not have experienced, and the "call of the southern route" is loud indeed.

They settle their bill and set off for Qumran and Ein Feshka on the shore of the Dead Sea.

Situated on the North Western shore of the Dead Sea Qumran is, after Jerusalem of course, one of the most significant places on our planet. Qumran is the place where a Bedouin boy found the "Dead Sea Scrolls" in 1947. And this was just one year before the foundation of the modern Jewish state of Israel. The remainder of that story now takes its place in the exquisite history of Israel and indeed of the world. For this Bedouin lad sold the pieces of material, that he thought were made of leather, to a cobbler in Jerusalem who had the good sense to show them to a local Assyrian Orthodox Bishop. This led to an academic study of the scrolls and the verification that they definitely contained portions of Holy Bible Old Testament books.

The Dead Sea itself is regarded as one of the wonders of the world, amounting to a notably deep cleft in the earth's crust containing highly saline water (literally super-saturated with salt).

This salt concentration is about eight times that of "normal" oceans like the Atlantic, Pacific, etc. and accidental inhalation can result in death. So you could end up with the dubious distinction of being a "dead human in the Dead Sea"! At nearly 400 metres (1300 feet) below "normal" its sea level is also the lowest point of the earth's surface. In its southern regions salt is commercially reclaimed from this sea and the presence of dredging and other equipment is evidence of such industrial activity. Because of this intense concentration of salts, swimming is generally considered to be healthy for the pores of the body and it is nearly impossible not to float here. In fact it is much easier than in any normal sea.

Phil is trying to swim there but he can only just stay in one place because a strong wind is blowing across the sea. It feels like a slimy substance against your skin, although you know it's clean and safe provided you don't get any down your trachea. There's no risk of being bitten by anything in this sea because the relatively high salt concentration prevents practically anything from living in it.

On both sides of this extraordinary sea one can see the immense contrast. For whether one looks at Jordan to the east, or the Negev desert to the west, either way it's arid. Like just about any desert however the Negev supports a rich variety of animal and plant life.

At frequent intervals along the western (Israeli) coast of the Dead Sea one encounters well-irrigated Kibbutzim with substantial agricultural and horticultural environs. The Negev mountains also provide spectacular scenery on this route and the relatively dry climate only supports the lowest bushes and a few species of trees.

Ruth and Phil stop for a while at Masada, 17 miles south of the Ein Gedi Kibbutz, and enjoy a much-needed snack with food and water for the hot weather saps one's strength. From the heights of Masada there's a panoramic view over the expanse of the Dead Sea, and beyond to the mountains of Jordan on the east bank. On this hot September day the Sea is partially shrouded in mist that is slowly blowing across the region. It is literally an awe-inspiring sight.

"Just look at the surface of the sea." Ruth's excitement is obvious and now they could both notice the transformed scene.

"These look for all the world like ice floes except it's too hot out there for ice that's not started its life in fridges and been strategically placed in drinks."

"No, I think this must be evidence of salt reclamation on an industrial scale."

They appeared to have sorted out what this was all about after all and agreed that ice floes were "off limits" in this area. Sections of the route gave cause for concern as the surface became quite rough and pot-holed. Our intrepid travellers also encountered wet mud on occasions, with no asphalt beneath it.

"Years ago I experienced something like this on the Hume Highway, between Sydney and Melbourne." Phil commented. "That was extremely muddy and again we only had a standard car – none of your four-wheel drives. We slipped around a bit but ultimately made progress forward and reached Melbourne in one piece."

This however is a very different country. This is Israel.

A little further down the road, on a straight and well-asphalted stretch between Hatseva and Yahav, running out from a side turning or yard there trundled this burly and scruffy-looking guy with a truck tyre over his shoulder. He gesticulates at them and obviously hopes for a lift to some destination, presumably some place where people could assist with truck tyres? Taking a considerable risk, they decide to stop and offer this man a lift to whatever place he needed to reach, down the road towards Eilat. Since he does not appear to have any English and they certainly couldn't converse in Hebrew or Arabic, dialogue isn't exactly easy. After about twenty minutes and upon reaching the outskirts of Yahav their passenger indicates that this is "it", he wants to be put down at this place, if you please.

Now, was this man completely genuine, utterly to be taken at face value, and coming "out of the blue" from the yard up the road and all he wanted was a lift down the Negev, by these naïve tourists?

In all probability neither Phil nor Ruth will ever know the true answer to this question or indeed to other questions relating to further events during the course of their honeymoon in Israel.

"Wonder who that guy was, Ruth?"

"Umm, reckon he could well be a regular truck driver but you know he could also be fluent in English and merely making a good and possibly well trained job of pretending not to understand a word. There's a real chance he could have been scanning all that was remotely of interest within this vehicle."

After the Jerusalem breakfast meeting and the Heathrow/El Al flight incident Phil and Ruth were now very much on their guard.

Whatever the answer may be to such interesting questions they now have only one target in mind. That target is to reach Eilat with no further excursions. The route takes them down through Votvata and Beer Ora. About half an hour's drive north of Eilat they pass the Timna Valley National Park and a short time is enjoyed there.

It's a particularly intriguing historical area, with copper mines that are 6,000 years old and remains of Bronze Age activities. There is clear evidence of workers' camps and cisterns. It would have been good to re-visit Timna later, but time is precious now and they didn't want to lose any opportunity of getting accommodation in Eilat.

Now they are in the deep south of the country and the first buildings that mark the outer suburbs of Eilat come into view. This city is located on a narrow strip of land, bordered by Egypt to the west, Jordan to the east, and situated at the northernmost point of the Red Sea.

"That's a sharp contrast, Ruth, one has to be especially careful with pronunciation when it comes to 'Dead Sea' and 'Red Sea'. These two seas could hardly be more different in nature. One of these seas, the Dead one we've been to earlier today, is just that. It is indeed completely dead. In complete contrast this Red Sea has life in abundance – full of fish and sea flora with a wide variety of species. Brings literal meaning to a phrase I've heard somewhere else: 'better Red than Dead' (oh, dear!)."

The town they now found themselves

enjoying has, like most in this part of the world, a marvellous history and in his time Solomon built a fleet of ships there. It is aptly considered to be the Acapulco of Israel and these days there's a hotel named with this slice of history in mind: "King Solomon's Hotel".

They stay at the Edom Hotel and visit several of the cafés and restaurants in this fascinating town, one of their favourites being the "Café Royale". Another visit Ruth and Phil were to make, one they would thoroughly recommend to anyone, is the Coral World Observatory and Aquarium that comprises a largely glass structure situated 100 metres off shore and running to about five metres subsurface.

In total contrast to the Dead Sea abundant fish are clearly visible in their natural habitat.

"That's as close as I want any of those fellows with the metre-length jaws to come, thanks." quips Phil. (Ruth did tend to agree with this also.)

Immediately opposite Eilat they can clearly see the Jordanian town of Aqaba, a large part of which is under construction, including a desalination plant.

The Edom Hotel is very comfortable and its guests enjoy the relative luxury of air-conditioning. This matches the car to which they had become so accustomed and it also provides such a contrast to the rather uncomfortably hot guesthouses of Tiberias and Jerusalem. On reaching their room they decide to enjoy some relaxation in the lovely air conditioning.

Phil lies back on the comfortable bed watching his wife who first showers and then sits combing her hair. He thinks of all the things about Ruth that had made him fall in love with her, especially her happy friendly way with people and of course her love for him. To Phil she is radiantly beautiful. She is, after all, quite a "head-turner" with her gorgeous sensitive eyes, fair hair, classic figure – and *that* smile.... Marriage to her had been the best thing that had ever happened in his life. He calls her over to him and the lovemaking between them that afternoon is just so tender. And for a little while here, before even thinking of dressing ahead of going out for dinner at the Café Royale, they sleep in deep contentment.

On their way down in the elevator an American guest recognises their English accents and expresses amazement that they are even in Israel at this time. Only just before Ruth and Phil left the UK Iran, in league with Al-Q'ida-linked extremists, had caused a serious international crisis that could well ignite the highly inflammable Middle East.

However, these two honeymooners are completely oblivious to practically any kind of danger.

Their final couple of days in Israel are imminent and, after a last gorgeous night at the Edom, they begin the long journey northwards once more. This time, however, their destination is to be Ben Gurion Airport for this is where they began an adventure that was to have dimensions never imagined before the trip. The drive north would take them over the desert diametrically—southeast to northwest, through Béér Sheva then to Jaffa, that is the southernmost region of Tel Aviv and in fact is the old city.

Ahead of such a journey, which is to include much desert road driving, they ensure that their car is filled with petrol at the point of departure on the outskirts of Eilat. Phil is busy manoeuvring in the forecourt of the filling station when:

"Er, what's happening?"

"What do you mean, what's happening?" Ruth is quizzical.

"Well, not to put too fine a point on it - the gear lever's waggling about like this and it's impossible to change gear all of a sudden."

On getting out of the car and simply looking underneath the vehicle the problem is obvious. The little lever that normally transmits gear lever movements to the gearbox is not able to do this right now, because it's dangling uselessly on the ground….

"Help, please." Phil asks a station attendant.

"What's the trouble?"

"Oh, yes, I can see what you mean. Huh, you won't travel far across the Negev with the controls in that state, will you? Well, we can't help you on this but I guess that the Avis Car Hire office just along there probably could!"

This is entirely amazing. Driving along and concentrating upon the vital search for a petrol station they had not noticed the Avis office that is all of 100 metres away and practically next door to the station. So, in they tread, letting the duty lady check through their car hire papers and then waiting a while for a technician. With the appropriate tools the technician has the lever back securely in place after a short time and then at last they are en route up the northern highway again, and the road to Béér Sheva.

Now they have completed several miles of this trip and are again on a fairly straight section of road, at which point they encounter their "northern route" hitchhiker. On this occasion it's a bit of a change from their burly and scruffy guy with the tyre from the "southern route". This time they can't help noticing a young and attractive woman in a particularly short and tight pair of ladies shorts. Her garb seems rather inapt considering the time of day and the location. Ruth is naturally the first to notice her... Another difference between this young lady and their previous hitchhiker is that she speaks good English and claims to be a student at Béér Sheva University. This is her desired destination - which is fortunate because at least she is on the correct route. But what is she doing thumbing a lift here in the first place?

Like many people when it comes to foreign languages this young lady can utter English clearly and understandably, the problems come when she is attempting to understand precisely what Ruth and Phil are on about. In any event they make what they hope are sensible attempts at conversation and Ruth becomes rather irritated because she even laughs at some of Phil's awful jokes.

They reach Béér Sheva at sunset, drop their latest and relatively glamorous hitchhiker, and make for the famous Bedouin open-air market that alas is on the point of closing. This is a shame but it is an education to see the remaining goods together with the hustle and bustle of an Arab market.

With a population of around 150,000 people, Béér Sheva is quite a sprawling town and it takes them longer than anticipated to pass through. In the gathering darkness they somehow miss an important turn without realising it, a turn that would have taken them to Jaffa more or less directly. Instead they come ever closer to the infamous Gaza Strip and need to stop near a streetlight (which itself is quite hard to find) to read the map.

"Oh, heck, how do we get out of here then?"

Once more Phil found himself worrying about road routes, in a strange country. "Phew, look at that." Further evidence of the military presence manifests itself by a tank transporter complete with battle tank rounding the corner on the other side of the road.

They manage to locate themselves on the map, decide upon the best strategy for getting away from Gaza and on towards Jaffa, the outskirts of which they reach with no further hassles. Although they believe that their hotel should be easy to find this turns out to be another mistake and they enlist the help of a young Jewish guy in an incredibly small car who clearly knew an excellent route to the hotel. His car is considerably smaller than their Fiat which itself is far from large! Grateful indeed they make their farewells to their local geographical genius, check into their hotel and once more enjoy a well-earned dinner. There is also enough time and almost enough energy to look around Jaffa and across to the lights of Tel Aviv (the modern part of the city). And so to bed for their final night's sleep in Israel.

In the morning they take things quietly, enjoying having breakfast out of doors beneath a magnificent canopy of flowering trees. This is nice and easy and conversation flows smoothly. They pack the car for the last time, drive to the airport and then regrettably have to leave their staunch little Fiat. Considering Phil had driven it over most of Israel the momentary gear-lever drop-out back in Eilat could certainly be excused.

For once, atypically for them it would seem the morning proceeds quietly and without incident. However, just as these two are passing through the Israeli security checkpoint Phil could contain his anger no longer and he verbally lashed out with: "You crowd of ******* *******!" At least two members of this country's security staff took notes but Phil was not detained. Doubtless this little incident became logged into Mossad's files for future reference.

At last they reached the plane itself with no one approaching them for "a discussion", and not a soul thumbing them for a lift. They could not see any signs of blokes with tyres over their shoulders, let alone girls with short shorts wanting to get to the airport or whatever. Also of course, when homeward bound, one does not have to go through all that security interviewing palaver. It must have been a close-run thing with security back there but no effort was made to stop their entry on board this homeward flight.

In a sense they now feel at something of a loss. Where are all the security people? Would someone strange and inquisitive join them for breakfast - or even on the plane or perhaps at Heathrow Airport?

What an anticlimax this truly is.

Chapter 5 Military Exercises?

The countryside is welcoming with a radiance of bright green and the evident thrust of new growth. Brilliant yellow splashes of daffodils almost dazzle you in the morning sunlight, occasionally interspersed with mauve borders and glimpses of bluebell carpets in the woods. This is April in England and spring is conspicuous everywhere.

Phil Kerridge is enjoying a pleasant if circuitous route through this countryside with its small and generally well-kept villages. He is not, however, entirely confident about exactly where in the world this is. He rapidly opens the driver's window and calls out to a guy walking in the village of Guifford: "Excuse me, could you please tell me if I'm on the right road for Birstington?"

"Ooh, yes, yew'll be orll roight if yew terns roight at the next craiss rodes, then left at the next. Go just past 'The Swan and Signets' orn yer roight. Then it's abewt fifteen moiles pratikally straight."

Rapidly translating in his brain, as fast as possible in case he wanted any more accurate information, Phil just said: "Thanks. Thanks very much for your help," winds the window up again and drives on.

The navigational instructions turn out to be very accurate and by 11 o'clock he's turning into the main entrance. The impressive wrought iron gates are fully open and it is a simple drive towards the gatehouse that is about 200 metres away. Here you are "invited" to pull into the small service area, exit and lock your vehicle, and check-in there. Actually it is not so much an invitation because the guys are, in fact, armed guards and that fact does tend to sharpen the wits (!)

Alan Tuckey, who seems to be the chief guard, manages to extricate himself from the soft-porn girly magazine over which he has been drooling to suddenly appreciate that someone (Phil) really does need attention. It is 11:30 already and this must be his first real official activity that morning.

"Oh yeah, interviews. Well, you droives abewt one hundred yards up to the central boulevard where you turns left. Then it's arewnd three hundred yards before you makes a roight turn into the main car parking area. There's plenty of spaice."

"Thanks, no problem." Phil now realises that the accents in this region can be pretty broad and in fact you often needed to listen intently in order to make sure you grasped everything that was being said.

Alan's comment "There's plenty of spaice." is definitely an understatement because that car park was *immense*. You could place there something like fifty battle tanks, all on transporters, plus several hundred "Saracens" (wheeled military vehicles) and you'd still have plenty of room left for hundreds of cars. And that is probably the idea, Phil muses to himself.

Having parked the car, Phil proceeds to the building where the interviews are to take place. This is a peculiar low-profile red brick building that looks practically insignificant. On entering the small reception area he announces his arrival:

"Good morning, I'm Philip Kerridge and I am here for the interviews."

"Oh, yes. I have you on this list. How was your journey?"

For a fleeting moment Phil is tempted to tell this lady a little about his encounters with "persons of a certain intriguing local dialect". But he thinks better of it and just follows her instructions for him to sit and wait in the little corridor set aside for this purpose.

Phil is now in his late twenties but even younger people are getting on to these interviews now. Beside him there sits an energetic-looking young guy sporting a head of that stiff hair which, Phil considers, projects quite a tough appearance.

"Hellow there. Mai neme's Jimmy McCabe, soh whoo are yoo?"

This "Jimmy" made his enquiry whilst smiling broadly.

"I'm Phil Kerridge and I'm pleased to meet you. I guess it doesn't take a linguistic genius to notice that you hail from 'north of the border'. Have you come directly from Scotland for this interview?"

"Noo," says Jimmy. "In farct althouw I took my first degree in Glasgow I'm still completing my

PhD at Cambridge University and coming here was quete a somple journey this morning."

Phil comments a little upon Jimmy's revelations, after all the two had only just met, and he proceeds to tell him some basic information about his origins. Starting with his Surrey birthplace, his London engineering degree and the lecturing job he's currently in. Suddenly, almost with a shock as these things always are:

"Mr. Kerridge? Would you like to come through and meet your interview board?"

If you have ever been interviewed for an executive job in the public services, or for promotion in the same, then you might remember that it's quite an experience in itself. As soon as you enter the interview room a veritable sea of faces beam at you from behind a long line of desks.

"Good afternoon Mr. Kerridge. Good to meet you - please take a chair." Phil decided to avoid the usual silly joke and didn't ask them where they'd like him to take the chair!

The usual pleasantries are exchanged including how he got there and so on. In fact almost anything except what the weather's been like or what colour underpants he preferred.

Obviously it's important not to be too fazed by the pressure of the occasion. The effort was to keep from being too nervous and to relax as much as possible whilst maintaining sharpness and clarity of mind.

On this interview board there sat three full professors, the Head of the College unit, a British

Civil Service administrator and (in this case because it's a military establishment) also a senior army officer representative.

Although Phil had experienced several interviews before, he had never been presented with an ordeal of this magnitude. Having felt naturally nervous before the event, now he feels faint, nauseous and sweaty cold. Here, in front of him but, of course, on the other side of the long set of desks, sit six very highly qualified men. Each of the professors has that deep searching look. It's as though they could see right into Phil's mind at one instant. There's almost no need to ask any questions because they already know all about his (parlous) level of knowledge…..

Dr. Gerald Scott is the Head of the College unit. He's a small man with a pleasant smile who's obviously very much at home wearing a light-coloured suit. As one might expect Dr. Scott also has *very* high degrees indeed - a fact that Phil had picked-up from the literature sent to him before the interview. Yet for some unaccountable reason this highly senior interviewer looks considerably less fearsome than any of the others. And this worries Phil even more because he knows that appearances are often so very deceptive.

Later on, over the years that were to follow, like so many people, Dr. Scott turned out indeed to have been an "iron fist in a velvet glove".

The British Army, who after all owned this place and presumably for whom everything here happened, is represented by Brigadier Stanley

Keeling who is resplendent that morning in full and very smart military uniform. "Heck. Would this guy be asking him if he had experience in the army, or enjoyed rugby football or competitive cricket?" Philip Kerridge knew full well the military passion for these traditional sports, but neither rugby nor cricket ever had been of any interest to him whatsoever...

After the Brigadier, the civil service "bod", one Alan Shesley, is the most neatly dressed civilian. He is the only man turned out in a smart grey three-piece business suit.

Many types of questions are asked and Phil is almost amazed at how ably he could provide apparently sensible answers. At least Brigadier Stanley Keeling didn't ask about any sports interests and Phil began to feel quietly confident. But Alan Shesley did have a standard request that he had to put to every candidate, he said:

"Before you leave, Mr. Kerridge, I have to ask if you would be prepared to sign the forms relating to the Official Secrets Acts. This a statutory requirement for anyone entering what is, after all, an official government job."

"Yes of course," Phil replied. What else could he or any of the other interviewees have said?

This is how Philip Charles Kerridge passed through to what he regarded as a super job at Birstington. Now at last he could really get down to his favourite teaching and research, with microwaves as used in satellites and radars getting prominence every day. His enthusiasm is infectious.

By that September he's well into the new job, and the first year, with plenty of "his kind" of electronics, went very well. Then he was suddenly exposed to some very interesting and unexpected questions:

"Colonel, can you please give us a clue as to exactly what a satellite down converter is, and precisely what possible relevance this may have to us in the military? We all began to think it must mean that the blithering satellites were either being shot down or brought to ground with some form of remote fishing net."

Here they sit, the usual group of nine army guys in the syndicate, all "bright-eyed and bushy-tailed", just waiting for some pearls of wisdom to somehow drop into their perfectly laundered military laps and magically enlighten them about this mysterious electronics stuff.

Captain Kirk Downleigh is an Australian army officer in the group, although the comment could have come from almost any of them.

Kirk, who enjoys all the jokes about "Star Ship Aussie Enterprise (or 'Stassie')", is a fair-haired and rugged sort of Australian character. He comes across as basically a nice guy with evident high intelligence. Such a high level of intelligence is not by any means always the norm for officers on these courses.

This pathetic "down converter" sort of comment is frequently made to the Colonel who joins various syndicates, so that there are then effectively two "masters" – the Colonel and Phil Kerridge. It's well known that no man *can* serve two masters and that certainly applies here.

Phil spoke to Mark Throughbolt-Smith about this problem. Mark is a senior member of staff who has been lecturing here for many years. Phil said: "Picture yourself as an army student in one of these syndicates and you've just asked this (cynical) question. Who would you direct it to? And who would you be trying to impress most, if not all the time, when he's there? Why – the Colonel of course – naturally."

Very enthusiastic, "academically bespectacled" and voluble, Mark Throughbolt-Smith represents the "old school type" and he can practically always be seen wearing a check sports jacket and grey flannel trousers. He has a tremendous sense of humour and most regard him as an expert on military radars of all types. Mark agreed that a serious difficulty existed here, but could not offer any viable solutions.

Sometimes the syndicated students actually seem "normal" and then they ask almost disturbingly intelligent questions of the academic (Phil). The reason for this is not difficult to spot, it's because his positive feedback to their precious Colonel, typified by Alisdair Goodhunt, is vital to them for their precious future careers.

One day, after yet another syndicate meeting, Phil made the comment: "Hello there, Alisdair, I must say that the group were noticeably on the ball this afternoon. Do you know what? They even got the right answer to that difficult one on satellite down converters."

"Really?" responded the Colonel, "Gosh. I must tell the General….!"

Now Philip attended a presentation, a regular twice a year event, that Brigadier Mike Pollard gave mainly for the benefit of these mid-ranking officers just starting out on their much-loved courses.

During each presentation Mike Pollard would always say: "You will be taught by excellent academics, many of whom have PhDs from British universities. These chaps also teach specialised undergraduate and post-graduate students and they do advanced research. At Birstington you will be exposed to the cream of scientific and technical academe. Therefore you cannot lose. This will be the making of you and you'll come away filled with deep knowledge of the specialised aspects of military hardware and software. And this is just what you need to reach the upper *echelons* of your careers."

There was only one thing wrong with this – it just wasn't true.

When you first meet Mike Pollard you almost always get the impression, frequently the case with officers, of being in the presence of an aloof, distant and remote man. But the more you got to know him the more everyone came to appreciate Mike as a bright, warm, interesting and highly approachable human being.

Few people had ever really taken much notice of

one particular word that Mike chose to emphasise during his talks. It was, interestingly, the word: "echelons".

Following one of these presentations Mark Throughbolt-Smith talked with Phil Kerridge: "Interesting use of that word *'echelon'* during the talk, didn't you think, Philip?"

At first Phil couldn't even recall exactly the context, or the timing, of Mike Pollard's use of the term. However, rather disinterestedly, he just indicated his observation of its use. Many years later the ramifications of this precise word would become extremely serious in Phil's life.

For Phil and many of his friends and colleagues at Birstington these courses for senior officers represent the worst side of the job by far. Their only raison d'être, in front of such officers' syndicates and so on, was simply the fact of their backgrounds and "academic prowess". And all this never did cut ice with professionals who needed teaching with full relevance to military requirements.

Fortunately life on the academic staff of an advanced college or university is not all courses, students and related problems. Out of the research side comes the need for attendance at, and eventually, active participation in international conferences. Having joined the staff of Birstington late that summer Phil realised that just such a major international conference, of importance in his research area was taking place in London that September.

The weather was beautiful in the capital city

and it was stuffy indoors, so after eating his lunch he tells a colleague: "I'm just going outside to take in some of this beautiful September afternoon sunshine and warmth. Do you want to join me?"

Phil's colleague has another appointment, so Phil strolls alone for a few minutes in the sunshine outside in Buckingham Gate.

Before long the inevitable elderly touring American couple begin walking in Phil's direction. You can always tell these types by their general appearance, with brightly coloured clothing and the camera ready for action dangling around the neck. Being friendly by nature Phil extends his hand to this stranger and generally welcomes both him and his lady wife to England.

Now, it should be appreciated that Phil still has his name badge on his lapel and, as it happens, this includes the word *"Royal"*. In fact the badge also has his full name: Philip *Charles* Kerridge.

Our American friend notices this badge and that does it: "*Weell*. Neow aah don't rightly know how to appropriately address yew, Sirr, but it certainly is a trait and a privilege to mait yew he*rr*e.

Hey, Madge, come and mait this guy right in frurnt of us and near his howm I guess – this being Burcking Ham Gate annowl!"

At first Phil naturally assumes this must be a set-up of some type. He'd vaguely heard about government agencies who might plant apparently innocent people to check out the movements of public sector (and other) employees. But this is just too naïve to be true – isn't it? Well, amazingly and as far as he can detect, this American couple appear completely genuine. They make for such stark contrasts in appearance: Madge and her husband in colourful summer outfits and Phil in his smart-but-grey business suit.

The guy introduces both himself and his wife, speaking slowly and steadily (being elderly) but with complete clarity: "I am Dwight Rayland and this is my dear wife of forty years, Madge Rayland. Madge, ain't yew goin' to mention about his mother deare?"

"Oooh, yes Dwightie. Ah simplie *must* tell him right now."

"Sir, everie tarme ah see yeuwr deare mother on the television ah thinks to marself: 'wow, and she's lookin' so neat in that pastel owtfit with perfect matchin' hat'. Tell me, please tell the both of urs, dores she actually go out and buy a nu owtfit fer each und evry erccasion? And as for yewr *Grandma,* weeel mie - she really is the neatest!"

By now Phil of course finds it extremely difficult to stifle the surge of laughter welling up within him. For a short while he had found himself attempting to picture his own little mum wearing one or two of the admittedly beautiful and highly tasteful suits and hats worn so elegantly by Her Majesty Queen Elizabeth II. These attempts lead Phil nowhere because *his* mother rarely even wore any form of suit, let alone a $5,000 pastel number.

Phil is doing his best to humour this delightful couple but obviously he needs to tell a few "porky pies" on the way. Various photographs are taken and a little further conversation is enjoyed. In his mind Phil has to admit that he just doesn't have the confidence to spoil their happy "discovery of a Royal". Although what will happen when they show the photos to friends and relatives back in the States he could only imagine. There's now probably a warrant in both countries (noting that special relationship) to arrest Phil as an impostor!

Philip receives copious "Good-byes" and everyone goes on their respective ways. It should be noted, however, that Phil *doesn't* manage to get to live in Kensington Palace... Later on, Phil's wife and his father fall about laughing at this story. Any such laughter most probably rapidly went hollow over in the States.

Unfortunately an awful down side to this conference was about to take place that had nothing to do with the amusing event in Buckingham Gate. Later during the conference there is an urgent message for the guy who is Phil's immediate superior and who had been attending. It turned out he had now left and Phil has to enquire about this urgent message. What happened was that, the professor leading the entire programme of new teaching and research, had experienced a terrible road traffic accident that left him in a coma in hospital. Within two weeks he died, so leaving not only a widow but also now a "rudderless" department. As so often a human tragedy spills over into a wider corporate disaster.

This college, annually consuming an average of £2-3 million (about $4 million) of British public money, is set in about 600 acres (243 hectares) of fine, open countryside adjoining a charming village and close by several more. Like most military establishments this one has its complement of drab, mainly red brick buildings. This applies to the officers' mess blocks and also the administration, teaching and laboratory buildings. There is, however, just one grand country house on the site that dates back into the 1800s. This is called Tampler Hall. The extensive grounds, complete with facilities for many outdoor sports, are flanked by sweet chestnut trees the scent of which pervades the area and is gorgeous in high summer.

Life in the adjoining villages is naturally in stark contrast to the rarefied atmosphere of the college, although several officers live in one of these villages or even further afield. Most college staff either live locally, or up to 20 miles away. British accents are notoriously highly varied and this certainly applies here. However, with (sometimes high-ranking) army officers, and also people usually based overseas, the accents heard in local shops could vary enormously at any time. "'Ow'r yew this foune mornin' then Fred?"

"Ooh, oi carn't sey Oi'm teoo badly yew know, Misses Martin."

Such "local" talk can literally be heard simultaneously with: "I should particularly like two kilos of those super potatoes and twenty slices of that gorgeous ham. But may senior maid will come in to collect it later on – or could you deliver? May cheque will be with you by the end of the month."

One also often heard, by people originating from nations located around ten hours east: "OK if I hev some of that pink cheese, pleese?"

Yes, this area is certainly rich with the accents of people from many cultures.

Whilst social life in the villages is akin to that of virtually any English village, centring mainly on the local pubs and the village halls, the "social events" in the officers' mess, or associated with the senior staff meeting room, are, of course, much grander. The high points of mess events are usually the Christmas and Hunt Balls and while officers are required to wear appropriate military uniform the civilian attendees can occasionally be seen in "white tie and tails". Otherwise, black evening suits and black bow ties are absolutely essential. The food is generally excellent but more often than not far too much alcohol is consumed. In fact the alcohol intake is greatly excessive on many occasions and trouble would frequently ensue. Lager-lout soccer fans in full cry after an exciting match have nothing on this lot.

Philip Charles Kerridge is familiar to most around Birstington as the guy who usually wears a smart sports jacket (sometimes a suit), even when lecturing. Women are generally attracted to him and on one occasion, at a naval officers' lunch time get-together for lecturers and all, one of the most attractive Royal Navy wives commented about his leather reinforcing pads on the elbows of his jacket. This observation was made in an extremely familiar manner with the lady sensuously fondling the leather material.

The middle-ranking army officers generally refer to Phil as: "that dark, swarthy guy with typical "high-tech" enthusiasm and a curious mixture of accents...".

Professor Paul Kajanski has the unenviable task of being Phil's immediate boss for most of his time at Birstington. Professor Kajanski, a Hungarian Jew by birth and childhood, is the epitome of charm and grace. The rigours of his background show, however, in his deeply furrowed face that attests to past agonies and enormous sadness. The result: "*two*" Paul Kajanski's. One is full of joy when he smiles and the other looks truly sad and even angry when he simply isn't smiling. When Paul smiles his face does not just light up – it positively radiates. His mode of dress generally consists of a suede jacket, shiny with age, and a pair of dark grey trousers that must surely have been purchased at the same store as Mark Throughbolt-Smith's.

During Phil's second year at Birstington an ugly rumour came to light. One morning Harvey Stockbridge, one of Phil's colleagues and without doubt a rapidly rising star, told a group of them:

"You lot had better wake your ideas up you know. You definitely need to get into fine-tuning those lectures."

"Why are you getting at us right now, what's happening? In my case the material I'm having to cover has literally been forced upon me and is beyond what I was given to expect when I even accepted the job." Phil reacted, not a little angrily.

"Huh. Well, rumour has it that the Head of the College is insisting that every Professor sit in upon sequences of lectures by his staff."

Since all the staff knew that Harvey "had the ear" of the Head of College, they began to think this might not just be an ugly rumour after all. Instead, there was a danger that this could really be true.

As things turned out Professor Paul Kajanski "invited" himself to pairs of every lecturer's sessions including, of course, Phil's. Given the "over-the-top" nature of Phil's syllabus he couldn't claim any sort of quality grasp of how best to cover the material. As a direct result the lectures (and therefore the Professor's comments) were nothing short of disastrous. Obviously Phil immediately set about repairing the damage to the best extent possible.

Then came a year of much worse personal disaster. This time it was beyond anyone's remotest expectations.

Towards summertime Phil and Sharon, his wife at that time, were overjoyed, the reason being, their impending parenthood. Sharon had been pronounced pregnant earlier in the year and the two, soon to become three, experienced a fine Mediterranean holiday that spring. Early in August Sharon gave birth to their daughter Annelise and the first few weeks seemed fine, except for the time-honoured struggles experienced by all new parents:

"George: could you or Elaine possibly come over please? Annelise is crying and then burping, and she hasn't eaten anything for two hours...."

George Maston, a close colleague and friend of Phil and Sharon's, and often also his wife, Elaine, proved marvellously indispensable people during that time.

Many weeks passed before several people increasingly realised there could be a serious problem. This was not so much with the baby, *but with her mother.* During those years many folk, probably most, had never heard of such a thing as post-natal depression. From that September the family of three, plus friends and relations, in Birstington were destined to feel the full impact of a mother's severe "PND". Sharon would of course become the principal sufferer but Phil would also suffer enormously as husband, father and breadwinner.

Within weeks, following panic amongst the local medics, Sharon was committed to a psychiatric hospital that was located about thirty minutes drive away, and she could not possibly look after Annelise.

This continued for three solid months and then, even after that hospitalisation, with Sharon home, things were bad, very bad.

One damp and forbidding autumn evening Phil made his regular journey to visit Sharon. He sat for a while beside her in the open ward area when suddenly she rose from her chair, took Phil by the hand, and introduced him to several fellow patients as her uncle! If this hadn't been so serious, it would have been really amusing. Phil was completely devastated.

The next day he talked about the previous night's "dreadful farce" to a good friend in the administration department at Birstington, and asks him:

"Rob: you've experienced some people who've been victims of terrifying mental breakdowns and similar ordeals. What do you reckon the prognosis may be? Be honest with me, I really want some idea because this thing is literally driving me *mad....*"

Rob's response did nothing to relieve the gloom surrounding Philip:

"Well, sometimes they recover to a large extent. But then again, in too many instances, they do not recover at all, not ever."

"With someone who has a physical illness or affliction, but who can sensibly communicate, it's absolutely different. In that case I could cope and even, to some extent, relish the challenge. But *not with mental illness.* If she doesn't recover I'll simply be the next in a psychiatric hospital, probably the same one as Sharon. We might as well put in for a permanent booking. And the terrible truth is that Annie, our darling little Annelise, would then have to be fostered."

The following spring both the pressure and the on-going crisis took their toll on Phil's health and he began to need the support of considerable medication. This also meant that his performance in the job shifted into considerable decline, which was precisely the opposite direction of course to the change that was needed so desperately.

The familiar figure of Jimmy McCabe strode down the corridor towards Phil at the College: "Phil, look, both myself and Rosie know what's happening and what you're going through. A major concern is obviously Annelise. Now, and please give this some serious thought before saying one way or the other, we want to offer to have Annie for as long as is necessary for Sharon to recover. You know Rosie is able to do this because she has just the right experience. If you decide to take up our offer then everything will be set in motion."

What an offer.....

Having slept on it, Phil of course decides to take Rosie and Jimmy up on their extraordinarily kind offer. Then Annie, with the entire entourage of baby milk-making and clothes, goes to their place.

Sharon is driven away to stay with her parents for however long it may take and Phil now spends his time staying at their house in Birstington village, and some time also at the officers' mess - over at Birstington College. He remains on strong medication and his lectures are definitely awful - as witnessed by an ex-student about ten years later.

Apparently one session went something like this:

Beginning of session, Phil arrives (students very

apprehensive). Lecturer Phil spends fifty minutes essentially telling them nothing but gibberish then thanks them for their "immaculate attention" and leaves. Sketches on the blackboard all showed electronic circuits that could never, never possibly work.

After the session Doug Southern, a civilian student, asked: "Phew. What do we all think of *that*?" Major Tony McEwan, a dour Scottish officer acting as spokesman for the course, apparently told them all:

"Aye, the mun's too ill. He nay should be even attemptin' teachin' us. Instead, if yew ask me, he needs a *very* prolonged period of rest and recuperation."

Yet the extraordinary thing is that Phil firmly believes his sessions are proceeding just fine.

During the ensuing summer Sharon returns home and it looks like for keeps this time around. Most things, importantly including health, improve very markedly in all respects and Annie also comes home to enter her crawling and walking stages. With this new dawn, this wonderful improvement in life's prospects, Phil's efforts towards research and teaching are redoubled and this steadily improving situation continues over the years ahead.

Affiliated to a place like Birstington, Phil knew that there were still many more exciting conferences to attend. In early September he is "detached" to a major international conference in Montreux, Switzerland. This was especially exciting because it was the first overseas trip he has ever undertaken in the course of his work. He took the conventional route by flying from Heathrow to Geneva, then bussing from the airport through Lausanne to Montreux itself, tracing a trajectory along the western side of Lake Geneva. The weather was sunny and warm, but any remaining thoughts about possible early morning swims in the Lake were rapidly dispelled when he was told, that it was so filthy and polluted, few if any fish are alive. Phil mused: "What's not good enough for fish is also not good enough for me..."

Harvey Stockbridge who had, in ten short years, risen from "teaboy" to principal lecturer at Birstington, was also there with his wife and family, doing the sensible thing by combining business with holiday pleasure.

"Well, we've not been too well 'cos of sickness and diarrhea. Reckon we've eaten too much fruit, which is so good and widely available over here." Poor Oswald doesn't look so well either. True, there is plenty of good fruit and wine in the region but it's so easy to unwittingly overdo things.

Now it is early on a free afternoon and Phil has decided to take the funicular railway up into the local alpine mountains. Phil purchases the appropriate ticket and waits patiently at the station's wide-open platform. And he waits, and he waits.... Many trains come and go but not one either looks like or mentions "funicular" and certainly there's no sign of the destination desired. Eventually he plucks up the courage to ask someone what's happening and they confirm that all this time he's been waiting—at the wrong platform... It turns out that the funicular uses a special platform that is some distance away. In any case it is now far too late to think about his intended trip - "flipping heck what a totally wasted afternoon."

Later that day, around eight in the evening, Phil experiences his first overseas encounter with temptation of the sexual kind. He is, innocently but probably naïvely, standing on a street corner very near to the conference centre (trying to decide what to do for the evening) when two women walk up alongside him and one suggests how he might like to spend the evening or even the entire night! She says: "Don't move. Just stay right here where you are. I'll be back in only a few minutes and then we can have some fun!"

Phil hardly needs to even think about it. He's never been approached so brazenly. He immediately returns to his hotel room, changes into completely different clothing, combs his hair differently and then spends the whole evening eating, (hiding), in a restaurant - lest the "dangerous woman" should return to bug him again.

This turned out to be the "highlight" of the Montreux trip and he is quite relieved to find himself back home safely.

The bad experiences of the past, however, make Phil restless and he'd always had a hankering for living in warmer, more adventurous, climes. He finds an advert for a lecturer's job at a university in Australia, applies for this and gets offered the position. After much planning, he takes the entire family there on a two-year detachment.

This proves to be a major undertaking but somehow they all make it and hugely enjoy two years in Sydney. The story of this "adventure" is for another day but suffice it to say here that, after those two years, all the family returns to Birstington. A significant milestone, no one's life could or would ever quite be the same again.

Back at Birstington and in fact doing the same job as before he went to Australia, Phil talks animatedly with Mark Throughbolt-Smith:

"Mark, we both know there's been real and inexcusable incompetence on the part of the military training and advanced educational planners - deeply influencing this college. I'm of the opinion that this has led directly to an increased weakening of the UK's already questionable position in world economic, governmental and military circles and to the strengthening of the perceived need for external 'assistance' in military and other security areas...."

Mark agreed, although he is noticeably wary of Phil now. After all, Phil has only recently returned from the Antipodes, a very different man from the rather shy person everyone was used to just over two years ago. In earlier years Phil had come across as a somewhat naïve guy where worldly things were concerned. OK, so he was pretty good at electronics but that just about told you almost everything. Now we have a guy who is much more forthcoming and clearly possesses strong views about serious international issues - views he forcefully expresses too.

Eventually Mark lays it on the line:

"Look, Phil, these views of yours are all very well and don't, please, think I'm against what you've been saying. But as signatories to the official secrets act, working for the British defence department, we must be very careful indeed. We know each other well and I've been around for considerably longer than you, Phil. So please take this as friendly advice: don't talk about this sort of thing outside the college at all. For that matter, be very careful what you state and how you put it even within this establishment. If you don't, if you act unwisely Phil, it could get you into a lot of trouble and goodness knows, your family has experienced more, much more, than their fair share of trouble over the years."

Maybe the discouraging aspects of Birstington act as "negative drivers", although there are certainly positive career reasons too, but several of the staff recruited back in those heady earlier days saw fit to leave after some years. In most cases they just took up other appointments within the British government establishments.

In at least two instances the other appointments were within the GCHQ establishment in Cheltenham. One of these guys, Gareth Evans, is an expert in the now burgeoning area of digital electronics and this would make him particularly valuable to GCHQ. Gareth is a somewhat bumbling, bespectacled, good-humoured, tall Welshman with straight dark hair and a very keen intellect.

When he accepted the appointment at GCHQ Phil asked him:

"Why leave now, Gareth? There's so much going on here at Birstington and surely an exciting future to be had?"

"Well, Phil, I don't necessarily agree with you here. At least this is not how I see things from my viewpoint. To be honest, I think the teaching here's awful because of so much incompetent planning and hence inadequate, miss-fitting courses. So I've taken the opportunity of extricating myself and getting on to this more exciting career path at Cheltenham."

Incompetent planning, thought Phil. Now, wasn't this something along the lines I was going when talking with Mark the other day?

"Yes, Gareth, I can see your point of view clearly. As for me, well I remain so excited about microwave radio and all that stuff. As you know I'm highly experienced in this sector that's so vital in electronic counter-measures, radars, earth-bound mobile and satellite communications."

So, Gareth goes to GCHQ whilst Phil remains at Birstington.

Now, GCHQ is a highly secure establishment, staff are indoctrinated from their first day there and you literally don't hear about their work at all once they have taken up their appointments.

If Phil, or anyone else, should ever meet them somewhere, then they will clam-up and will not speak about their departments in any way.

~*~

Plenty was going on around the world throughout the final quarter of the 20th century and into the first quarter of the 21st - plenty of expanding high technology.

By 2008 for example it became clear that GCHQ was to receive an additional £12 billion "investment" via the British Government. The purpose was to enable this establishment to develop software which would mean it could tap into ***every*** phone call, ***every*** e-mail message and ***every*** web site visited —potentially by any individual in the UK. By October 2008 the first billion pounds had already been committed.

And Birstington's expanding facilities strongly reflect the immense and accelerating activity externally. Until 1990 the Cold War remained at its height, with both the Soviet Union and the USA competing for military supremacy and, in conjunction with the military effort, for electronics and communications technology advancement. The impact of increasingly digital electronics expanded in its significance for almost all military operations. Coding for security as well as code-breaking techniques also accelerated and all of this is now essentially electronic.

During the final decades of the 20th century the

USA, the UK and many other countries in the "free world" enjoyed massive government funding, principally for defence purposes. Well, the reasons for the funding are stated this way at any rate. Financial provision is enormous in the USA with the emergence of a president, Ronald "Ray gun" Reagan, who was passionate concerning "The Threat" and who presided over the notorious Star Wars programme - more correctly termed the "Strategic Defence Initiative" or "SDI".

At Birstington, Phil is able to join the audience for special lectures about "The Threat" that were almost always given by USA colonels or generals. Films are also occasionally shown and one of these is "The War Game". This film dates back to the 1950s and it was originally made in black and white. A large audience assembled for its Birstington screening. In the 1950s an attempt had been made to get "The War Game" out on to general release, but audiences became so petrified with fear that eventually the film was banned for showing to the general public because of the prospect of general civil unrest.

Now Phil and most of the audience would understand why. This is somehow the most frightening film ever made, mainly because it is so thoroughly and horribly believable. It steadily and inexorably gets into the nuclear holocaust, with all the appalling aspects of that for ordinary families - including the effective take-over of one's vomit-ridden dwelling areas by: rats, yes hordes of rats.

One thing about the wretched courses for mid-ranking officers is that everybody at least gets the chance to visit private companies that manufacture for the military and also the "BAOR" (British Army of the Rhine). This entailed being bussed to an air base to board a Hercules transport aircraft that would "whisk" everyone to Germany. It was NOT like regular air travel. You didn't get comfortable waiting lounges, duty free, customer care or cabin staff, etc. Instead there was the constant loud whirr of the Hercules engines that, to Phil's ears, was a most forbidding noise. On boarding, about the last of these aircraft that Phil ever entered, there was also the unmistakable stench of vomit (oh, wow, vomit - again). Momentarily he thought: "has the real 'War Game' actually begun already?" Again, you didn't get conscientious groups of cleaners going through the aircraft and making sure that everything was in tip-top, clean-smelling condition - ready for the passengers. Of course there were no fare-paying passengers as such on this type of trip. There was just a horde of international army officers together with Phil and a smattering of other academics.

Everyone was there on duty and the army types were probably even used to this obnoxious stink.

The Hercules gradually rose into the night sky and rumbled its way on the familiar route to the destination air base in Germany.

The "Arrivals" process was of course much faster here than with the regular airlines. After all, everyone here had already been thoroughly checked, kosher in every way. So, they were all very soon being transferred by bus out of the air base and into Germany proper. It's an interesting experience travelling in a foreign military bus within Germany. You find yourself stop-starting along city streets, many of which must have seen awful carnage during the war. There are frequent instances where the grimaces on the faces of people, particularly the elderly, express direct hostility and tell you all about their understandable attitude. Although Germany, as everyone knows, directly caused both world wars, one can appreciate the feelings of the people even today. Now this leads to an interesting maxim:

"Even in a democracy one cannot necessarily blame the actions of governments on the people who voted these governments into power in the first place. Neither can one fail to understand the hostile attitudes of the ordinary person even many years after official hostilities have long ceased."

Admittedly the situation today is much more complex and people always need employment, some of which arises from government, military and security sources.

One aspect of these visits to BAOR that remains indelibly imprinted on Phil's mind particularly clearly is the lunches. As usual with too many military organisations there was, back in the 1970s and 1980s, an inordinate emphasis on booze – the "grog". Many senior personnel in the British defence establishment are indeed assessed, at least in part, by the quality of an officers' ability to "take the grog". Someone once famously stated that: "an army marches on its stomach". Experience led Phil to submit that perhaps this should have read, for the mid-1900s: "an army marches on a lot of booze in the officers' stomachs"... Nowadays lunchtime boozing is seriously frowned upon in the services.

Visits to private companies involved in defence manufacture are also interesting. Birstington staff are regularly greeted with surprised looks and: "Good grief - what are you doing here? Where have you been all these years?"

Phil sometimes met old pals during these visits, people with whom he had worked over the years, and it is another neat way of keeping up with contacts. On one such visit he managed to find a little time to talk with an old colleague who told him something of considerable importance, and little known at the time. "Did you know," said Robbie, "anyone with a reasonably sensitive receiver and converter can read your computer screen (yes, right now), from distances up to around 50 metres down the street or in the adjacent block?"

This is an immense and embarrassing surprise to Phil because he really should know all about this highly meaningful fact.

Robbie continued: "This form of eavesdropping has become somewhat more difficult over time, especially with more effectively shielded computer boxes nowadays - but it certainly can be done. Unless perhaps your office is shielded throughout with aluminium foil (like the kitchen rolls)."

Much later, this knowledge would become very important for Phil's new wife Ruth.

Now that we are well into the 21st century many of us are acutely aware that things are in fact much worse than this - much worse than even a "man in a van" sitting in a driveway watching everything that appears on your computer screen.

When these or any other visits involve travelling between Birstington and London one favourite route includes the M40 motorway and this means travelling through an escarpment taking the highway through a range of hills. At the top of this escarpment there is a clear view of a radio tower, bristling with microwave dish antennas all around it and providing the facility for vast numbers of simultaneous phone, Internet and other communications traffic.

Today, much of this traffic is handled by fibre-optic cables but the microwave radio links also continue to be used. It's an interesting question as to just how much interception - how much "listening-in" takes place of the traffic on these links. *And* who on earth might want to do this?

As everyone did their jobs and led their lives during the Cold War years, the period from 1970 to 1990 in particular, so the international security activities were growing uncontrollably. And the associated agencies still continue in strength today - many years after the collapse of the Soviet Union and the end of "The Threat". As we all know so forcibly there is an even greater threat nowadays, namely *international terrorism*. And this is so very much more dispersed and uncontrolled than the Soviets ever were. The security agencies are still definitely required, but with a different emphasis. Nowadays it's people who are fluent in Arabic or perhaps Korean who are mainly needed rather than necessarily those who know their Russian.

The first journey ever for Phil to *the* superpower (the USA) became available to him in early-summer, about two years following his return from Australia. What's more it was to be Dallas, Texas and that was a really exciting prospect. This followed the acceptance by a conference committee of a paper he had submitted earlier, so he virtually had to go. Earlier that year one of the professional magazines featured the Dallas skyline on its front cover and Harvey Stockridge managed to access his copy before he got to it. Harvey placed the names of certain characters from the TV soap "Dallas", people like Sue Ellen etc., strategically on various hotels and so on. Oh, where would we be without a sense of humour?

The trip itself began by flying British Airways from Heathrow to Kennedy Airport. Kennedy was awash since heavy rain continued to fall all day and Phil had about a three-hour wait before his American Airlines flight to Dallas/Fort Worth.

Whilst waiting he was approached by a guy named Chris Tailton:

"Hello. Do you mind if I join you? My name's Chris Tailton and..."

It turned out this guy was a member of the staff of "Georgia Tech" (the Georgia Institute of

Technology) and Phil suddenly realised that he was being head hunted. By the end of this extraordinary informal interview it was clear that he could be offered a job at that Institute. Questions remained: "Was this a complete coincidence – or how on earth could Chris Tailton have possibly known that Phil would be at that place at that time? Was he being traced?" Already, the superpower gave Phil the distinct impression of being in another world. No wonder they called it the "new world", and little wonder Dvorak composed his symphony of that name.

Yes, the power and grandeur of that music is appropriate indeed.

The only thing is: how about that "coincidence"? The American Airlines' departure area at Kennedy is pretty large and it's stretching credulity to imagine that Chris Tailton, with his "speal" just arrived there to "magically" coincide with Phil. No, something sinister happened again here. Doubtless there were people abroad who wanted Phil out of Birstington...

It was late evening when the PanAm jet landed at Fort Worth and what a climatic contrast this was for, as soon as he was out of the air-conditioned airport complex, Phil was hit by the heat and humidity. The temperature was well over 80 degrees Fahrenheit and the humidity exceeded 80%. "Why is it that I almost always seem to end up in hot places?" Phil asked himself. Fortunately he really liked the hot weather, provided there was air conditioning available for indoors.

Aiming for downtown Dallas, he took the normal transportation which was locally known as the "Surtran", being an invented name combining SURface and TRANsport. This amounted to a bus that went from Fort Worth airport to Dallas city. Another form of rubber-tired surface transport, common everywhere now but relatively new at that time, was the "hoppa bus". Never having heard of this, and pronounced with a strong Texan accent, there was no way Phil could comprehend what it meant and this fact (bearing in mind he's an Englishman) was a tremendous source of much mirth here.

The hotel reception staff were frequently pulled out towards the front desk whenever Phil was around and he began to find this, at least, a little unnerving. It turned out they just want to hear his rather noticeable English accent – that's apparently quite rare in downtown Dallas, Texas.

Ice-cold IBA root beer is a tremendous treat in the heat of downtown Dallas in the middle of the day. In 1963 Dallas acquired world fame for a terrible reason, namely the assassination of President John F. Kennedy by gunshot from that notorious dormitory block which is still clearly visible. Phil managed to find time to visit Kennedy's memorial there. This represents another sharp reminder about the violence that lurks just beneath the surface of much of today's life, which can affect any one of us directly or indirectly at any time.

Phil Kerridge's talk at the conference was going to be heard by several hundred people and this was easily the largest audience for him so far in his career. His presentation, and indeed to his knowledge all remaining presentations that day went along just fine.

Following the conference Phil re-routed himself through Dulles Airport, rather than Kennedy, for the return leg because he wanted to briefly visit the National Air and Space Museum in Washington, DC. This was achieved and was well worth the worsened jet lag later. He shot some beautiful pictures at that museum and this is a definite thanks to the helpfulness of several super Americans there:

"Can I take the shot for you?"

"Would you like me to balance the camera here, so you can take that?"

Now it is back from superpower-America to non-superpower-UK. But there's always that "special relationship" that keeps the two countries closely entwined in a form of non-consummated marriage. In spite of the European dimension this continues to strongly influence trading, and many other aspects of corporate life.

It was now two years after his return from Australia and Phil had a new boss, one Professor Henry Maitling (Professor Kajanski having retired). The greying Henry Maitling is fairly short in stature and of stocky build. He is a Cambridge University Don and a brilliant mathematician. Henry signalled Phil into the prestigious office and said:

"This is very good. You are progressing along

fine. The report we received on those two years in Sydney was really very good - not absolutely excellent but very good all the same. Your research is going really well and you have a book published. Provided you continue like this, we intend putting you up for promotion, based on a board interview to be held next year."

For Phil this is of course marvellous news. After all the pain of the early years followed by the admittedly intensive and exciting push over the past five. Perhaps this would at last show how, just getting on with life, and not thinking about promotion can lead to just that. The real opportunity for recognised advancement is here for the taking.

When it came, the lead-up to the promotion interview of that April was almost like thirteen years ago all over again. The main difference was that now Phil's confidence is tremendous and the interview goes extremely well. An independent corroboration of this came four years later from one of the guys who was the external advisor on the original interview panel. Furthermore, this guy had been specially selected by the British Civil Service. He was amazed and extremely disappointed to hear that Phil had not been successful.

Yes, crestfallen, but by no means completely discouraged, down but not out, for some strange reason all positive expectations proved unfounded in the end and the bid for promotion failed.

Once again Phil is recommended for promotion interview, in fact the very next year, and the board is to have a different composition this time. Ahead of this new attempt the Head of the College arranges to see him in the research environment. Dr. Gerald Scott is highly enamoured concerning the quality and depth of Phil's research and his immediate superior also confided in him that he virtually had it made provided he just maintained his performance during the interview. If anything, his performance in this new interview is even better than the previous year. But, yet again, he is not promoted.

Somehow, perhaps because of the intense secrecy of the security apparatus, it seems that Phil's bosses and even the Head of the College are actually unaware of the elaborate plot to ensure that he would certainly not ever be promoted. The "promotion interviews" were in reality just wind-ups. Far from it, he must somehow be removed from the college and from the defence establishment altogether.

By now Phil is experiencing his own, personal, kind of "ultimate deterrent" and other events beyond his control are beginning to strongly influence Birstington and possibly even threaten the continued existence of the college.

By the next New Year, armed with damning evidence that promotion is still several years away if ever, he decides that he must definitely leave this wretched place at the first real opportunity.

The security people would have their way, on this one at least.

Chapter 6 Selling Out

"We believe, and we're confident that most people want and accept that responsibility has to reside with you, the people."

"Surely individuals, each sentient human being like you and I, perform best when standing on their own two feet. Don't we all function much more effectively when we have an involvement, a sense of real ownership, a stake in the organisation in which we work?"

These kinds of exhortations have become a mainstay of the political rhetoric of modern times. It got under way in the late 1970s and grew in momentum with Margaret Thatcher when she triumphantly won that ground-breaking UK general election in 1979.

And the rhetoric took root most fervently in the old "specially related good mates": namely the USA and the UK. From 1997 onwards Britain's Tony Blair and America's George W. Bush strongly continued this relationship, most notably with the "war against terrorism" and their attitudes towards the Iraqi dictatorship that culminated in the early 2003 military campaign in Iraq.

By the 1990s the rest of the world had discovered the benefits of privatisation and this became an irresistible trend. Privatisation had become virtually the watchword of economists and politicians across the globe. Even communist China and the former leading nation of the soviets, i.e. Russia, would all but cease to function were they not to embrace private industry and to encourage increasing amounts of overseas investment. Countries like Cuba and North Korea, which doggedly continued to avoid this trend, have continued to suffer very badly in economic terms. And this is most probably a major reason for the "entente cordiale" that, for a time, developed between North and South Korea. This relatively new relationship may yet develop into one that is positive for both sides after such a long estrangement.

It was a warm August day, several years before dramatic political changes were to shake the world. Phil was in conversation with Mark Thoroughbolt-Smith whilst the two shared drinks at the officers' mess bar in Birstington. Phil said:

"What about the effects of all this privatisation stuff on us here? Won't we begin to feel some of the wind, even possibly gale-force, associated with all these intense changes?"

"Well, yes," said Mark, "It will have to influence this place to some extent I suppose. At the very least all of us should keep up to date regarding what is going on and prepare to alter our aspirations accordingly. Some of us, of course, might even decide not to stay the course. At least a few may make up their minds to dare to leave for pastures new....".

This comment caused something of a pause

because Phil was literally in the throes of considering just that. He was indeed actively planning leaving Birstington - yes, daring to plan on *leaving Birstington.*

After an uncomfortably silent number of seconds had elapsed Phil said:

"I reckon that, as time progresses, all this will lead to a fundamentally altered culture. I say this because there's a tremendous spectrum of capability across the peoples of every country, especially our so-called 'advanced' countries, and this situation just has to mean problems are being stored up for the future. What do you think about this Mark?"

"There's everything right with the idea of individual responsibility and those who can - those who really do have the fitness and the ability - should definitely be urged within their countries to follow their own careers, even to run their own enterprises. The serious difficulty comes when any of us looks, for even a fleeting moment, at those who truly cannot. It's a huge issue for those who for whatever reason are not fit or able to run their own lives satisfactorily, not even enough to re-train. These people belong to what is often called an 'economic underclass' and this is where open human care must come into the picture. As things are today the growth of this underclass is a catalyst for crime and violence."

Once again there was a lengthy pause because Phil was reflecting upon just how strongly Mark's point came across. And in fact both Phil and Mark had other appointments to keep which meant that any further conversation on this vital subject would have to wait until another opportunity. Such an opportunity came two days later, when Mark and Phil found themselves together over morning coffee.

"It's interesting." Phil began to talk about what was happening locally and indeed everywhere in the western world. "Looking back, over perhaps the past two decades or so, it seems to me that sales of electronic security systems have rapidly increased worldwide. I mean from a small, and often personal level, all the way up to the national or international scale. However, the actual extent of personal security - how really secure individuals feel - does the absolute opposite.

Don't you think there's obviously a link, Mark?"

"A prime reason for increasing electronic, and also indeed very basic, security is of course the encroaching crime everywhere. And as we were saying the other day the 'underclass' element expands so that, together with the constant perception of affluence elsewhere, the propensity for crime and violence increases."

"Well," said Phil, "everyone is concerned about crime and you only have to look at people's homes, vehicles and business premises to see the extent of alarm systems. Twenty years ago it was a rarity to see an alarm system almost anywhere, except perhaps a secure warehouse. Ten years back the industry was in its infancy but expanding rapidly. Now it is a major global industry."

"It's 'Do you have some change, Mister? Can I have just a little money—for some food please?' beggars are seen with increasing frequency on the streets of most, perhaps all, large towns and cities around the world and not all of these beggars are on drugs. Naturally, the existence of drugs and the fact that crime and begging are associated with the drug culture impedes many folk from offering anything to the beggars."

"Maybe it's just as bad," Phil said, "when kind old ladies, and I know some, give them money and some of those beggars are quite likely to spend that cash on drugs."

"Yes," responded Jimmy McCabe, who had now joined in this conversation, "..and how obvious it is nowadays that beggars are on the streets, even in a city like Bristol. A few days ago we were over there and I stopped to ask one of them: 'If I brought you some food would you accept that?' The rapid reply was a definite 'Yes' and, rightly or wrongly, I took it that he honestly did need food and probably wouldn't exchange it for drugs. What a contrast this makes with the affluent section of society in Bristol or anywhere else for that matter!"

Phil came in again at this point with, "Yes, and all of us here, including everyone with university or government-related jobs, represent a major fraction of the affluent society. What I mean is that it doesn't have to be the privatised outfits. There's surely a kind of irony here?"

(Isn't it interesting how, when a conversation reaches that point at which the individuals concerned appear threatened, even if just slightly threatened, we have usually reached "the conversation stopper of all time.")

In the UK, for example, this social feature emphasising self reliance and individual responsibility is probably the main reason why the Conservative government led by Margaret Thatcher, and the subsequent one headed by John Major, came into power and stayed there for so long. The Conservative governments exercised political power in Britain for eighteen years. Although admittedly winning the Falklands War doubtless helped the Thatcher government in the early 1980s because at that time unemployment was relentlessly rising.

Compare their main opposition over that period, namely the British Labour Party. This party placed social issues and support for the underclasses very highly on their agenda, but remained in opposition for those eighteen years. The Labour party's policies demanded finance with relatively large public (i.e. government, i.e. tax-based) spending and the people did not have the stomach for any more of this. They (Labour) were also burdened with leaders such as Michael Foot and Neil Kinnock and these guys exuded rather less charisma than the now Baroness Thatcher. It was only when Labour (now "New Labour") made radical changes to their policies and embraced the market economy that they eventually succeeded in wresting power from the previous Conservative government. That was when Tony Blair's charismatic New Labour party won their landslide election victory in May 1997.

Interestingly, although the "old" Labour party repeatedly lost British general elections in the 1980s, Neil Kinnock and his wife Glennis subsequently secured comfortable European Union positions for themselves, i.e. "when Brussels calls, money talks."

One evening in autumn 1994 Phil entered his favourite pub in the area, the "Farmers' Arms", where he struck up what amounted to a continuation of the conversations he had previously enjoyed over at the college. Only this time it was with the guy who owned the local fish-and-chip restaurant: one Dan Binkley.

"Maybe, from now onwards through the 21st century any government, and indeed any political party, can sensibly only enact legislation and provide scene-setting through economic policy?" Phil suggested.

Dan was more forceful, responding with: "But gusherment intervenshun is still abshulutely necesshary to shupport those who jenuinely can't look after themshelves – the 'underclasshes', if you like." His voice was, as usual, slurred as a result of his high intake of neat Scotch whiskey.

Now Phil didn't accept this as a solution because he considered that it would inevitably lead to the downward slope towards communism and totalitarianism with powerful demagogues leading centrally commanded economies. So he came up with:

"What is absolutely necessary is a turn-around of attitude. We must have effective entrepreneurs but we must also have, along with this, people, they should often perhaps be the same people, with caring attitudes and actions. It's a matter that amounts to no less than turning around the moral fibre and aspirations of an entire culture."

It was clear that Dan did generally agree with this sentiment. The two finished their drinks and retired unsteadily to their respective homes.

A guy named Norman Tebbit, who was a minister in the UK's Thatcher government in the 1980s, once used the phrase: "On your bike" and by this he meant "be mobile and get out there to find and retain work". Naturally the phrase rapidly gained notoriety including, most unfortunately, the crude slang meaning amounting to "Get away" or "Beggar off". It would have been great in many respects if he'd meant that people should use bikes more, rather than the polluting road vehicles that most of us drive almost everywhere.

Back at Birstington it was another morning coffee time and the perennial subject of privatisation came up yet again with Phil on another of his "hobby horses". He started by making the following provocative statement:

"The term 'nanny state' has always struck me as being particularly interesting," said Phil, who continued: "I think the message would have been received quite differently if phrases like 'centrally organised' or 'big brother' were used instead. It does seem completely acceptable to consider that any government cannot always know best what to do. In business it must be the businessmen themselves who run things. However, there is another side to the coin. The very phrase 'nanny state' is quite benign and carries a kind of caring message. So the question must be raised as to who organises the caring side of things? Is it all going to be down to small local, and frequently charitable, organisations? Can the state effectively continue centrally running, for example, health care which is ultimately the responsibility of the Department of Health?

Will the often scandalously greedily-run private nursing homes continue to flourish? Putting it bluntly: is your health up for business grabs? These are very serious questions for all of us to ponder, wherever we may live."

This time Harvey Stockridge became involved in the conversation. He said:

"Privatisation, to many folks, sounds as though it will 'solve every ill' and in the 1980s at least it was definitely trendy. It represented a break with the past – the absolute opposite of the now-discredited nationalisation. It was: away with the old quasi-socialist, lack-lustre publicly owned organisations that were all products of the 'nanny state'. In with the new expanding private concerns, some completely new ventures but also several privatisations of previously public, government-owned concerns. Notable examples in the UK were British Telecom and British Gas. Privatisation means competition which must be good and healthy for everyone, with the added benefit of improved attention to the customer."

Harvey continued:

"Also privatisation means that ordinary folk, 'the people', can now at last have a share, a financial stake, in the newly privatised companies. And don't you just love being in control? In practice, of course, it is the *institutional* shareholders that dominate and exercise control. I mean banks, insurance corporations and other large firms. And these institutional shareholders carry the main sway by far. By coming together in strategically appropriate circumstances these shareholders can force major changes and often mount hostile takeover moves. Frequently some will be foreign-owned and what started life as an 'all-American' firm can quite easily finish up being owned by a Japanese conglomerate, for example."

"Beyond straightforward privatisation then there's the general trend towards increasing 'corporatisation'. That's a dreadful word, I know, but I really refer to the evolution of large international corporations. Such corporations tend to wield gargantuan power and, unless controlled to at least some extent even in a modern market economy, this can lead to dangerous monopolistic situations. The world-renowned New Zealand-based speaker and author Barry Smith repeatedly warned us all about this creeping and insidious 'corporatisation'."

Most of his colleagues respected Harvey not only for his electronics abilities but also for his knowledge and grasp of world situations and events. So they listened intently as he continued on this vital theme:

"You see, it all has a lot to do with 'the New World Order' and this involves conspiracies that have been with us all for centuries. You know, only a few people are in any way aware of the situation and its dangers. A lot of people are suspicious regarding the integrity of the phrase 'New World Order' but it seems that the first high-profile public mention of this phrase may have come from Past-President George Bush when, in 1991 during an announcement following the end of the first Gulf War, he is on record for using the phrase publicly. Was he, we might wonder, so heady and flush with the success of the war effort that he perhaps went farther than intended in making this specific quote? And if you want to know more about this New World Order and the conspiracies behind it then you can be sure that our good 'Kiwi' Barry Smith will oblige."

Mark now chipped in with:

"Yes Harvey. And for most of the 20th century the world has been living with greatly contrasting massive power blocs. With the USA and Europe leading the 'free world' and the USSR and China operating as the major communist power blocs. However, wouldn't we need strong globally cohesive and internationally secure communications so as to achieve and secure such a situation?"

Harvey Stockridge responded with: "I agree Mark, but we must look at the tremendous strength of the USA. The world's major high-tech and innovative nation is now indisputably the United States of America - *the* superpower. In this country there is a vast private industry sector with hundreds of thousands of companies, ranging from tiny 'one-man-bands' to enormous internationally operating corporations, like Boeing, IBM, Microsoft, Wal-Mart and so on. However, less understood is the fact that there is also a massive government infrastructure employing a large number of people and costing hundreds of billions of dollars to maintain. Until the early 1990s far and away the greater part of this expenditure went to defence, and the USA still is easily the largest contributor to NATO."

There could be no doubt but that Harvey was right about all or most of this. And Phil Kerridge had a deep knowledge concerning aerospace so he reminded the small group about America's tremendous strengths in this major industry:

"In aerospace, that's aircraft production and space activities, the USA has been in the forefront since at least the 1960s. Big airframe manufacturing names, like Boeing and Lockheed-Martin, are *the* major international players. These giant corporations sell internationally on the civil aircraft side to the even larger airline transportation companies, like American Airlines, Delta and United Airlines in the States and also most other airlines; Air France, Japan Air Lines, Air New

Zealand, Qantas, etc. Both also sell military aircraft. With the practically *'cosmic'* scale of investment needed, hundreds of billions of dollars, the space effort was always going to be led and funded by government. Following various launch successes in the 1950s and early 1960s, and driven by the 'space race' between the USSR and the USA, the National Aeronautics and Space Administration (NASA) was formed. Within NASA, the Apollo programme started in the early 1960s and it is well known that this led to the successful manned lunar landing in 1968. In that era it would have been almost unthinkable for anyone to dare ask a question that, wittingly or otherwise, criticised *costs.* In 1981 we had the very first shuttle mission and what an awesome experience it was to see the television pictures as the world watched the lift-off and that magnificent landing. In fact the landing phase made the deepest impression on me because the whole thing is, after all, a glider at that stage. It's a very heavy glider with high-speed touch-down to boot! No surprise it requires parachutes to slow it down to a stop."

The first low point came with the Challenger disaster in 1986. Although many successful shuttle missions have since been completed, that 1986 catastrophe reminded everyone that rocket launches, including the shuttle, could never be taken for granted.

One of America's most experienced and respected astronauts commented, soon after Challenger: "At the launch pad and for the first 30 seconds or so into launch it's like sitting in a vehicle boosted heavenwards by an immense uncontrolled bonfire. There can never be effective safety control during that initial phase of the mission." Then came the terrible loss of Columbia in 2003. This time the effects of tight budgets and poor project control led to heat-shielding tiles coming adrift during launch. This, as we all know so vividly, led directly to the subsequent re-entry failure, the break-up and the final disaster.

Prior to Columbia the Space Shuttle had proved especially useful for satellite release and manoeuvring in space. However, an expert in matters concerning launchers had already warned all of us not to become lulled into a false sense of safety: the probability of yet another disaster is at best one in a hundred and that makes another debacle almost certain because over 100 shuttle missions were originally reckoned to be required for the international space station construction.

The space Shuttle "Atlantis" blasted-off from the Kennedy Space Center on 8th July 2011 for the last-ever shuttle mission. Following this mission the world-famous Shuttle programme became history and (like the end of the Apollo Programme back in the 1970s) many dedicated and highly-trained staff faced lay-offs and uncertain futures. An awkward time-gap of several years had opened-up before – hopefully – the next phase of the manned space era might begin. In America at least manned spaceflight is certainly a multi-decade roller-coaster ride.

The USA has also for many years been operating big government organisations primarily concerned with "security", notably the Federal Bureau of Investigation (FBI) and the Central Intelligence Agency (CIA). Whilst many a movie had told the world essentially about the FBI, it probably took Watergate, during 1972-1973, to reveal something to the general public concerning the CIA's activities.

Until 1989 the USSR (the Soviets) were still prominently in existence and most people outside and inside that intensely military alliance considered them to be a potent power. Indeed, the specific meaning of the phrase "the Threat" referred to that provided by the USSR and a substantial nuclear capability was available. This was the essence of the situation for forty-one years, from 1948 until 1989. The USSR had its security near-equivalents to the USA's FBI and the CIA – principally the notorious KGB.

The USSR rapidly disintegrated, several of its former constituents are in dire economic trouble and we still cannot rule out conflict even in the near future.

During the early years of the 21st century it became very clearly apparent that the ex-KGB Putin was going to rule Russia with effectively a rod made of iron. In fact, almost a decade into this new century it would appear that Putin is prepared to wage economic war on western nations—particularly those that depend increasingly on exports from Russia's oil and gas industries. And this certainly includes most of Western Europe.

Russia is most decidedly back on the map regarding aggressive tactics and this involves the country's intelligence apparatus.

The People's Republic of China opened up vastly in economic terms during the 1990s and early into the 21st century. But despite winning the right to host the 2008 Olympics this nation continues as a centrally planned economy and dissent in any form is still crushed by the state police or the military. The PRC's apparent new economic openness could represent a subtle danger by placing something of a veil across the face of the Western trading nations. For example, late in 1998, the PRC announced that severe restrictions on telecoms trading were going to be put into place, thus essentially back-tracking on the previous open global trading. So, a China that could still prove potentially dangerous continues to lurk just beneath the apparently benign "free-trading" surface.

On the other side of the coin it is highly doubtful whether another "Tiannamen Square" would be tolerated today, most probably leading instead to a massive civil war.

At the Birstington College an early-autumn wine-and-cheese party was well under way. Most senior staff, military and otherwise, attend these events and generally enjoy them greatly. With all such events there was however something of a hidden agenda and they were used to "sound people out". Probably most of us do this, even with informal parties in our homes, but when you are talking about "parties" in corporations or universities, let alone at military establishments, there's no doubt about the fact that almost everyone's looking, checking, searching and generally making up their minds about everyone else they meet.

At its most severe, senior people are almost certainly trained to check for adherence by their opposite numbers to codes of ethics.

They are also acutely aware of the fact they signed the official secrets act...

During this particular party Professor Paul Kajanski and Brigadier Mike Pollard were indulging in intense conversation. Paul openly said:

"Do you know Mike, now we are well into the New Labour and politically correct era many people, including influential persons in 'high places', could be forgiven for believing that 'the West has won' the battle between the centrally controlled state systems and the democracies of the 'free world'. Whilst certainly free market economics had taken root globally this has hardly been followed, as yet, by any real re-orientation of several major, essentially totalitarian, nations. It is well known that the gap between rich and poor also continues widening, in practically all regions of the globe and regardless of the political stance.

Do you think that this might be the true legacy of simply being human?"

What a deeply meaningful statement followed by an equally meaningful question. *And* this to the Brigadier no less. Admittedly Paul and Mike had come to know each other pretty well during the fourteen months that Mike had been at Birstington. But even so, this was a heck of a potent topic to come up with.

After a moment's thought Mike waded in with:

"Well Paul we now have a world in which 'free' market economies reign supreme. Almost everywhere there's a continual growth of new companies across a wide range of industries. Many of these are in 'high technology' of one form or another, mostly electronics and things like telecoms services. There's a corresponding increase in mergers and acquisitions, with big corporations gobbling up smaller fry in which they have a strategic business interest. This is often directly related to the corporatisation feature. The overall result is: rich pickings for anyone interested in 'industrial espionage', and that's yet another growth industry in itself. *However* I'm sure that you will understand Paul if I restrict myself from saying anything further about industrial espionage because there are literally massive security implications......".

From this point onwards Paul and Mike's conversation ranged across many matters, although of course none of these even slightly verged upon industrial espionage or international security.

It was a few days later at the college when two VIPs were ensconced within a soundproofed office that had been carefully "swept" for possible eavesdropping "bugs". General Terence Goathead and Dr. Gerald Scott, Birstington's military boss and college head respectively, held an extremely important one-on-one meeting. This concerned nothing less than the entire "culture" of Birstington from the security viewpoint and the position of the academic (and related) staff. Almost uniquely for such meetings, right from the outset Goathead insisted that they mutually swear allegiance to the "crown and country". He also insisted that neither should ever breathe one word or even any idea about this meeting to anyone. And this must include even their wives and families.

To bring Gerald up-to-date Terence outlined the current status and anticipated development of the international security apparatus, with particular emphasis on electronics and telecoms. Then Gerald made the following extraordinary and frightening statement:

"I'll bet none of our people, including our most senior professors, even have an *inkling* about the extent to which their activities and day-to-day conversations are being monitored and analysed internationally."

Terence Goathead and Gerald Scott concluded their exceptional rendezvous with an agreement that there was nothing for it—the electronic eavesdropping and interceptions would continue because the USA was the prime mover, and not the immediate administration of the UK. Terence again reminded Gerald about the paramount need for secrecy and the conversation came to a natural end. Gerald was in fact extremely uneasy and he wondered whether the same could be said for Terence?

There was yet another dangerous aspect to the burgeoning privatisation of the 1980s and this was leading to precariously unbalanced economies in which service industries increasingly took precedence over manufacturing. In the west, certainly European countries and the USA, supermarket and hypermarket chains, other types of shops and trade outlets, specialised training organisations (including defence), telecoms and other utilities, are all still benefiting from privatisation and the forces of the market economies to a much wider and deeper extent than manufacturing industries. It's as if we could end up with a world where the western nations have this enormously disproportionate emphasis on service provision, whilst the rest of the world's nations (including developing nations) increasingly focus on manufacturing. An exception is initiatives like call centres shifting into India. When the developing nations' plant-based industry is owned by a western company the bland term generally used is: "off shore", i.e. the same term employed when investments are made outside the country of origin of the investor.

Unfortunately, all this leads directly to unfettered exploitation of the working people in those factories located in third world countries - and so the wheel goes round, and round…

Life was mostly pretty nice for the "innocent" academic at Birstington during the 1960s and 1970s. After you'd finished with (more precisely: been finished *by*…) your syndicated group of officers you were free to amble off and get into something interesting, such as research. Or, best of all in reasonable summer weather, a swim in the on-campus open-air heated pool! For this purpose the definition of "summer" would theoretically be any time from early April through October. Unfortunately the swimming didn't happen every day because there were serious research activities and teaching prep to do. There were even occasional deadlines to meet. One of those deadlines concerned research group meetings and these were held on a regular monthly basis, chaired by Professor Henry Maitling who by 1980 was fast approaching retirement.

Henry Maitling intercepted Phil Kerridge in the corridor and asked:

"Phil - have you completed the minutes of our last research meeting? We do need them for the next meeting you know."

Phil had to admit that, as usual, there was an oversight and he had not yet got around to writing-up those "fascinating" minutes. So it was "goodbye" to his eagerly anticipated lunchtime swim because he knew that time was so short and indeed he only had a few minutes to draft out those wretched minutes....

A full afternoon was always "devoted" (*"committed"* is a more appropriate word...) to these get-togethers and it often seemed as if the meeting would have to happen anyway. This would be regardless of whether it had been previously established that no one, absolutely no one, had anything to report. The vital nature of the meeting as such was further emphasised by the realisation that it could never, not ever, finish early:

It was four-thirty in the afternoon and everyone knew essentially all the business of the meeting was now over. Everyone except Henry Maitling, that is. He could always be relied upon to "find" something, however trite or insignificant, something to "fill-in" the final hour or so of the day.

On several occasions the research team members had, by any standards, completed everything required of them during the meeting and they genuinely just wanted to get back to the work (well, the swimming pool in summer) but still they were "kept at school" until 5:30 p.m.

"All right, you can all go home now. But that's after you've written down one thousand lines stating: 'I must *always* let my Professor have the entire afternoon'!"

Well, look, that's what it felt like anyway.

Owned by the Defence Ministry, a UK government department and functioning primarily for the armed forces, Birstington cost the British taxpayer several million pounds sterling annually (more in terms of millions of US dollars) at 1980 values. Various rumours of complaints concerning the value-for-money of the establishment were heard over the years and this reached its high point with a letter that appeared in one of the more lurid Sunday papers, in 1981. If this letter had been written by any old Tom, Dick or Harry then little notice might have been taken, the rumours might have continued for a while but life may well have continued on pretty nicely at Birstington through to most staffs' retirements.

However, the author of the letter was none other than Michael Tridem. Mike was a Labour politician who was mainly famous for his pronounced "affected" accent and his taste in large, polka-dot spotted bow ties.

The British Prime Minister Margaret Thatcher and her senior aide Cecil Parkinson conversed at the Prime Minister's official residence; 10 Downing Street, London:

"All right Cecil, show me this wretched letter if you must but please bear in mind my hectic schedule today."

"Here you are, Margaret, this is a copy of the precise letter text from Michael - sorry, Mr. Tridem."

"Whilst my government as we both know is hell-bent - whoops, let me correct that Cecil - I should say 'totally committed' to the privatisation programme in industry, this thing about the training college really is an awful nuisance and we're only talking about a few million quid after all."

"Yes Margaret," responded Cecil, "I fully appreciate it's less than a thousandth of BT's annual turnover but we now have a public relations problem on our hands because Tridem is notorious – my turn to apologise – 'very well known' and the Sunday Realm is widely read by the proletariat. We must be seen to be doing something about this."

Cecil's Prime Minister chose to ignore the oblique reference to the "proletariat" and asked him, "Well whatever happens we can't term it privatisation because this would not be appropriate for a military training establishment, where on earth is this Burstytown anyway?"

"It's *Birstington* actually, Margaret. But if that's all right I shall talk anyway with the appropriate senior people to get the ball rolling on this one."

What an extraordinary thing, after all the years wondering, after all the rumours, it seemed Birstington's fate was going to be decided following the publication of a "hate letter" in a wretched gaudy tabloid paper. Moves leading to inevitable change had been set in motion following a meeting between the Prime Minister and the Party chairman, with the p.m. never even having heard of the place, let alone how its name was properly pronounced or spelt.

From the standpoint of those on the ground, the staff and indeed senior students, all that filtered down during those days were stronger rumours than ever before. But everyone could see the early signs of a crucial "change in the weather" and all the staff knew that a storm would soon break. By the following year, 1982, there was wind about a possible joint operation involving the college and perhaps a research institute, but developments were slow at first and time passed. By 1983 it became clear that an arrangement to take up the "academic operations" (that's teaching and research) was in the offing. It looked like Birstington might become a part of a major technological university in the UK.

Now this was not going to be a matter of Birstington becoming purchased, "acquired" by those taking an active interest. The college was located on land owned by the British Crown for a start. It's always a complicated process acquiring property from the Crown and it usually turns out very expensive.

So this is not privatisation as such, there could be no thoughts of any "outsider" making a purchase of Birstington's interests in terms of assets. Instead the advantages to the interested party were entwined within the academic teaching and research strengthening.

An on-going sequence of five-year rolling contracts was decided upon as the best route and as a result can you believe the term chosen? Margaret Thatcher's sincere hope is that this doesn't blow your mind (it did for most of those involved in the early/mid-1980s):

- *contractorisation* - - - (!)

There followed many meetings, much exchange of information and then, in 1984, (which was by any measure extraordinary timing—remembering George Orwell's book and film "1984") the contractorisation was completed. Staff who had previously functioned as civil servants were now university staff.

The snag, from the staffs' viewpoint, was that from now onwards things would be more concentrated, it would be more of a sweat shop, informally dropping in to the research lab every now and then would have to be better organised. "Quickie" swims in the middle of the day would happen less frequently.

But staff activities and day-to-day conversations would continue being monitored and analysed internationally - and that's definite.

Chapter 7 Chilling Out

"Don't buy it right now. Look, there's a new, substantially improved and much more advanced model coming along shortly - you'd be wasting your money on that unit so why not wait for the super new product that's just been launched?"

What a classic scenario, so characteristic of the late-20th and early-21st centuries. Never mind the fact that by not purchasing particular items you need now, for your son or daughter, yourself or your business, you will be disadvantaged because there's always "something better round the corner". So you resist buying that brand new multimedia computer, or that gleaming new car because you've discovered that something providing better value-for-money will hit the market running in a few months' time.

"Darren, shame about your 'Pentium ZZ-based' machine - the one you bought just a few months' back - and I hear it does everything and more that you and the family could want. I warned you about this before your purchase and see how right I was. Now available, and well within your budget I'm sure, we have the Alpha-Super personal 'Hyperform' computer and you can go see one of these in action at PC World this week. Remember, this is the one where you can easily become a part of the active scene because true 3D holograms are projected out of the display. You can even project the 3D images into your backyard remotely, so they could be 'wrapped into' a BBQ for example. The Alpha-Super is, needless to say, fully compatible with the latest Internet developments and can be configured so the 3D images may be included on your Web page or blog."

"Well, Darren, although we've resisted the Alpha-Super so far as you'll have noticed we do have a Ford Millenior in the driveway now. This is a car I've had my eyes on for some time as it features that much- publicised 'anticipation command function' or 'antcom'. With 'anticipation command' the entire vehicle responds to up-coming changes in the environment, like road conditions and weather ahead on your route. We now find that, well before we are approaching a region involving heavy delays, the car is either automatically re-routed, or you are given other options. You can even stay on your original course and enjoy the gridlock if you want. Naturally it's all linked-in with the Sat-Nav —either GPS or the new European Galileo system. Another advantage with antcom is this: as, say, the outside temperature is *about* to drop, an event that maybe several minutes away, so everything relevant within the vehicle is readied to track the changing conditions. In short, you are *never* taken by surprise."

"You know, Wilf, have you ever given a thought to the wider implications of all this - this obsession with gadgetry and gizmos to do this and that for us?"

"Darren, I must admit that I tend to just accept things as they are, live a day at a time so to speak. If life has enabled me and my family to seriously consider and go purchase some of these marvels of modern science, then I think to myself all right, that's fine. But I also just start wondering what's going to be around tomorrow?"

"Huh, well there's a well-known saying that 'tomorrow never comes' and this certainly applies to our era of the ever-extending, ever-improving, high-tech gadgets. And, Wilf, it's not regular guys like us and all the other millions who are affected as individuals and families. This continuous change must also be a challenge at the managing boards of companies, and also senior government levels."

Darren and Wilf are both employed on the executive staff of Tekanalytics Limited—a UK-based high technology consulting firm. Whilst the smiling fair-haired Darren is somewhat out-going in nature, the relatively tall and dark-haired Wilf is really the opposite, being much more conservative. It shows particularly in their choice of clothes: Darren tends to go for sharp suits and colourful neckties, whereas Wilf is usually seen wearing a plain tie if any tie at all and just a neat jacket and pants.

Darren is right. Companies and corporations, from one-man bands to multi-billion dollar global players, government departments, transnational inter-governmental agencies - are all deeply affected by the "high-tech race". At this level, beyond the guy-in-the-street, it is computers and communications that are the most important tools and for several years this fact has been clearly recognised. The two have come firmly together now: computers need communications, and communications could not operate without computers. Whilst the prices of individual PCs and things like printers have fallen dramatically during recent times, with extraordinary improvements in value-for-money, corporations tend to need top-of-the-range systems. Just putting all the hardware and software together for this IT stuff remains an expensive service.

New and cleverer software must be mounted onto today's more powerful computers. And you must have the new and cleverer software if you intend staying abreast of your competition (if you don't - the only way is down - and out!). Assuming that you cracked the "Y2K millennium bug non-challenge", you must still stay ahead in the software race. Your competition is all the time being urged by Bill Gates' Microsoft to get out there and buy that latest operating system or new application software.

In the big government departments, and the even-bigger international security agencies, the requirement is for ever-more cunning ways to *code* information and for massive databases with sophisticated *"find"* facilities. If you happen to use at least a fairly modern computer then you will know that the edit/find facility is one of the most useful available. In this way practically any sequence of characters (usually just a word) can be systematically and reliably tracked down. When you have finished the first run of typing almost anything, you can then perform several carefully chosen edit, find operations. In large international systems this simple requirement has to be taken to a high level of sophistication.

A guy named Phil Kerridge, now the Managing Director of Tekanalytics, overheard most of the conversation between Darren and Wilf. Phil said:

"Most of us 'ordinary mortals' are also interested in the used products market, both as purchasers and as sellers. There's the 'trickle down' effect where the wealthiest are selling off their 'old' used items - from shoes to musical instruments and cars - whilst other, less well to do, members of the population are only too pleased if they can purchase these cast-offs. Car boot sales often form the main outlets for much of the lower-priced used products, along with traditional methods such as local newspaper and local Cable TV ads—and of course eBay. Relatively high-value items, such as the computers and cars, are more likely to be traded in for new or at least newer products. Although having said this it is increasingly likely you will not be able to sell your old computer or gas-guzzling car at all and instead will be forced to have these items trashed along with many other unwanted items like white goods. It all leads to the urgent challenge of waste management on a global basis."

"Purchase is obviously easier for relatively inexpensive items and impulse buying will often come into play with many lower priced goods. However, when a major purchase is involved and hundreds through thousands of dollars or pounds are at stake, the purchaser is likely to wait until a better match to his or her needs comes on to the market. The only exceptions to this are either an apparent bargain or literally a one-off opportunity. If you have reason to believe that an opportunity like this for your purchase plan is unlikely to be repeated in the foreseeable future then you will almost certainly buy."

Wilf butted in with: "So you're saying that no-one should ever buy new?"

"No Wilf, somewhere people must be buying new - otherwise eventually there can be no used items. The competition nowadays is so intense that it can be a project in itself for anyone to properly research the field and draw up a short list of trade outlets through whom to consider purchase. The most fundamental issue is of course whether to purchase a particular item directly from the Internet or via a high street shop. However I have to leave the area on some urgent business now so don't you two go on discussing this kind of thing for long. Look, there's work that needs getting done."

We are, quite literally, ever-increasingly spoilt

for choice both in terms of competing products and competing trade outlets.

"Pete, can you hold the fort please while I trek down to the 'Hyper' to take delivery of the new car for my wife?" said Jerry.

"Hang on, Jerry, what's all this about the 'Hyper' offering small cars?"

"Tell ya about it when I'm back, Pete. Then you'll be able to drool over the superb little beauty then too."

Pete and Jerry also work for Tekanalytics. They specialise in data analysis, Internet operations and administrative activities.

An interesting aspect of life today is that we're rapidly approaching a critical point where the time interval between the introduction of new products cannot sensibly be reduced and yet still provide a viable market for the manufacturer and all related trade outlets. Most major manufacturers of computers, related software, cars and home entertainment units have already realised this is happening and two-to-three years tends to be the typical gap between new "releases" of products. So, innovative new ways of selling, like that car Jerry's wife is going to have, represent further exciting marketing approaches.

From now onwards geography has less and less influence on the purchase of reasonably small goods and also less influence on the origins of the suppliers of physical goods, software and services.

You are as likely to be buying your electricity,

for example, from an American or French-owned corporation whether you actually live in America, France, or the UK. Also you could be placing a phone call or making an Internet connection using, say, a BT link - although you are geographically located in Portugal.

Pete said: "How about considering buying a new car overseas and then having it shipped back home?"

But Jerry countered with: "That's all very well Pete, but the trouble is you've got a vast amount of paperwork, not to say conversions (from left-hand to right-hand drive or vice versa) and so on. By the time you've finished the price differential is eroded enormously. So I've decided to buy second hand again in spite of what I understand Phil and Wilf have been saying."

The situation is obviously different when considering a large physical object such as a car or your home. But even in these cases a strong international flavour is almost certain to be present.

Where great differences, immense gulfs, do exist is within cultures and from one culture to another. In any country the less-well-off underclass will hardly purchase anything unless it's something they regard as absolutely indispensable and can somehow afford. This applies even if it's by barter (and that's increasing too). Basic food and clothing obviously and desirably come into this category.

Unfortunately, practically all forms of drugs (alcohol and cigarettes as well as narcotics) also tend to be regarded as "absolutely indispensable" because of the addictions suffered by a disproportionately high number of these folks. This of course characterises the well-known downward spiral that leads only to worse situations.

The tremendous problem of the underclasses pervades virtually every corner of the globe. In those regions where the problem is worst or, in which there's basic poverty on a massive scale, the dynamic high-tech trading is naturally at its lowest ebb and only slowly growing if at all. This includes most of the Third World nations and several of the developing economies. And in many of the advanced economies, notably North America and Europe, trashed old IT hardware ends up in countries like China, Korea and India.

This is what is often termed "the digital divide".

It is afternoon tea-time and Darren has now returned to the office. He wants to add some comments about global situations:

"It's a tragedy that, were it not for the extremely low-wages for skilled factory workers in many of these countries, people in Western nations could not possibly be the beneficiaries of 'competitively priced' products. Today, as you read this book, hundreds of thousands of people are working in assembly factories, in places like China, India, Mexico, the Philippines and Thailand, to make products or provide call centre services for you and me, Wilf. These amount to sweat shops and wages are a tiny fraction of any 'low wage' in Calgary, or Birmingham, or Sydney, or Brighton, or Paris."

"There's no chance of any of these Chinese, Indians, Mexicans, Philippinos, or Thais as factory workers ever remotely thinking about future purchases of any of the products made in the plants in which they work. And even if they were given such a high-tech product the cost of learning to use it and the overheads involved in running it (certainly for a half decent car) would be prohibitive."

Right through the ages, until after the Second World War, a slow pace of life was evident almost everywhere on earth. Sure, in industrialised nations quite a few people owned a car and/or watched TV but in most countries this was very much the exception rather than the rule. It's worth remembering that in those days all TV was black and white. Indeed you could also buy any car as long as it was black!

"Jerry, what sort of computer did your dad have in 1955?"

"Look, Pete, I know this must seem incredible to young people today, but in 1955 people simply didn't have computers. The entire concept of a computer was different in those days. Large rooms were needed to house machines that were much less effective, much less 'powerful', even than the $500 PC of today. Now there's another thing to remember. The 1955 computers cost millions of dollars (small fortunes in those times) and only outfits like large banks, insurance companies, well-funded research organisations and government departments could possibly justify the investment."

Pete went, sort of, cold and quiet because he's finding it almost impossible to imagine a "computerless" culture. After all, the 21st century is absolutely dependent upon these machines and most importantly networks of them – most notably the Internet of course.

"How did you live, how did you work, in the 1950s? There must have been virtually paper mountains of Himalayan proportions if you wrote everything out by longhand and filed it." Pete is trying to recover his composure.

"Well, most of the written material was typed with completely mechanical or electric typewriters. But this is the interesting thing, Pete, somewhere along the way a wretched 'paper fancier' invented something termed a 'line printer' that really amounts to a sort of automatic typewriter that's driven by the computer itself. The first printers produced what could often be enormous quantities of fan-folded paper and this scene led to strong criticisms and sarcastic jokes about 'the paperless office'."

"Unlike the old, pre-line-printer days when the operator determined how and when paper should be inserted for a print run, these days complete computer-controlled sequences of print production can be set in motion and left with a minimum of attention.

This roughly describes a newsprint plant and, with such a de-skilling of the required workforce, what a gift the computer age has been for the media moguls."

"Here's something else, Pete, - something which crucially defines just how far the computer age has come to deeply influence all our lives. We have these extraordinarily powerful machines sitting on our desks or on our laps in the car, train or plane. As they stand, alone and unconnected to any telcos, they are incredibly useful. However, once we connect them together using some local connection or the Internet, then we are into an entirely different ball game. Now we have the marvellous facility of exchanging e-mails or surfing and maybe 'downloading' from websites.

However, there's a definite downside (as well as a downloading; ho, ho) to all this because in communications terms we are now exposed to the world. Our computers are now almost inextricably tied into the international eavesdropping operations. We are greatly enhancing the opportunities for 'electronic spying'."

"But," Pete responded with an element of panic in his voice;

"Surely on this basis all our telephones and faxes are also under similar surveillance?"

"Oh yes," said Jerry in a sombre tone; "As I said it's all linked with this coming together of computers and communications. Although admittedly if we just concentrated on the communications side that's sufficient because all telephone and fax calls are indeed regularly intercepted and analysed on a global basis."

"So we're stuck, aren't we? Even if we didn't have our marvellous computers we would still be subject to covert surveillance?"

"Well, Pete, and I know this will surprise you as well as most people, but the rather ironic fact is that we may find ourselves needing our precious personal terminals, our PCs etc., even more in the face of this 'global eavesdropping threat'. I say this because there's a special technique called 'encryption' which is a way to reduce this problem, although it will probably never be completely successful unless techniques based upon quantum physics become a reality."

"*Encryption*? Sounds like something to do with the churches of the middle ages. You know: 'caught in the crypt' and all that... What the heck is this encryption thing and how does it work?

"Probably without realising it you're on the right track here Pete, because the word crypt refers to an underground cell or vault, generally beneath a church and invariably used as a burial place."

"The modern English word originates from the Greek *kruptos,* meaning hidden. And this leads to exactly what encryption means—hiding the real message so that it is extremely hard for anyone to unravel it. The 'en' prefix in encryption is the active syllable like *en*rolling for a course of study, or the 'em' in *em*powering meaning being provided with the power. The encryption of something, usually a message of some type, requires electronically scrambling it so that superficially the result looks like rubbish."

"This is where computers really come into the scene since you take the actual message, long before even thinking about transmitting it, and intensively process it digitally for encryption. Computers work digitally anyway so this is a 'natural' for them. You save the original message under a password. The computer then jumbles the message up and places all sorts of digital codes around it and the result is the encrypted version."

"The passwords are only known to those people whom you want to see or to hear you and can be changed by pre-arrangement. Obviously it's sensible for these arrangements to be made either personally, on a face-to-face basis, or provided in a phone conversation or possibly even hand-written and posted by ordinary mail."

During the late 1990s the Clinton administration in the USA came under pressure to drop the present government controls on encryption technology. An office known as the Economic Strategy Unit had reported these controls could cause the US economy to lose tens of billions of dollars ($35bn to $96bn) through most of the first part of the 21st century.

A group of twelve leading members of the Democratic party had also written to President Clinton urging that the obsolete encryption policies, affecting exports, should be overhauled. This group claimed that the US government could not control the proliferation or direction of technology in the digital age. Meanwhile, shady deals had been done regarding Chinese satellites and launch vehicles…….

One could equally argue that no government in the world, possibly no trans-national organisation either, could ever now think seriously about controlling where modern digital technology is going. It is, as they say, all down to market forces – globally.

"Jerry, you know all that fuss in Washington DC about the controls on encryption technology? Well, from what you've just been saying, I reckon that all current and future Presidents, of whatever political hue, will also come under intense pressure, probably irresistible pressure, from the national security people not to yield, don't you?"

"Yes, I agree with you on this one Pete. And even if one of them does apparently give way then you can safely bet one thing – those security outfits will be hard at work finding ways of counteracting what otherwise appears to be quite a problem for them."

"Another thing is that several years ago the national security people attempted unsuccessfully to have a special encryption chip, known as the 'Clipper' chip, declared mandatory for all superficially secure North American communications. This was pretty arrogant of them because, as things turned out, these security 'police' already had the ability to break the coding on this chip!"

"Does this all emanate from the USA alone,

Jerry, or have any other nations also got on to the encryption control bandwagon?"

"Heck no," blurted out Jerry bluntly. "The UK's GCHQ actually succeeded in the late 1980s in compelling not only the UK government but also European authorities to downgrade the encryption of the latest digital mobile cell phones. The original coding was so sophisticated that even the highly capable GCHQ couldn't break it. Maybe this says something, something rather sinister, about the weaknesses, or at least the vacillations, of the European political structures?"

"Also, on the other side of the world, a resident of Western Australia was claiming that he'd developed encryption software which was unbreakable. Security officers who had initially disbelieved this story, arrived unannounced at his Perth office and promptly prevented him from obtaining several export sales. Staying 'down under' for a moment, the security apparatus in New Zealand has also, as recently as the mid-1990s, succeeded in blocking export licenses for encryption software."

Jerry and Pete agreed that the general environment will be dominated by the need to always be at least one step ahead of the "opposition" at all times. They also agreed that this is good news for the encryption software technologists, but most likely bad news for the rest of us because we have to pay.

Meanwhile, across the world, high technology accelerates ever onward and it's all a game of leapfrog. And specialised consultancies, often small firms, germinate, grow and expand to meet the growing multitude of users' pressing needs. The national security people will be well aware of their activities, too.

Chapter 8 New Horizons

"Seen the ad in today's 'Telegraph', Sharon? That's it, the insert by Scott & Ackleman in London. As you see they want a Market Researcher with knowledge of electronics and telecoms. Do ya' know what? I think I'll have a crack at this."

So began a saga that took Phil into new vistas entirely.

After the usual wait of a week or two, an interesting looking letter popped through the letter-box and on to the mat at home in Birstington, England.

"Well, this is good news so far. Those Scott & Ackleman people have offered me an interview in London. It's for 2:30 p.m. on Tuesday and I can make that."

Ahead of the appointed date Phil and Sharon booked into what was billed as a superb comedy show, bearing the title "Daisy Pulls it Off" which was then being performed at the Globe Theatre in Shaftesbury Avenue - strategically located in London's famous West End. Whatever the outcome of the interview, they had good reasons to consider they would owe themselves a night out in the "big smoke".

Since they lived only a few miles from a main line rail station with frequent services to London the "standard" procedure was followed: namely drive to the main line station's car park, followed by the train. Phil and Sharon reached Britain's capital city with plenty of time to spare and that is always wise for an interview. To reduce post-lunch drowsiness they bought two packs of sandwiches and black coffees at a roadside café and they ate these as the clock ticked towards 2:15 p.m. Now it was time for Phil to make his presence known to Scott & Ackleman.

"Phil Kerridge? - Let me show you into the interview room."

The obligatory leggy secretary girl wiggled her way along a corridor, opened the door and this was "it". Phil was committed in there and the interview had effectively started.

"Good afternoon, Phil," said one.

"Hi, glad to meet you," drawled the second guy.

It rapidly became clear that here were representatives of the company from both sides of the Atlantic Ocean.

"Phil, I am Cedric Baxter, Managing Director of Scott & Ackleman here in London, and this is Hardy Kleinman, Vice-President of the corporation and, therefore naturally, he is located at its headquarters in New York."

Phil thought: 'Gosh, big time, they've now got the 'Seniors' doing the interviewing of little ole me.'

It's funny how you notice certain small things - have you heard about body language?

Well, throughout the entire interview Hardy Kleinman sat, with his feet propped upwards on the rather nice (antique?) desk, smoking a big cigar. Also, on the wall was, resplendently displayed, a painting of Cedric Baxter playing the piano... "Was this for real?" Phil thought.

Or was Phil being cast in some theatrical play over in Shaftesbury Avenue?

The interview started awkwardly.

"You responded to our advertisement for a researcher and you based your application upon your knowledge and capabilities in electronics, etc. Am I correct?" The little New Yorker came across as somewhat harsh and as though he had other ideas up his sleeve.

"Yes, that's correct. I confirm what you have just stated and that's why I'm here." Phil responded uneasily.

"Well, I'll be absolutely straight with you from the start. We have considered your background carefully and have concluded that whilst you are not really cut out, as we see it, for hi-tech market research - not yet anyway - we think we could use you for hi-tech business presentations. You see, you may or may not be aware that Scott & Ackleman, as well as providing high quality research reports, also run equally high quality seminars, geared for business and marketing professionals. You gave a technical presentation down at Dallas a year or two back?"

Now this sort of approach always upset Phil. This business about their being "absolutely straight" with him. They haven't even been particularly straight so far and the interview's only just begun!

Phil: "Again, yes, but how did you find out about that. It wasn't in the CV that I sent in?"

"OK; we have our 'scouts' at many events worldwide and this was one of them. We got a good response about you for a range of reasons. Anyway, sorry about the researcher job, but let me tell you a little more about our Seminar Leader contracts."

The little guy, still with his feet on the desk, and frequently puffing at his cigar, proceeded to take his interviewee through the structure and financial compensation associated with the seminars. When you think about it for even a moment this would not take Phil on to a new job and if he took this up he would have to somehow combine it with his existing career. Or alternatively change career by some other means of course.

It turned out that the first seminar series they wanted developed was in the field of fibre optics and this was certainly a growth area at the time. It was not Phil's main speciality but this wouldn't present any real problem.

"Cigar and feet man" even talked about how he liked to enjoy the "good life" within each major city and he clearly believed that this would somehow further attract Phil to the idea. No question, this guy was not by any means the most savoury character Phil had ever met. But this was business.

"Might you possibly be interested in this

prospect? We don't expect an immediate response, especially considering that we have definitely sprung this one on you this afternoon. Please let us know in about a week because we need to start planning. One further thing, if you do decide to take up this challenge then we would require you first to attend an existing Scott & Ackleman seminar to see how we run things. Cheryl will provide the details."

"Thank you." Cedric made one of his rare interjections. "We look forward to hearing from you within a week Mr. Kerridge, if that's acceptable?"

"Yes, gentlemen, I will seriously consider your proposal and will let you know my verdict within the appointed time frame. Thank you for interviewing me, even though it was not for the job as I believed."

Phil left the interview with mixed feelings. On the one hand he had not even been interviewed for the job he had sought. But, on the other hand they had put to him a seemingly attractive "alternative" proposition.

No way could he allow his distaste for Hardy Kleinman to cloud his judgement—and in any event, Phil quite liked Cedric.

"Hello Phil." Sharon greeted him with anticipation - trying to read his body language before he opened his mouth.

"Hi there darling. How did it go is the usual question I guess, but in this case all I can say, for the moment, is that it was a most strange event."

Phil told his wife about the interview "panel",

how "all-British Cedric" contrasted with "Cigar and feet Yankee" Hardy—the totally unexpected shift of emphasis for the interview, the prospects and indeed the sense of disappointment. Clearly Phil didn't quite "pull it off" even if "Daisy" might in the show they were going to see later on.......

They decided to take a wander around town, followed by a "Kentucky fried" as an early-evening snack. Had the interview gone better, with the prospect of a new job at a good salary, they'd probably have gone for a decent meal out. But on this occasion they literally didn't feel they had the stomach for this. However, they had pre-booked for the theatre so no way were they missing out in these terms.

Theatre-going is expensive and the seats they had booked were not the most comfortable, being squeezed in "the gods" i.e. closest to the ceiling in this Victorian London venue. "Daisy Pulls it Off" had been billed as a wonderful comedy (a bit like that interview earlier really), and it certainly lived up to the reviewer's comments all the way through. As far as Phil was concerned everything was terrific, until about twenty minutes from the end when terrible abdominal pains set in and he was sitting there in increasing agony.

This was the second disappointment of the day and the question was—were the disappointments in some way related? Phil struggled down the winding staircase of the theatre, out to the cab rank and, after what felt like an eternity, into a cab that his wife had hailed. All Sharon and Phil wanted to do was get a train to their home city but Phil must have looked awful because the cabby asked in a clear and urgent tone: "Do you want the 'ospital, maite?" He almost replied "yes", but thought better of it and made for the station and a very uncomfortable two-hour journey followed by an even more uncomfortable (and strictly illegal) drive as car passenger finally to home and indeed to his much-needed bed.

Was it the effects of the interview? Was Phil allergic to intense puffs of cigar smoke? Perhaps it was those lunchtime sandwiches, or the Kentucky fry, or the cramped theatre seating? Maybe it was some combination of those things, but the main thing was that, following a period of tender loving care, the 'ole boy was as they say "right as rain" again.

Phil decided to give the Scott & Ackleman seminars thing a go and, having told them so, his experience of a "typical" seminar was arranged. As with most of their seminars these were generally led by an American "expert", being a Senior Executive from one of the big multi-national corporations. This seminar, spread over three days, was all about IBM computer networks and various features such as standards, terminal equipment, connections and costs were covered in detail. Frankly, it was all extremely boring and tedious and Phil found it extraordinarily hard to remain awake... Yet it was even more important for him to stay awake than any of the delegates - because he was there on behalf of Scott & Ackleman and indeed they were footing the entire bill! Thank goodness the weather was dry and quite sunny. This at least meant that one could walk in the adjacent park for exercise and "refreshment".

The only thing was that none of the many American tourists Phil encountered took a scrap of interest in him. It was a cold winter's day, his lapel badge didn't include the word "Royal" and nobody approached him to chat and take photos. This was *so* unlike that September in London several years' back.

A tremendous amount of effort was now put into preparing the seminars he was to present on fibre optics. Sets of 35-mm colour slides were standard requirements and every delegate had his, or her, own copy of extensive notes. The time for the seminars came whilst Phil was still employed at Birstington so all this was regarded as "external consultancy". Everything was now fully prepared and ready. As it happened, with much nervous energy, the response was good for a new seminar and he was clearly on-track as a "Scott & Ackleman seminars man".

Shortly after that first seminar, in March of the following year, yet another key event unfolded.

"Hello, is Phil Kerridge there?" Sharon took the call initially and, as it happened, Phil was in so she passed the phone to him.

"Yes, hello, it's Phil Kerridge speaking - who is this?"

"You probably won't have heard of me before. The name's Jim Kidd and I run a consultancy partnership known as Econotech. We specialise in the high technology sector and provide consultancy for companies and government. It's nominally worldwide but in practice mostly European. At the moment there's myself and a guy called Phil but we are under pressure and reckon we need to expand. There's obviously a lot to tell but just in the short term we have to complete the research for a study on fibre optics, for which we are under contract from Scott & Ackleman (hadn't Phil come across these people before?) and we are wondering if you might possibly be interested in assisting us?"

Now this immediately rang bells in Phil's ears. Jim Kidd must have found out about him and his fibre optics seminars by talking with those people in London. So, clearly not only did the delegates like the seminar but the contractor was also responding with a high regard for his performance. Intriguingly there's another "Phil" there too….

"It's good to have this contact with you, Jim, and it's easy for me to understand the Scott & Ackleman link because of these seminars that I run for them. Could you let me know more details about the research study? At some stage I shall need detailed information about it so that I can go away and think before coming to a decision."

"Now, Phil. I'll be honest in every way by telling you now that time is pressing in that we are greatly behind with this project and if we can come to an agreement, meaning that you take up subcontracted work with us, then it would all have to happen this summer."

Now, Phil was still based at Birstington College and the first thing he needed to check was permission for external consultancy at this level. This was granted, after seeing all the details he was keen to proceed, and by the end of the summer Econotech had their material. Econotech and Phil Kerridge got on well together and by now they knew what he could do. A September phone conversation between Jim Kidd and Phil Kerridge was particularly promising:

"Phil, you and I both know that you are looking for a move - a change of career. Bearing in mind we are well familiar with each other's capabilities now, Phil Short and I have discussed the situation and we should like to put to you the possibility of your joining us full-time. Having said this, there's much we should discuss even if you are slightly interested at this stage. Do you know, we haven't even set eyes on each other yet?"

This was true. Although much material and many phone conversations had taken place, so far none of them had ever met. This was mainly because Phil was based in the "deeper south" of England and Econotech's headquarters was in Majorfield, well to the north east of London, nearly five hours drive away in total. In 21st century life we all just accept the use of fax, mobiles and e-mail for efficient local and global communications and it's hard to appreciate that, in the mid-1980s, few companies and offices had fax and essentially no one had even thought seriously about e-mail in the sense of day-to-day use. So most of us were stuck with just the usual fixed line phone and regular paper mail. There were relatively few mobiles in those days and the ones that were around were usually known as "bricks" because their size and shape was very similar to that of a building brick.

"Seeing that you can gain fairly ready access across to the M4 motorway, and noting that Phil Short and I have to be near Heathrow Airport on the 25th of this month, is there any chance of your meeting with us at a hotel near the airport that evening? Could I suggest the Hotel Marnier Heathrow? We could all have dinner together and get into discussions as deep, and as extensive, as we all feel necessary."

"Great, Jim, I've just checked my commitments and found that 25th is free in the evening. I'm not sure about the exact position of the Hotel Marnier so can you send me directions please?"

"We're not too sure either, Phil. Neither of us has ever been to this one before. The best thing would be for you to give them a bell and ask them to post you a map. That should arrive with you in good time for the meeting."

Looking back Phil came to believe it was sheer arrogance on his part, but this all seemed rather "grand" and kind of "business sophisticated". It was beyond most of his experience to date but if he was setting sail on a completely new business-orientated career then presumably this was the kind of scene to get used to.

Driving up the M4 motorway towards London, listening to a tape of Sade singing her "Smooth Operator" hit, Phil found the hotel with no difficulty and parked the car. The "smooth operating" receptionist discreetly directed him towards the two executives and this was how the very first meeting between Econotech and Phil began.

All three present at this meeting wore the conventional conservative business suits and appropriate fashionable neckties. Jim Kidd seemed an amiable kind of a guy: fairly large build, slightly rotund facially, dark thinning hair and clean shaven. He spoke unusually softly and it became apparent that this was usual for him. Phil Short was of about the same height as Jim, but there any similarity ended for Phil Short had a much fairer complexion, sported a neat beard and spoke more loudly.

As with any initial meeting like this, where all parties have so much to discuss, it was always going to be an extremely interesting event. And it was a long evening.

By the end of that dinner date at the Hotel Marnier everyone had come to the mutual conclusion that Phil Kerridge probably did fit potentially well with Econotech's immediate and future plans. Now both parties needed to "sleep on it", reconsider, and hopefully take things on further. During the course of the evening a salary had been mentioned and there's nothing like the sniff of money to sharpen one's wits – is there?

It was not long before Phil followed up with another meeting to "check things out" independently.

This time it was a lunch meeting with his accountant friend, a tall, dapper golfer named Martin Heyford, and the aim was to sound out Martin regarding the sense and credibility of this proposed new career move. Martin was a good friend who had good financial experience relating to small firms.

"Well, Phil, you've not exactly been happy at the college over the last few years, have you?"

There was absolutely no denying that one. How could anyone remain content in an organisation where they have been applauded for performing so well and yet, following no fewer than two most effective interviews, they still have not been promoted?

"Yes Martin, as we both know Birstington has to be over for me. I appreciate that this will appear somewhat arrogant but, in my opinion, they, the college, are the losers here. What I am concerned about is the risk of falling foul of the old proverb: 'out of the old frying pan and into a new fire'. What do you think about the manner of Econotech's approach so far, and that salary?"

"All of this seems fine, Phil, very much 'par for the course'" (Martin was an excellent golfer, but would probably have used this phrase even if he was a "rabbit"). "Eventually, all being well, in a few years time, you'll probably get offered a seat on the board and in Econotech's sphere of high technology activities the sky should be the limit for growth."

That sealed it. Enough thinking and discussion had happened and it was time to complete the deal with Jim Kidd. This was done with only minor trimmings to sort out, mainly matters of timing.

Only one thing nagged away in Phil's subconscious: was he really being a "smooth operator" in all this? Only time would tell…

"Henry, I have something most important to tell you." Professor Henry Maitling was the Head of Department at Birstington and Phil's immediate boss. Obviously courtesy demanded that he must be informed first and ahead of any formal letter of resignation, which would be the first ever for the more than fifteen years he'd been there.

Now, in spite of those appalling promotion non-results Phil had always studiously got on well with Henry. Better, in fact, than many of his colleagues. Even so, Henry's reaction came as something of a shock:

"Don't do it, Phil. Believe me I've seen several 'tech types' getting involved in the management of small firms and it's terrible. There's masses of bureaucratic paperwork, much of it frankly menial, and you're always having to keep such a wary look at the 'bottom line'. The biggest bugbear is cash flow – controlling that is a tremendous problem."

One could be forgiven for imagining that Henry was somewhat against this move but why was he *so adamant*? Why was he so strongly opposed to Phil's intentions? This took Phil entirely by surprise because he had anticipated that Henry would be glad to get rid of him in many ways. After all, didn't Henry realise how deeply the non-events of the past three years had affected this lecturer?

Much to his credit Henry made strenuous attempts to dissuade Phil from his intended path. Having tried the negative aspects he now swung into the "positives" of Phil prospectively changing his mind, although after Phil had said:

"Henry, as far as I can see there would never be any real chance of promotion in the foreseeable future."

"I think there's a good chance of this, for instance we would be prepared to shift you into a different research team….."

But it was already much too late and nothing Henry could say would ever change Phil's mind. After fifteen years he was determined to leave Birstington for good. "Wild horses" wouldn't hold him back now.

From a now most disgruntled Henry Maitling he was saddled with agreeing to a series of part-time tutorials and exam marking until the following June, but otherwise he was free to join Econotech and that started officially on the very next New Year's Day.

The place (i.e. Birstington) buzzed with interest over what was happening to Phil Kerridge. Some pointed out that whilst the college's work was being contractorised, which amounts to a sort of privatisation, by joining two others in what would remain a tiny firm he was "going very much private".

When you've achieved something new and hopefully enduring, something that has as far as you can see advantages for you and your family, Christmas and New Year celebrations take on extra spice. This was definitely true of the coming season. There hadn't been a season like it since Christmas 1976, when the wider family had to take on board the fact that their youngest would be in Australia for all the following two years.

On each occasion, albeit for different reasons, misgivings existed about many things. Australia meant sacrificing otherwise frequent family get-togethers, but at least they planned returning in the future and job security seemed virtually guaranteed.

But this was different again. When you decide to "go for it" within a small business team there's no doubt whatsoever, you risk either achieving solid growth and an excellent future - or else disaster.

Whatever people may say or think when you are involved as an employee of a "micro firm" job security is no better than when you may be employed by a large company stuck with operating in a declining market. There is however one big contrast: in the tiny firm you are a "big fish in a small pool", and wielding some influence over events, whereas in the large but troubled company you have hardly any influence at all.

The most powerful attraction, perhaps a fatal attraction (?), was the fact that Econotech operated in a range of growth industries centred around electronics, lasers and telecommunications. There was even a product licensing side and the firm appeared distinctly robust in every respect.

It seemed that, however small or large you might be, functioning within the glamorous and exciting growth sectors of advanced technology - you just couldn't possibly go wrong, could you?

What a contrast this new job turned out to be. Talk about being baptised with fire. Whilst Phil had been kept busy and generally worked hard when at Birstington full time (apart from the swimming pool etc.—that is!), here at Econotech it was one deadline after another. Before you'd completed one major research effort for Scott & Ackleman you were obliged to rush out proposals for new ones - brand new studies. Sending out as many well-focused proposals to as many likely clients as possible was decidedly the name of the game. By "well focused" everybody meant good quality but also hitting areas of industry and associated technology with relatively high chances of success.

With any kind of change, business or personal, there will always be ups and downs and the new (for Phil) Econotech venture was no exception. How often is it appreciated that one's health plays a considerable part in the dynamics of life? A health factor was almost catastrophic in one particular instance.

"Phil, Bampton & Harway want us to meet with them at a business-critical brain-storming day in a grand-sounding place near Buxton, Derbyshire. It's 'The Bondales Mansion' and the dates are 2-3rd June. Can you make those days?….. You can, great, we'll set up plans ahead, decide our strategy, and make arrangements harmoniously with Bampton & Harway. I'll be back in touch with more details later." This was Jim organising yet another meeting.

Now Bampton & Harway, a major "Footsie 500" quoted materials-based company, were in the midst of a massive re-organisation, much of which involved electronics. Econotech and Phil Kerridge had previously encountered Bampton & Harway in a most unusual manner.

Several years before, whilst he was still at Birstington, a director of the firm contacted Phil personally. It was, however, many months before this could be acted upon and by that time he was working for Econotech. So a meeting was set up among the following four people: two of Bampton & Harway's directors, Jim Kidd and Phil Kerridge. They had all agreed that a hotel in Oxford, they chose the "Glove Box Hotel", would be the ideal venue for all concerned so they met there for lunch.

During the preamble to the meeting a giant of a man bearing considerable presence ambled through the hotel. This guy was well over six feet in height and it soon occurred to Phil that here was none other than David Dimbleby, one of the late

Richard Dimbleby's sons, and well known across Britain as a highly accomplished TV broadcaster. Having said this Phil generally found it is quite unusual to encounter any "celeb" during one's everyday acvities.

At this meeting everyone came to know each other and got on well and this led directly to the "Bondales Mansion" invitation.

The purpose of the coming brain-storming day at "The Bondales Mansion" was to explore, in detail, the demands of the marketplace and get right through to determining likely directions for company strategy.

As the 2nd June approached Phil began to feel apprehensive. This was nothing to do with the business of the event itself, he felt totally confident about that. It concerned his state of health. In the past he'd suffered the agonies of hay fever, but this was hardly a problem at all now. As this June dawned, things steadily worsened, and by the time he'd reached the Buxton area it was obvious that at least a severe head cold was rapidly developing. Such a health state hardly portended well for the big meeting and this was terrible because he realised that he was not going to be able to make himself understood all day. As a result he hardly spoke once during the meeting.

One thing that never ceased to amaze Phil in much of his life was the extraordinary insensitivity of one's fellows. OK, this does not apply to all of them of course but once people become deeply engrossed in a particular subject they often lose all sensitivity to others around them. When you have a severe head cold you'll know you've got one all right. Also, the noises, splutterings and nose blowings should surely send some form of signal to others around you. This is not least because they'd rather be some place else - well away from your virus-spreading mission.

The intensity of Bampton & Harway's mind-bending 3rd June all day meeting must have been devastatingly gigantic, because apparently no one noticed Phil's awful cold. Here was a guy who was "red hot keen" on practically all things electronic and certainly including materials, here was a guy who would have given his right arm to have been inextricably involved in that meeting. Yet the poor fellow literally couldn't function. And apparently *nobody* noticed why. This is how he found out "the truth about the people at that meeting".

"Phil, can I have a word?" It was coffee time the following morning, with Jim and Phil still at "The Bondales Mansion", preparing to leave later that day.

"Of course, Jim," Phil spluttered. "What's it about?"

"Well, I hate having to tell you this, but the Bampton & Harway directors and senior staff are pretty fed-up with your lack of performance. You hardly said one word yesterday at the meeting, yet you were seen talking with someone afterwards."

How Phil regretted saying even a few throat-straining words with anyone following the dreadful (for him) meeting. His reaction was to explode at Jim, which is indeed a tremendous risk because anyone could be sacked on the spot for less.

"Jim, haven't you or any of those ******** noticed anything?"

Phil barked; "Did any single one of you have the slightest appreciation as to my state of health and the, now definite fact that, if I'd any sense at all, I would never have set out for this dump on the 2nd ?!"

"Why on earth didn't you say something early on in the meeting?" asked Jim incredulously.

"Because I, wrongly it seems, believed that grown men might have some recognition of the obviously low state of health of one in their midst, even if their recognition was vestigial!" At this point, ignoring his now rapidly cooling coffee, Phil stalked out of the room and into the outside air.

Now this could only, at the most, be a walk around the grounds of the hotel and needless to say he was in a terrible state. This awful row didn't exactly help his persistent cold, either. After some minutes he returned to find Jim at exactly the same table where he had left him - except that now he was standing upright staring blankly at a wall. Naturally in Phil's mind there were apprehensive expectations including the possibility that this could be "it". This really could well mean curtains for Phil's brief excursion into high tech consultancy. Was this wretched encounter surely signalling the end of a brief chapter with Econotech, a chapter that started with such strong promise?

Fortunately, Jim had had time to think and come to understand what had actually happened. Deep down he must have felt sorry for Phil, but it's passé to show this in business. They walked around the grounds together, sort of "kissed and made up" (not *literally* of course!), agreed that this was a terribly low point and decided to push on because each had so much to give in this still-exciting business. So, Phil drove home in a less-depressed state than could well have been the case.

Unfortunately it's a Herculean task attempting to redress the balance - to correct an awful misunderstanding - and no one entered into this process with Bampton & Harway. As a most distressing result it must be said that there was no further contact with them.

Before all this, back at Birstington, everybody wondered whether things could just continue this way, with Econotech's consultant staff spread geographically across a considerable swathe of England.

As it stood there was a large triangle with Majorfield forming the apex, Birstington at the bottom left corner and Bishop's Stortford (one hour north of London) forming the third corner down and to the left. The company had one each of its three staff at these places.

Sharon and Phil had "put down roots" in Birstington and any prospect of a move would be keenly resisted. However, by the end of the first year the portents were not good and it began to look as if Majorfield would be the preferred centre of the Econotech universe. Options included possibly going it alone or attempting to find another, closer, job. Phil did try for other possible positions and got to the point in one interview where apparently he scored a record mark in the psychological and intelligence/sociometric tests. At this stage, with limited experience, the prospects of creating a startup firm were never seriously considered. Not even remotely...

So the home in Birstington was sold and, come September a year later, a reluctant family moved into temporary accommodation in a village in the nearby countryside. This small village was about thirty minutes' drive from Econotech's headquarters in Majorfield. Having already seen several likely candidates for a more permanent home, the family settled on a beautiful $500,000 property in Durham Avenue, Majorfield and, following the usual selling procedures, residence was taken up well ahead of Christmas.

"Welcome to Majorfield, Phil and Sharon, this, it would seem, is the beginning of your local country experience." Jim was waxing somewhat lyrical at this lovely dinner party that he and his wife Mary had put on for them. They waded into mushroom soup followed by a finely cooked chicken-based main course with delicious sauces. As the wine also flowed so the enjoyment increased and a great deal of laughter could soon be heard reverberating around the Kidd home.

Jim continued, talking directly to Sharon: "Well, Sharon, as you already know so well, life is noticeably different when you're working within a small firm and they don't come much smaller than Econotech with its three-man team. Perhaps there's not that much difference in terms of the extent to which one works, but the pressure is always substantially greater because each of us is acutely aware that we absolutely must perform in order to keep the entire enterprise afloat. But don't you miss the students, Phil?"

"To some degree (no pun intended) yes of course I tend to miss the regular appearance of the 'little nuisances'. One thing about working as a teacher or lecturer is that you are confined to quite a strict time regime. The nearest 'equivalent' in business is when you have a series of closely-packed meetings to attend, each of which requires preparation. Naturally I also miss the mid-career officers with their arrogant requests, often in feigned ignorance: '...Mr. Kerridge, what on earth *is* a travelling wave tube when it's around?

Does it have anything to do with some new form of military transport?' As you might guess this kind of infantile behaviour would usually be followed by laughs and guffaws at the lecturer's expense!"

Phil continued (oh, yes, well into his stride all right now): "A distinct downside to 'the lecturing life' is the quite severe restrictions it places on the taking of vacations. You can't just leave and go away for two or three weeks and take advantage of 'off peak' holiday prices, unless you're fortunate enough to have a lecture-free term. I wonder how many non-teaching people appreciate this serious restriction for teachers and lecturers?"

Jim chipped in with: "Of course, even in business, especially in a small close-knit outfit like ours, none of us can just decide we'll 'up and go' on vacation or whatever. All the time that any one of us is inextricably involved with researching and completing a study, whether for Scott & Ackleman or for some other client, the key word remains 'inextricably' and that decidedly ties the executive to the job until it's completed and delivered to the entire satisfaction of the customer. Although I must admit that we can all plan around the projects and it's probably better to go away on holiday at or near the start of a project, rather than always wait until after it has been completed."

"Fine, Jim, and in the planning at least we can make a reasonable attempt to have the breaks at times so that we could take advantage of the 'off peak' prices. After all it's only when one's children are young and still at school that one must be tied to peak time vacations." - Phil was keen to round this subject off at this point.

Having just about worn the "socks off" vacation discussions the conversation turned to many other things, including golf and other non-business pursuits that one can attempt to follow whilst blending in with the demands of a heavy schedule in the usual week. A most enjoyable and informative dinner party ended late that night and the Kerridges returned to their home in Durham Avenue.

Getting to know one's neighbours is a major part of settling into any new home and its surroundings. On one side of their Durham Avenue home lived Brenda and Geoff Masters. Geoff was a retired senior accountant who had worked with one of the best known insurance companies for the latter years of his career. The couple were keen gardeners, not entirely Phil and Sharon's scene, but they were extremely decent folk with whom anyone should get on well.

It wasn't difficult to guess the nationality of their equally friendly neighbours on the other side of their home: "Ronnie, any chance of taking me downtown - I need some boxes of candies?"

Yes, Marilyn and Ronnie Kaylie were Americans living over here in England with their families. It seemed that Ronnie was attached to some American organisation and was in the UK for a sufficiently long period of time making it worthwhile to purchase property. Both were of medium height, in the five-and-a-half to six feet range and Ronnie was a particularly well built guy—exhibiting almost athletic strength.

Marilyn was a slim and attractive woman with long blond hair, whilst her husband had a noble head of dark hair and a sallow complexion.

One day Phil just in passing asked Ronnie, as

he would anyone, where he worked and what his business was.

"Pardon my asking you what you do for a living. I'm always interested in other people's lives because they're almost always bound to be more interesting than mine." Nothing like going for it direct, Phil was right in there.....

"Well, I can tell you I work at a US base called Charteridge but because of the security I can't tell you more than that and I'm sure you'll understand. I am trained as a civil engineer and I've worked on civil engineering contracts for the US government. However, I don't use any of my training in the job these days." Phil thought this must virtually have been Ronnie's necessary stock answer.

When you work for any government or security organisation, or with a private security company like a "private eye" for that matter, you are very constrained indeed concerning what you can say to any outsider. Having been with the British Ministry of Defence and, admittedly many years ago now, signed standard security agreements, Phil felt that he understood this situation, even if it *was* practically the conversation stopper today. He could not, however, resist coming up with the following comment:

"Oh, you work at that place with all those giant golf balls then? They always suggest to me a sort of 'listening spheres' farm...."

"Yes, you're right about how the place appears, Phil, but I couldn't possibly comment upon your description. Sorry guy, but we'll have to leave any discussion out of it because I'm bound not to talk about my job literally to anyone. Do ya know this includes all of my closest family and friends, including even my wife Marilyn."

Now, its basic human nature isn't it? When practically anything in life is stated as being "secret" it's somewhat like "must not touch" or "don't go near that". It's "that's dangerous" or "you mustn't look at this". Human nature ensures that you will be all the more inclined to get searching in an attempt to find out as much as you can.

Wasn't it the biblical Eve who first yielded to that temptation to eat of the fruit? And several people around the world have spent considerable time and effort researching secretive organisations.

Throughout most of Sharon and Phil's first year in Majorfield, Econotech continued operating with its staff still dotted about and not located in a single office. But at least now everybody was within twenty minutes' drive of the headquarters.

Eventually, the company decided upon the route of taking on a new sales and marketing "guru" (Tony Creswell) to add to its staff, employing its own administrative secretary, becoming better equipped and operating from a specific fixed base. Only in his early thirties Tony Creswell came in from a large company. He was "your ultimate high-tech marketing whizz", a lively personality and a family man with a prominent mop of brown hair. Sandra Johnson, the new secretary, was au fait with high-tech terminology and terrific at dealing with clients. She was in her late-twenties, attractive with shoulder-length blonde hair, had a confident manner and was a rapid yet accurate worker.

These new people were taken on over a period covering several months and Econotech became established in its rented premises close to the centre of town. It was not only the premises which were rented, practically everything, from office furniture to cars and computers, were either rented or leased so that the company owned only a few assets.

But at least Econotech had plenty of work on, an enviable team of highly skilled staff and had become appropriately computerised.

Chapter 9 UKUSA

"Is that Phil Kerridge?" This was the unmistakable voice of Sally Probert on the phone, and immediately Phil thought it must be something to do with the fibre optics seminars that continued strongly.

"Good, Phil, with your fibre optics seminars going along so well we should like to talk to you about the possibility of developing a microwave technology seminar also. Just to gauge your initial reaction may I ask if this is something in which you have sufficient background for credibility and to generate the seminar material?"

"Yes, certainly Sally. This is really my first subject ahead even of fibre optics. No doubt about that, it seems exciting and would be right up my street. You may also know that I've prepared several microwave industry studies for Scott & Ackleman over the past three years."

"Fine, it's excellent to have such a positive response from you about this idea, Phil. First we would need an outline and we naturally have to come to an agreement regarding fees, etc. May I leave it to you to get the ball rolling on this one?"

"No problem, Sally, my schedule over the next few days should enable me to prepare this for you and get a draft in by the end of next week. How does that sound?"

"That's fine Phil, I look forward to seeing your draft."

Now, Scott & Ackleman are well recognised for their high-quality *business-orientated* seminars. Indeed the fibre optics seminar had always been focused on the business side and technical features were treated with "kid gloves" and often superficially, bearing in mind the audience's demands. So naturally this new concept of the microwave event was developed along the same lines as any business-orientated seminar.

This was always much more of a challenge to Phil than a deeply technical course. He is totally at home with highly detailed treatments of this area of high technology, having lectured to post-graduates on the subject both in Australia (where he constructed brand new courses) and at a major UK University.

However, some of the material required could be gleaned from the industry reports they had researched over the previous three years. Armed with this material and by sensibly introducing new topics, a suitable draft, and eventually, a full set of notes and teaching material for the seminar was completed. Here was a thorough seminar carefully designed for the usual Scott & Ackleman spectrum of delegates: industry people, marketing VPs and decision-makers.

All concerned, the client (Scott & Ackleman) and staff at Econotech, were confident this material fitted excellently the requirements of the anticipated audience.

Meanwhile, back at GCHQ in Cheltenham, several *technical* staff were lined up to attend this ground-breaking seminar. Every candidate had to check thoroughly with, and be vetted by, a keen young man named David Ward, GCHQ's internal security advisor. David reported to the Organisation's Senior International Security Advisor— *Nigel Penley.*

When you are commissioned by a company like Scott & Ackleman to deliver seminars you find yourself treated rather like royalty as far as accommodation is concerned. In this case, in the same way as for the fibre optics events, Phil stayed at the extremely plush Buckingham Plaza Hotel in central London.

"Would you like room service, sir?"

"Have you stayed with us before, Mr. Kerridge? We feel confident you will thoroughly enjoy your stay here. Although we could just possibly be biased we do consider this is a really top class hotel."

Breakfast in one's room is something of a "must" when you're in quite a hurry since you're leading a seminar and it's beginning tomorrow morning. What's more, it's a brand new seminar. So, Phil completed the appropriate section of the card to hang outside the door and hoped that breakfast would arrive practically on time (this can, and has on occasion, become hair-raising when they're even a tad late).

"Thanks, Cynthia, that's fine and the room looks in good order." Scott & Ackleman always seemed to employ female staff to oversee and act as one's friendly hostess for these occasions. Usually they were quite glamorous and Phil could see that this frequently distracted the delegates at the seminars - just possibly on occasion Phil also (!).....

Now the seminar itself began. The usual introductions: "This is Phil Kerridge, your Seminar Leader. Phil's background is........".

The morning got under way.

Any experienced seminar leader is well used to various "noises off" and murmurs from the audience. But this was somehow different. Phil was confidently performing in his usual manner and this was an approach that had won him considerable acclaim and occasionally excellent responses in the past. And yet he believed he could detect background sounds and also some body language indicating disapproval. It's extremely deflating, more particularly when one should have the audience in the palm of one's hands. And remember this is Phil's strong home ground in terms of subject matter.

"Dr. Kerridge, may we have an urgent word please?"

This was coffee break on the first day and here was a "gang" of delegates who gave the seminar leader the distinct impression they could lynch him unless something changed dramatically. "Look, we are sorry to have to say this..." (Phil recoiled, his body going limp in anticipatory dread) "...but, is this just introductory material, are you moving into much greater depth after coffee?"

Here was *the most* horrendous reaction Phil had ever experienced in over twenty years of conscientious teaching high technology, much of it microwaves. Worse still, he didn't know what to say at all. He was completely and utterly stuck for words—or actions.

"Why, can you please tell me precisely what the problem is? As you know, in conjunction with Scott & Ackleman I've put together this business-orientated seminar for you. I presume you are acting in an executive or managerial role...?" Poor Phil was struck dumb with horror once again because, looking at the name badge of this guy, he could clearly see that he was in fact a highly technical section leader at GCHQ.

It turned out that Scott & Ackleman had, without even warning the leader, put on a seminar ostensibly for highly technical staff, including designers and systems engineers, but openly allowing Phil Kerridge's original materials to go through, all of which were clearly designed for business people!

Phil was remembering all the work that had gone into this event. He could vividly recollect all the occasions when it would have been very easy for Scott & Ackleman to notice, and comment, that the material was insufficiently technical in depth and the horribly ironic fact that, a highly technical event would have been considerably easier for him to develop. You can imagine the difficult and frosty atmosphere pervading the remaining hours and days of this ill-matched and ill-fated seminar.

Now Phil did not, and still does not, believe that Scott & Ackleman are stupid in anyway. If they were stupid then they would have to be extraordinarily ignorant because the issue at stake amounts to "shooting themselves in the foot", and no reasonably adroit business person would do anything that could lead to that. No: something else was definitely at work here and it had to be something covert, subtle and probably sinister.

Could it be connected with the fact that several GCHQ staff were amongst the delegates? Perhaps Scott & Ackleman had allowed a GCHQ senior executive to overview the main strands of the seminar during preparation i.e. well before the event? If there was some conspiracy within the "establishment" to "get rid" of Phil Kerridge (well, the microwave expertise of the guy anyway) then this GCHQ senior executive could have OK'd the material, knowing full well that it didn't meet the requirements of the staff he would send. Then, never mind Scott & Ackleman's business, let alone Phil's reputation, this should do the trick – it would be "goodbye Phil Kerridge," at last.....

There was just one other significant point about Scott & Ackleman at this time. Whilst hunting through paper files at Econotech's head office, Phil glanced through the administration file on that client. He found a damning letter which finally told him (and anyone else privy to the history) everything anyone needed to know about Hardy Kleinman, Vice-President of the corporation and that "cigar and feet on desk guy" who'd been one of Phil's interviewers three or four years' back.

Remember that Phil had received several excellent responses to those fibre optics seminars?

Well, this letter actually stated, yes there it was, incredibly in black-and-white, that "..as we all know Phil Kerridge's fibre optics seminars never did come up to expectations. He didn't develop...".

Well now, Phil didn't need to read any more. This put the cap firmly on everything to do with that outfit. This was literally lies, damned lies, and completely provable lies too.

The security people had succeeded in seriously damaging Phil Kerridge's reputation in all respects.

Meanwhile they had also sacrificed the reputation of Scott & Ackleman for quality technical seminars.

"Both Phils and Tony - we need to meet in order to discuss a most important matter." Jim was requesting what was obviously to be a truly milestone meeting between all senior staff. This meant: Phil Short, Phil Kerridge, Tony Cresswell (the new sales and marketing "guru") and Jim himself.

"None of us seated here is wealthy. I guess this is why we are all sitting here in the first place....". And nobody was going to argue with Jim about that one. "If any of us were sufficiently wealthy, and by wealthy I do also mean cash-rich, I am confident that he would see wisdom in investing a substantial capital sum into Econotech. However that is not the case and it rarely is the situation in any small concern. This means that if we want to expand and develop our business further, through, and well past 'critical mass' then there's only really one way and that's by attracting venture capital. So, I propose that we embark on a systematic process of approaching selected venture capitalists until both parties find a match. It is the purpose of this meeting to fully discuss this approach."

Econotech ended up having interview meetings with four "possible" and eventually just one of these looked like an excellent match. The firm had the name: "Multidim Investments". Everybody came to the conclusion that "Multidim" must be short for "Multidimensional" and hopefully not how "dim" i.e. thick-witted the organisation was!

"Hi Tony," Jim enquired in his best "calm yet earnest" voice. By now Tony Brasher, who was to be their manager at the venture investment company, was becoming well known to all the staff: "I hear that things have moved on quite a bit recently?"

"Yes indeed Jim. In fact I was about to contact you because we are now in the position for setting up a meeting so that we can go through the signing which must be completed."

This seemed fine—it was good news for all concerned. On the appointed day all the senior staff packed into a car to make the five-hour journey into the City of London where Multidim

Investments' head office was located. They arrived mid-morning, meaning that they were in good time for the meeting, and proceedings began. Ahead of this crucial event Jim had naturally enquired about the likely amount of time the entire process would occupy and had been told that generally these things take about four hours or so, all told.

Now, the prospects of around four hours sitting round an enormous boardroom table seemed onerous to everyone present. But in the actual event they remained incarcerated in that place until around 8 p.m. There were small difficulties with all sorts of details in the agreement that was being drawn up and countersigned and various people around the fund manager's offices had to become involved.

"Gentlemen. We've managed to get this far through the document but our small firm's sector financial manager had some questions. These are now all cleared satisfactorily. Sorry again about this tortuous process." Well, at least Tony Brasher was keeping everybody updated about everything. Delays in locating many of these folk accounted for the long period of time.

Obviously, setting off from central London at 8 p.m. and with a five-hour journey ahead would mean that the car-load of Econotech's staff could not reach home until the early hours of the morning. So, each performed the phone contacting needed to let their loved ones know what was happening including the fact that they had agreed to stop over for the night at a "half-way" hotel.

Now Tony Brasher was by all accounts practically ideal for a firm like Econotech because he was not only an acclaimed fund manager with a good track record, he was also highly knowledgeable regarding this high-tech sector because he had worked with a major telecomms company for many years in the past. Tony clearly knew much about the industry and its vagaries and Phil Kerridge quizzed him on several things at their very first meeting. There was no doubt about it Tony seemed to be an excellent "find". It is, however, worth mentioning that the guy had an unusual appearance.

He was of unusually short stature, being around 140 centimetres (under five feet) in height, with ginger hair and a full beard. The result was that he looked positively gnome-like!

When you have venture capital, assuming that your manager has at least some idea about how to run his business, he will make sure that senior management meetings take place on a monthly basis with him essentially chairing these meetings. This goes on at least through the first and often the second years. Needless to say Tony adopted this approach and Econotech enjoyed excellent management steering from those meetings.

At one meeting an unusually exciting announcement was made: "Gentlemen, good news, we have completed a deal with 'MXX Corridor Strategies' and this provides for us to support them in attracting North American investment into the region." Jim was understandably pleased with the result that he and Phil Kerridge had achieved during their negotiations. "We have some research to do first, but the main thing about this project is that we get to go to Massachusetts - all paid for by the sponsor."

"MXX seem keenest on fibre optics and we have to be guided by them so our initial objective is to set up visits to as many appropriate 'targets' as we can find in fibre optics within the State of Massachusetts."

There followed something of a hiatus of activity on this project and both Jim and Phil Kerridge set off for Boston in late November.

Mountains of snow were clearly visible as the plane touched down at Boston Airport and Phil (who hates cold weather and snow) was becoming seriously apprehensive.

The two got through passport control, collected their baggage and Phil *almost* managed to get through immigration. Being a totally honest kind of a guy he had set down in detail, to the letter, notes about the content of the CD-ROMs he was carrying. At this point he was equally clear, when asked what information these disks contained, that they contained files including some with military significance. Unsurprisingly this feature caused eyebrows to become raised... He was asked to take these over to a nearby office which was clearly staffed by—FBI agents! One of these guys took on Phil's "case" and understandably wanted to see the full file contents of all saved files. He remarked that if it was found this was potentially sensitive material it (or even Phil) would have to be held back and neither the files nor Phil would ever get any further into America... As it turned out the material was *just* sufficiently on the safe side and all seemed to be well.

However, unfortunately at this point Phil suddenly lost his cool and shouted out: "What a crowd of ******* you all are! It's just jobs for the boys isn't it? All this stuff about international security when everyone knows the likes of the National Security Agency and so on are just there to provide jobs for people who are incapable of doing an honest day's work anyway. And the NSA has a downright sinister side through which much insidious snooping is performed. I don't like you lot one bit!"

"You had better remain exactly where you are standing Mr. Kerridge. You will know that you are within a hair's breadth of being detained in this country. We will log this incident as potentially serious and you will probably hear from our Department eventually." This was the sombre response of one of the agents.

Around thirty minutes later the same agent returned to Phil - who was now sitting down nervously - and said: "OK. We've had enough of you being here anyway. Be on your way for now but watch your step very carefully."

Needless to say Jim lambasted Phil concerning his behaviour: "You know what you did in there Phil? As the guy said you came within a hair's breadth of detention in the USA. This could so easily have been your last few minutes of freedom here - and your last few minutes of employment in Econometrics." Feeling very contrite, Phil apologised profusely.

Once outside the airport Jim and Phil were greeted by Gary who was their contact working with the sponsor (i.e. MXX back in the UK). Both Jim and Phil knew Gary well, having worked through other projects involving him over the previous three years. He was a regular pleasant guy with the kind of face that always looks as though a smile would break at any moment. Gary was very easy to get on with and Phil put this down mainly to his great sense of humour.

"Hello there you two Brits." It was reassuring to encounter the smiling face of "our" Gary. "Welcome to Boston, USA, and did you notice that it's the winter?... Did you have a good flight?"

Phil said: "Good to see you again too Gary, and yes, the flight was fine. Par for the course we guess. When you stop to think about the huge numbers of flights daily into and out of North America and Europe which is increasing all the time isn't it amazing that standards are kept so high? Clearly the vital global airline industry does well to maintain such a high quality and standard of service. We don't have any complaints about this Manchester-Boston flight - don't you agree, Jim?"

"Phil, a 'little bird' has told me that you love cold weather and snow." Oh, here goes Gary's wicked sense of humour again.

"Oh yes, fine, huh? We saw the 'snow mountains'

around the airport but it's only late November and surely there's likely to be a break in the weather, with milder conditions for our visit here?"

"Well, I'm not at all sure about that, Phil, because the forecasts are pretty pessimistic. And let me tell you both something: having got to the hotel four days' ago for the next forty-eight hours it was literally impossible for anyone to get into or out of the place. In fact the whole of south-eastern Massachusetts was paralysed and that's rare here because they are well used to highly inclement weather most winters. This time the snow was nothing short of incredible.

We've had level depths of around two-to-three feet everywhere. As usual the drifting meant that ten feet or more was the case in many locations."

"Oh, sounds absolutely terrific Gary. From the heart we really do feel sorry for you with that awful and annoying experience over your first few days. - Jim, can we get back to the airport and book the next flight back to the UK, or better still to Orlando in Florida?!"

Everybody knew that Phil would not be exactly delighted with this snowy news….

Although it was cold at least by now the ground conditions had cleared.

Everyone had some spare time and Gary proceeded to escort the party around some of Boston's historic environs. There are many colonial houses and, set as they were now amidst the beautiful colours of the late fall, this was marvellous to see and have described. It's always amazing how so many of the coloured leaves on the trees will survive even the most drastic weather.

For the first phase of this mission the trio were located about one-hour's drive from the State capital Boston. This is right in the midst of the industrial region. Much of Massachusetts is populated with high-tech companies such as Artel Communications, Gandalf Systems, Madison Wire & Cable and of course the massive Raytheon Company. In many respects Massachusetts competes with California's Silicon Valley as the major high-tech industrial state and this has been true since the early 1960s. Although by now industry is spread rather more widely across the USA, California and Massachusetts remain vital concentrated hubs for industrial and scientific enterprise.

The Westford Marriott Hotel was comfortable enough, well appointed and well equipped.

"Jim, how do you feel about coming out for a jog and then a spell in the gym followed by the swimming pool? We can't work and eat all the time and keeping fit is most important for 'key executives'."

Phil was generally keen on health and fitness, yet not by any means freaky in this respect. At any rate Jim declined with: "No, thanks Phil. I'll just settle down and watch some television before dinner I think."

Gary wasn't interested either. "What a thoroughly obese and dull lot Phil thought."

So it was just Phil who made his own way and

got on with the exercise, etc. At least this way he would guarantee a good appetite and he would also feel less guilty when sitting in cars or at tables within companies later that week.

The next day involved a packed programme in spite of the fact that no corporate visiting was involved. Instead meeting rooms had been booked at the hotel and the morning was given over to presentations. Phil gave his well rehearsed one on fibre optics technology and the industry. Another guy presented a "picture of the political landscape", amply illustrating his political bias, and company opportunities in the geographical area, and a senior manager from MXX Corridor Strategies talked in more detail about various developments in the UK. Gary had been hard at work getting invitations out to a large number of industrialists from Massachusetts and surrounding states.

As usual, these occasions prove useful for contacting and, in this case, hopefully attracting people to the UK.

Everybody spent a hectic morning the next day - phoning firm after firm to set up visits and ending with a reasonable programme.

By now Gary had dispensed with his rented car and yet all the people had to get around many miles to reach various companies.

"Hello there, I'm Harry Weston. Wonderful to meet you." This guy was unmistakably British, with quite a "posh" accent and a designer suit. And yet he lived way down south in New Orleans. In fact, several years later, Harry Weston was severely displaced as a result of Hurricane Katrina. He lost his home, almost all his possessions and worst of all his health seriously declined.

For now, in Massachusetts, Harry Weston was happy to drive around practically wherever anyone wanted to go. It transpired that Harry had an arrangement with MXX whereby they could call upon him and he would do this sort of thing - provided it was logistically possible and fitted in with his programme. Clearly Harry and the MXX people knew each other from "way back" and this was a friendly business arrangement.

"Where would you like to go today?"

"Well, first off we'd like to say it's good to meet you also, Harry. We have a schedule of visits and these take in corporations spread over an area of around a thousand square miles of south eastern Massachusetts. But the first one is only about an hour's drive from here I think. We have a meeting set up with them for 10:30 so do you think we can make it OK?"

Harry thought he could have a crack at this one and indeed the "posse of staff" reached them on time. Two further meetings were conducted during that day. Harry's driving was superb and the fact that Phil, Jim and Gary had a chauffeur relieved everyone else from troubling over the highway traffic. As a direct result everyone arrived fresh for each meeting.

The next day was different again. A breakfast meeting had been arranged with the Vice President of an illustrious firm and this went well. After breakfast Jim phoned base in England:

"What did you just say Sandra?"

"A guy from a firm named Microwave Facilities Corporation has phoned us in England and asked to speak with Phil Kerridge because they would like to explore the possibility of some research.

I hope you're sitting down when I tell you Microwave Facilities is actually based in Massachusetts and is around ninety minutes' drive from where you are right now!" Sandra Johnson sounded quite excited which was extremely unusual for her.

Jim contacted Dirk Hanson at Microwave Facilities Corporation, Dirk being the guy who had phoned Sandra the previous day. Dirk must have thought Jim was having him on, that this was some highly unprofessional ruse. Somehow Jim managed to convince him that he and Phil *really were* in Massachusetts and could see him virtually right away. Fortunately Dirk could also find a short time slot in which to see these two "surprise" English executives and they obtained enough information from which to formulate a proposal when back in the UK later that week.

Meanwhile Gary was left behind - phoning like crazy. As a result another couple of meetings were arranged for the afternoon and after that everyone made their way to downtown Boston where they had booked into the Ritz Park Hotel. Being relatively old and traditional this hotel reeked with character whilst at the same time being extremely well appointed. In general appearance the Ritz Park presented a real contrast to the Westford Marriott. There were also far more tourists here and far fewer business types.

Having booked in and eaten dinner, Phil returned to his room and noticed he had generated quite a lot of dirty clothing. Time was now much too short for having the hotel deal with this, so he decided to take his laundry to a local "laundry-mat" (same as a "launderette" in the UK, for example). This turned out to be an interesting experience.

Surreptitiously, Phil carried his laundry through the hotel (including the lobby) in a business-like bag so that nobody could have any inkling as to the precise nature of the contents. He asked a disbelieving cabby if he could take him to the nearest laundry-mat, the cabby eventually agreed and there he was: marooned in that "do-it-yourself" laundry. It was all really strange, but with some difficulty Phil obtained enough soap powder to put into the hopper of the washing machine. The rest was easy. Here it is: clothing into the main container, close the lid, select the washing program and switch on. Clearly everything was working fine and you could hear all the motions happening until ultimately the bell rang signifying the end of the wash and final dry cycles. Over to the machine, take the clothes out and surely all's fine. The only thing was that nothing, absolutely nothing, appeared washed clean. Indeed it was dry – but it was dry anyway when Phil had last set eyes upon it, which was about an hour ago!

After due considerations and much inspection it dawned on Phil that he'd put the soap powder in the *adjacent* machine because, to the uninitiated, it was not clear which hopper served which machine.... However, for some reason the container of the machine that had just housed his clothes was still rotating. So, Phil took his chance: chucking out soap powder from the wrong hopper as fast as possible and transferring it into the machine with all his clothes now in again. This was how Phil's clothes emerged at least half clean by the end of the evening...

The next day some further meetings had been arranged around Boston but this time Harry could not oblige with chauffeur support, being unexpectedly called away on urgent business. So Jim rented a car for the purpose of travelling to these meetings.

"You know Jim, looking at the traffic, bearing in mind you have to drive on the other side of the highway and taking into account the complex road systems – I reckon I'll never drive in North America. I've driven left-hand drive cars before, but in relatively quiet regions."

"It's not so bad at all." Jim replied: "Most of the demands are similar to those back home and it's amazing how one adapts." By now it was the heavy traffic period and most vehicles were travelling at less than walking pace on the freeways around Boston.

The very next day once again they had the luxury of "chauffeur Harry" but for the last time because this was their final day in the States. The outside temperatures had remained stubbornly below freezing all week, with Boston recording only eighteen degrees Fahrenheit as the maximum on several days. However, the forecasts all indicated that the weather would worsen even further later that day. Their flight was early evening and everyone hoped that conditions wouldn't lead to any problems either on the freeways or at the airport.

"Please tell them to get a move on because I've just received severe weather warnings for this area." Harry urgently waived Gary back to the car, waiting outside the firm where the final meeting was in progress. At least all their luggage was now in the car.

"Come on you guys. All of us appreciate that business comes first in every way - but the forecast is ice storms for this area and through to the airport."

"Ice storms?" This was repeated practically in concert!

"Yes, that's right, I've only ever been through one and I don't relish enduring another. They're much worse than the hail storms and so on you get in Britain. With these ice storms the precipitation amounts to chunks of ice easily as large as your hand falling out of the sky.... Obviously these can and do penetrate vehicle windshields and therefore such storms are highly dangerous. That's why I was rushing you along."

The airport was reached without an ice storm,

although Jim and Phil watched Harry as he drove away, back down south to the warmth of New Orleans and hoping so much that he continued to avoid any weather problems. Take-off for the England-bound plane was only a few minutes later than scheduled and, after a smooth flight, they landed back at Manchester, UK.

Over the following few days Phil and Jim completed the proposal for Microwave Facilities Corporation (MFC) and mailed it to Dirk Hanson. They felt that all the details were accurate and should be attractive to the customer, including the price that was surely reasonable by any measures. Phil knew this corporation's product range and overall strategies extremely well so this was a bonus.

However, after all this and in spite of the fact that MFC had gone to the trouble of contacting Econometrics first, they still failed to get the contract.

Worst of all was the following fact. Although they tried they just could not get any feedback from MFC as to the problem. Often, following such feedback, one can re-negotiate and develop a contract that both parties can live with. But in this instance they faced a brick wall. Many years later the reasons behind these types of problems would become crystal clear - especially when there's an organisation involved in microwave, satellite or related areas.

On top of all this Phil and Sharon's marriage was clearly rapidly breaking up. As everyone knows this, so sadly, is the process that too often happens these days. "Tell me about it." as they say.

At first the future for Econotech looked decidedly rosy but dark forbidding clouds began to form on the far horizon. Firstly the large contract with a major motor manufacturer came steadily to a natural close. Due to the intense work performed almost continuously on that project virtually no time had been set aside to successfully obtain any follow-on work and into the bargain a global recession was setting in. Very soon Econotech found itself with no ongoing work and nothing imminent either.

All of the time the company was located in Majorfield's prime business district its overhead expenses were burgeoning and could only be met as long as income flowed in at a good rate. Now that new business had all but dried up Econotech was "on the wrong side of Mr. Wilkins Micawber" and within a few months the firm's bank insisted on a shutdown.

To cap it all Phil Kerridge had left the company to set up his own consultancy firm, known as Tekanalytics, within which he had some legally-binding subcontracts with Econotech.

Many quantum leaps above the levels of the Econotechs and Tekanalytics of this world, the relatively close relationship between the UK and the USA—that special UKUSA relationship—would remain absolutely vital on so many fronts, ranging from business through to political and indeed therefore *security considerations…..*

It's "funny" how impersonal relationships that are usually based upon mutual interests often persist whilst personal relationships tend increasingly to break down…..

UKUSA, Israel's Mossad organisation and the inextricable security apparatus associated with these were to prove extremely critical to Tekanalytics and therefore also to Phil and Ruth Kerridge.

Chapter 10 Special Relations

"Phil, what's this special relationship thing those politicians talk about from time to time? Do you think it has any relevance to us ordinary folk?"

As a senior executive with Tekanalytics Limited, Wilf, who has excellent technical knowledge and capabilities but knows far less about international stuff, is now getting deep into a discussion on the merits and demerits of the special relationship that remains politically correct when looking at UK/USA relations. Tekanalytics is an industrial consultancy firm specialising in high tech industries and the vagaries of this relationship are of importance to firms like theirs.

Phil: "Well, Wilf, over the decades at least following the Second World War much has been made internationally of the somewhat euphemistically termed 'special relationship' existing between the United States of America and the United Kingdom. By the way, the term 'Great Britain' is not exactly synonymous with the 'United Kingdom' because the latter includes, since 1922, Northern Ireland. So *that's* a pretty crucial distinction and one which the USA would *definitely* want defined accurately…."

"I guess the concept gained momentum with

the massive assistance the USA provided during and after World War II. This obviously included the war effort itself, with America's large-scale military actions in Europe. It also embraced the Marshall Plan under which around $13 billion was directed towards a wide range of European nations to assist them in the post-war re-building of their economies over the 1948 to 1951 period. Counteracting communism was a major driving force that led America to launch this Marshall Plan or 'European Recovery Programme' as it was officially known. And in those days $13 billion was a truly gargantuan sum, being roughly equivalent to the total annual turnover of most of the world's large corporations added together back then."

As might be expected, the United Kingdom and France were major beneficiaries of this European Recovery Programme and they were also the principal coordinators. It is interesting to observe that in 1948, i.e. at the very start of this Programme, the State of Israel was inaugurated. Now, following the end of the War, Britain's voters had seen fit to despatch Winston Churchill, who led the Tory-dominated War effort, in favour of a new socialist government led by Clement Atlee. It all seemed such a good idea – "Churchill prominent in the War effort but let Atlee's people now lead us in winning the peace".

However, that particular socialist government proved to be ineffective because of the classic socialist combination of good intentions but so often poor capabilities in practice. The UK was suffering from continued food rationing and the rampant nationalisation of "key" sectors of industry. Also, in the months preceding the State of Israel's inauguration the UK government's then foreign minister, a guy named John Treadwell, appeared to conduct his briefings in a somewhat anti-Semitic manner whilst he was discussing the situation with an Israeli who visited his office in London. Somewhat amazingly this episode was actually documented on film and the archive remains on record.

Everything, well almost everything, becomes clear in the "wonderful" light of hindsight. The post-war economic failure in the UK, which can only be laid at the feet of the hapless Atlee government, has to be seen in the context of the UK being a joint recipient of the Marshall Plan financial support. Add this to the UK's poor record of handling the problem of the Jews in Palestine both immediately after the War and during the first years of independence, and you have the makings of a greatly strained UK/USA relationship.

Whilst Britain essentially squandered its portion of the "Marshall money" on doctrinaire nationalisation, nations such as Germany (and also notably Japan) continued marching forward economically whilst Britain got left behind.

Phil continued: "This special relationship, this commonality of purpose, remains firmly in place today in spite of the advent of the 'Common Market' and more recently the European Community. From the USA in the late-1990s a politician named

Newt Gingrich publicly urged the extension of the relationship economically, rather than entering into a 'much more dangerous and risky Euro-based future for the UK'. It is frequently suggested that an attachment to the North American free trade area (NAFTA) would be more advantageous economically than remaining committed to the Euro 'gravy train'. This lends even more credence to the idea that the UK is in essence the informal 51st State of the Union."

"As things stand Britain is effectively being pulled strongly in two opposite directions: one to the East (Europe) and the other to the West (the US). At this rate it can't be long before the country is ripped down its middle! Come to think of it 'ripped off' could be an unfortunate use of words here!"

"However, with the early 21st century weakness of the Euro there is amongst most of the population a clamour for Britain to withdraw from the EU as soon as possible."

"By the way, sometimes people are understandably confused about the number of States which formally comprise the USA. The answer's fifty but occasionally people include the Federal District of Columbia and get fifty-one as the number of states. This is wrong because the sixty-nine square miles of the Federal District of Columbia is a *District* and not a State. It's usually abbreviated D.C. and it's the address of the Capitol: the White House is in Washington, D.C. A cardinal sin in the USA and elsewhere is to confuse this location with the *State* of Washington, which is approaching a thousand times the area of D.C. and as the crow flies is over two thousand miles away on the pacific coast, bordering with Canada."

Wilf now interjects with: "This is all very interesting, Phil, but often I cannot even understand the speech of the Americans. Their accents are frequently strong and they tend to use words in situations that are foreign to other English-speaking people, like us. The words 'neat' and 'bummer' are two that spring to mind. How does this simple fact square with the 'equality of language' aspect to which so much attention is placed?"

Phil again: "Look, neither of us is a 'Geordie' - a Brit from the Newcastle/Sunderland region - and as we all know they often sport very thick accents. They tend to use words in ways that seem strange to us. Can you say in all honesty, Wilf, that you always understand a Geordie?"

Wilf had to admit that he could hardly *ever* decipher what a Geordie was saying, and he therefore also admitted defeat on the American accents non-issue.

Following the American civil war, well over two centuries ago, English became the main language within North America. By the 1920s the USA came to dominate world trade and so English has become the main language of business globally. Although both Germany and Japan are also major players on the global industrial scene the USA's current strengths and legacy have made this English language so universal. Estimates put the number of native English speaking people at around 330 million worldwide, and there must be more than twice this number for whom it is their second language on which they are highly dependent. This means that well over a billion people across the globe can speak some form of English.

Wilf: "Is this all there is to it, then? Are you trying to tell me that everything's down to this English language, and virtually nothing else?"

"There are other underlying things, Wilf, such as the importance of the British Empire. Old maps of the world clearly show lots of red areas and these meant British-held territories. This of course metamorphosed to form the Commonwealth during the second half of the 21st century. But the common language spoken by both Americans and Britons is—English. Another aspect influencing language development was the geographical disposition of the UK and the USA, with the former located on the Eastern side of the Atlantic and the latter on the Western side."

"Also, where do you think the headquarters of the United Nations (the UN) is located? And which nation is far-and-away the largest contributor to the North Atlantic Treaty Organisation (NATO)? The answer in both instances is the USA."

"Like any relationship this one has not been without its strains which on occasion have become particularly marked. Examples abound: the first year or two of the Second World War when

America was late entering, America's actions in South East Asia (Cambodia, Vietnam) and to a lesser extent Grenada, the Bay of Pigs crisis, the bombing of Tripoli in a vain attempt to remove Colonel Gaddafi and his associates. Now a major, and growing, source of discontent between these two bedfellows is the issue of *security installations and their shadowy operations*."

"Incidentally, when you talk about the UK being America's 'informal' 51st state I'm glad that you apply the qualifier 'informal'."

But, Wilf immediately asked: "Why do you say this?"

"Well, we've both been to the States and we know what it's like when you've to complete – they would say 'fill out' – your immigration and customs forms. This usually happens during the final thirty minutes of the flight, doesn't it, and it's quite amusing watching passengers 'scratching about' for their passport numbers.

Some even attempting to remember their date of birth! On the customs form there's an irritating and confusing little slot where you're not supposed to fill anything in (American: 'out') and plenty of people fall into this trap. I myself have done it before and I'll bet you have too. Generally at USA customs they don't mind that too much.

My point is that it doesn't matter whether you're British, French, German, Chinese or Turkish etc., you've still got to fill out all that information just because you're an 'alien'(!)"

"I hear what you're saying Phil." said Wilf, "But

it's not so much on the personal level that this 'special relationship' operates, is it? It's surely of greater significance when you get to the political and international levels."

"Take the Falklands War for example. When you get events like the Falklands conflict, interesting things happen under this special relationship. The Argentineans' attitude to those cold and inhospitable islands, which they call the Malvinas, was that history indicated (or so they believed) the Malvinas belonged to Argentina. However, these islands had been occupied by Britain for many decades. So the conflict evolved and in the early 1980s the war began, with the UK sending a task force all the way down to the South Atlantic. At first, the USA acted as intermediary and publicly expressed antipathy to any idea that Britain might go to war for the Falklands. As usual nowadays much travelling diplomacy took place, with America's General Alexander in the hot spot this time."

"Now, there's no doubt whatsoever about the strategic importance of these islands - not least regarding global 'security' bases - that are mainly driven by a USA-based organisation. So after all it was in the interests of both the USA and the UK to ensure that the Falkland Islands remained British. Recapture by Argentina would be unthinkable because of the considerable security risk, especially with the military junta who were running that country at the time."

"Throughout the period following the

Declaration of Independence and right up to 1941 America and Britain functioned and traded essentially as two totally independent states. This was, after all, the long era of fierce national identities which really stretched way back thousands of years, to the ancient Chinese, Greeks, Egyptians, and so on. Everything changed once America entered World War II, particularly after hostilities had ceased."

"After their painful recovery during the late-1940s the European and southeast Asian nations steadily regenerated their cultures, their social fabric and their industrial bases. This continued throughout the 1950s and has only recently showed signs of stagnation. Germany and Japan had nothing to lose and everything to gain because they started in 1945-46 with totally ruined economies and deeply damaged relationships both internally and externally. This situation combined with the inherently skilled populations, with many creative people eager to play their parts in moving things onwards, provided an excellent basis for industrial expansion and all this led to the success of both these formerly aggressive and warring nations."

"Now, here's the classic scenario of these two nations, both losers in a terrible war, but both indisputable winners of the commercial and industrial peace. They achieved this by acknowledging the essential need for excellence in innovation as well as in marketing."

"Of the original, pre-1939, 'innocent' nations America remains immensely powerful because of its massive size and strength combined with great cultural talent."

Phil interrupted Wilf and tried to summarise the situation in this way:

"Here's the nation that survived the massive financial 'Wall Street' crash in the 1920s. The country that ensured that, by invention and more especially mass production, the world had cars, aircraft, typewriters, transistors, computers and indeed tremendous advances in defence and space technology. By entering World War II in December 1941, triggered by the infamous shock Japanese raid on Pearl Harbour, the Americans and their allies not only secured the peace but the War effort itself led to tremendous strides in technology, many of which could not have been foreseen."

Phil went on to point out that the USA also achieved progress by acknowledging the absolute need for excellence in technology innovation as well as bringing the right products to market. This is in basically similar mode to Germany and Japan but on a much larger scale and without the post-war devastation.

He commented further:

"Many of the important technological developments were American and the bulk of armament production took place in the United States. Battle tanks and other military vehicles, bombs, and (of major importance) fighter aircraft were borne across the Atlantic on aircraft carrier ships. Of absolutely critical importance there was also radar to detect enemy aircraft and other movements, and increasingly advanced military communications. Jamming techniques were also brought into action in order to confuse the enemy's radars."

"On the other side of the rapidly gelling special relationship, the UK also contributed key advances towards the war effort. Crucially, radar was invented by the British physicist Robert Watson-Watt in the late 1930s and this led directly to a radar network covering the south and south-east coastlines of England by 1940. This proved invaluable during the Battle of Britain that took place that year."

"Then just before Christmas 1947, in what were then the famous Bell Labs in New Jersey USA, a team of scientists made notes in their laboratory log about their latest development. Using a crystal of germanium, the forerunner of silicon today, they achieved an amplified electrical signal. The discovery was exciting enough to this team that was led by a man named William Shockley. It was also of tremendous significance to the world as a whole because this was the first transistor ever (the device, not the complete radio set) and this is absolutely pivotal to today's electronic world."

"I see," stated Wilf, in a decisive manner: "Technology, ever-advancing hardware, was the key to the war effort over 1939-1945 and clearly technology like transistors and microchips continues to evolve and represents the bedrock of the industrial economies today."

"Very eruditely put, if I may say so Wilf. But

there's yet another, rather more subtle aspect to both those wartime activities and current needs. We all know about software, at least practically everyone realises it's something to do with what you run on a PC. Far fewer people appreciate that most modern commercial software is inherently insecure. Whilst you are just running your computer in strictly stand-alone and truly personal areas, where you can be reasonably confident that no one else will illegally access it, then there's little concern about the security of your files and so on."

"There's just the possibility of someone determined enough reading your screens full of information by scanning from perhaps fifty metres or so away. But that does indeed require a highly determined and aggressive approach, targeting you or your immediate environs specifically."

"The main thing is that the advent of the Internet and its proliferation has changed everything and so there's an increasing demand for security via what is known as 'encryption'. This is your passwords and all that. It also crucially includes your virus, spam and spyware protection software such as AVG, McAfee, Norton, etc.

And, interestingly enough, this encryption idea has its roots deeply in World War II efforts. So it's certainly not the march of sheer technology alone that led to success for the allies during the War."

"It's also very much down to the intellectual effort and specifically mathematicians."

"Early in World War II, the German war effort

developed a coding machine, known as Enigma, with which they proceeded to 'encode' all their military messages. The simplest idea of coding is probably Morse code, where sequences of dots and dashes are used to replace letters of the alphabet, but coding techniques are continually becoming more sophisticated. With the German Enigma machine an entirely new basic setting was made each day, implementing a sequence known only to the originators and the (German) recipients of messages. The interception of enemy radio messages soon told the British that coding was being used and there was an urgent need to crack that code. A brilliant team of linguists and mathematicians was assembled at Bletchley Park in England and, working round the clock, this team cracked the German code as early as 1940. This was of course remarkably early in the War."

"Following this it became possible to find precisely the plans for the air offensive operations and also the Germans' North Africa campaign, therefore contributing greatly to the allies' War effort."

"This was something, something big, which Britain managed to accomplish without any external aid – not even from the Americans."

"Today, with powerful and pervasive computer technology, almost all encryption is run on computers. And this requires top-ranking mathematicians and software experts."

America has an extraordinary spectrum of people making up its population. Many have flocked to this "new world" nation from all corners of the earth, taking advantage of the unique entrepreneurial environment, or the powerful scientific heritage manifested in the universities and research organisations. Many people from vastly differing ethnic backgrounds have made their mark here, and indeed several have also made their fortunes. But "first generation" Americans continue taking strong leads: historical examples include John D. Rockefeller who revolutionised the petroleum industry and a notable modern example of a highly successful American is Bill Gates who runs Microsoft.

As the 20th century drew to its close and the world entered the third millennium America was an increasingly cosmopolitan society. At the outset, when the continent was in turmoil over two centuries ago, serious conflicts continued which were mainly between the indigenous North American Indian tribes and the incoming (mainly) Europeans. In those early years however there were few if any people from beyond Europe - an exception being the Spanish-originating Mexicans. The appalling slave trade, mainly in the 1700s and 1800s, ensured that plenty of Negroes entered the scene and became an integral part of American life although this was not, sadly, by any means always a peaceful process. This is a situation that continues right up to the present day.

During the second half of the 20th century an influx from both Eastern Europe and Asia steadily grew to make a highly significant impact on most aspects of American culture. Today, notably on the West Coast but also elsewhere on this continent, Caucasians are found in the same areas as Spanish and Orientals of virtually all types. A natural blending-in has taken place and continues to evolve.

In the main, Negroes tend to stick within their own communities but thankfully some "break out" intellectually to become professional members of society.

All these trends go deep into all aspects of the country and its culture: academe, government, and industry. There's a theory that many of the children of mixed-race marriages tend to be more intelligent (or at least more "successful") than those born of parents having the same race. And there is some strong evidence indeed to support this theory. When you look at the performance of mixed Caucasian/Oriental marriages, for example, very often they turn out to be notably well ahead of the pack. Without a shadow of a doubt many of the brilliant Americans today have family names like Chang, Chuo, Kuo, Khan.... It's by no means universal (neither Gates nor Rockefeller sound exactly oriental!) but it seems the proportion's growing.

It is not only at the human/cultural level that one gains an appreciation of the American lifestyle. It is also when one comes to look at mobility and the absolutely vast world-leading network of highways: freeways, interstates and toll roads. In recent years there has been something of a trend towards smaller cars but there were two problems with this new approach. Firstly it is of course strange to Americans and doesn't fit society's basic attitudes and secondly it is a fact that most of these cars have to be imported.

Wilf asked what really amounted to a particularly critical question:

"Isn't America, to a large extent, independent industrially?"

OK, good question so Phil had a stab at answering this:

"When an economy which is heavily dependent on motor manufacture starts seriously importing cars, as happened in the States during the 1970s and continues today, you soon see the dangerous results in the factories owned by the likes of Ford, Chrysler and General Motors. The effects of the almost daily increasing imports of these small fashionable 'autos' were devastating for the indigenous American motor manufacturers. By the time several of them had come out with new smaller models it was too late. The damage was done and the effects remain in evidence around places like Detroit, Michigan. Meanwhile, overseas manufacturers such as Volkswagen of Germany and Toyota of Japan are happily shipping cars across the Atlantic and the Pacific to their advantage and to America's most distinct discomfort."

Phil continued:

"By the 1990s a reaction had set in. This gigantic car-owning democracy began to appreciate that 'gas' (i.e. petroleum) was still pretty cheap compared to the general cost of living. So it increasingly seemed reasonable to ask: 'Why not go for some form of 'gas guzzler' once again?' This they did, but now there was a new emphasis: off-the-road types of vehicles, four-wheel drives and so on. Jeeps, rovers, land cruisers and the like all became very fashionable in both the USA and the UK. However, please note just one thing: most of these types of vehicles gulp-in gas at rates even faster than the older guzzlers of the 1960s..."

"With the gathering global fuel crisis nowadays the need for much more economic vehicles is vital. Cars like the Toyota Prius which uses a computer-optimised combination of petrol and electric and vehicles like the Honda FCX Clarity that is powered with a fuel cell are becoming effectively flagships of a new automotive crusade."

"Apart from railroads (American for what Europeans call a 'railway') there's one other piece of the jigsaw regarding regular public transport – and that's the airlines. Given the large distances involved in travelling across most states and certainly interstate, aircraft are a good option and frequently the only option that can meet either business or pleasure requirements of timing."

The extent of flying in the very busy skies above North America is much larger than anywhere else on earth. Anyone who's ever stopped at an airport like Chicago, Denver, or Kennedy (New York), or Atlanta etc., will appreciate that it's little short of mind-boggling in terms of scope and level of activity. The terrible events of September 11,

2001, followed by the fuel crisis have of course slowed down both the airframes and also the airlines industries. And now we have the ongoing implications of the recession.

However, mainly considering Boeing and Lockheed-Martin, the USA still leads the world in aircraft manufacture. Also it is hardly surprising that several large international airlines such as American Airlines, US Air and Delta are American corporations. Most of these operate transatlantic routes as well as making large numbers of internal North America flights.

Calling upon his intimate knowledge of the aerospace sector, Phil expounded about this side of the American experience:

"The space effort of the USA is probably even better known than the aircraft manufacturers or the airlines, at least outside the country. From the Mercury and Gemini flights of the early1960s, on to the giant Saturn launcher that launched men en route to the moon in the late 1960s and 1970s and then the era of the Space Shuttle. All this was driven by the Cold War that had begun between 'West' and 'East' way back in the late-1940s. This coincided with the famous time when, with characteristic drama, Winston Churchill observed that: '..an iron curtain had fallen over Eastern Europe..'. The USSR, headed by the demagogue Stalin, had become a totalitarian state that essentially squared up with the Western Alliance, headed by the USA."

"Out of the Cold War's ever-developing weaponry came steady improvements in the rocket technology needed to launch missiles and indeed, ultimately, to take humans into space. The choice of living and working in America, made by the world expert German rocket scientist Werner von Braun, gave the USA a practically unbeatable advantage in this critical field. Whilst each side, the USSR and the USA, developed and deployed more and more long range missiles with nuclear warheads parallel to this we first had the unnerving Russian Sputnik, then man in space (notably the Russian, Yuri Gargarin). This was inevitably followed by a continuing sequence of American satellites and astronauts. By the mid-1960s American capability had reached the point where a manned journey to the moon was distinctly on the cards and in 1962 President John F. Kennedy made his ground-breaking speech to Congress in which he determined that an American would be the first to set foot on the moon within the decade. After several successful launches of the mighty Saturn V rocket it is well known that Neil Armstrong and Buzz Aldrin achieved this ambition by landing and walking on the lunar surface in 1969."

"The Cold War continued unabated and soon both sides boasted enough missiles each to obliterate the other many times over. It was (deliberately?) called 'Mutually Assured Destruction' but the acronym actually came first and military commanders fitted the words around the letters. Everyone agreed it was MAD but, like any drug on which one can become hooked, as long as the Cold War lasted, the MAD situation just had to continue.

During the 1980s the technology associated with this military stand-off reached what was in retrospect an important climax. President Ronald Reagan announced the development of what was then termed the 'Strategic Defense Initiative' or SDI. This was nicknamed the 'Star Wars' programme because it required the development and deployment of space-based defence systems capable of carrying high-power lasers which could literally knock out all offensive enemy land, sea and air systems."

"The Soviet premier at the time, Leonid Breznev, did not take particularly kindly to this announcement - claiming that, not only their offensive, but also all the USSR's defensive systems would immediately be vulnerable. Notwithstanding, Star Wars research and development went ahead during the mid-1980s and towards 1990, with Gorbachev now in power following the death of Breznev."

"Then as everybody knows the Soviet Union collapsed, leaving Russia and the Ukraine as the dominant nations (the latter country retains an immense nuclear arsenal). However, what is not at all well known is that Star Wars very definitely continues; with a five billion dollar programme including satellite-controlled laser guns, infra-red detectors and the grandiosely-named 'space command'. And *international 'security' installations play a vital role in this.*"

"Again with the luxury of hindsight, it turns out that the Soviet Union's economy was skewed to such a massive extent in favour of the military that all other sectors were suffering scandalously. Whether or not the government of the USA (or its security apparatus) was aware at the time, the fact is that the effects of Star Wars became effectively the last straw for the USSR economy."

"For around a decade the Russian-led Commonwealth of Independent States (the CIS) looked as though a new, 'Western-oriented' and truly democratic-trending nation-state was growing healthily in west Europe and Asia. However, once President Vladimir Putin attained power it rapidly became clear that Russia was en route to an immensely strong comeback—a frighteningly resurgent Russia making massive economic and political gains from its large oil and gas resources."

"In spite of recent 'cosmetic' political changes Putin, he of the cold light-blue eyes and scary earnest face, runs the nation with an effective rod of iron and continues to place increasing pressures on foreigners in positions of any responsibility in Russian industries—such as BP for example. The possibilities for exerting economic and political pressure on western nations are now there by means of steadily escalating gas prices, in particular."

"In common with many countries there are, however, underlying fault-lines in Russia that may yet upset the Putin applecart. The activities of the Mafia and of 'wild-card' people like Vladimir Zhrinovsky should always be watched. You never know when such people might see a potential opportunity in their terms and seize the moment."

As things stand, not only in America but also most of the world, the emphasis now is on rapid reaction forces rather than immense power blocs facing each other in some MAD scenario. It is the capability for rapid response to crisis situations like the two Gulf Wars, Desert Fox over 1998/1999, the Serbian situation and the War against Terror campaigns (such as Afghanistan) that exercise most military minds nowadays.

Phil added:

"For three decades, through the 1960s, the 1970s, and the 1980s, the expenditure in the States and many other countries had risen inexorably. This in turn meant that substantial sectors of many a nation's industries were geared to military requirements. A wide range of firms gained their living entirely, or mainly, from contracts led by the appropriate government department, but this wasn't all ending up in technology as such because significant 'spin-offs' came to benefit commercial products. The special relationship with the UK, being America's number one contact in Europe and elsewhere, meant that a large amount of technology sharing occurred between the two countries."

"This sharing included increasing elements of high technology. Also, over the years a steadily increasing amount of 'security apparatus' was vested in Britain (and other countries) by the USA."

Both Phil and Wilf thought this was particularly interesting because the Cold War was over and surely the requirements for bases, which had been specifically developed with the Cold War in mind, would now reduce considerably? Fine, events like the Gulf Wars and so on would surely demand considerable security networks. But commonsense says these must be on a much smaller scale than what had been demanded when the USSR was in full fling.

But Wilf wasn't at all happy about the trends regarding "security investment", so he asked Phil:

"But hasn't there recently been observed some gradual reduction in the bases following the end of the Cold War? The 'Threat', that military stand-off between the two original superpowers, is now surely removed except for this resurgent Russia and the bases were originally geared-up for that Cold War, weren't they?"

"Quite the contrary—absolutely no sign of any reduction and in fact general increases," replied Phil emphatically. "The fact is that American 'security' bases continue to be expanded and ostensibly made more sophisticated at an alarming rate."

Wilf, now in a very sombre mood, eventually managed to croak: "Well, Phil, the nature of our firm's business makes it even more likely that security interceptions of our communications would be much more frequent and probing than for most people. So surely they, the security people, will be pretty keen to put pressure on us - even making every effort to get us closed down."

Meanwhile Phil had made efforts to visit GCHQ, with the help of his various contacts, and he accepted an invitation for a meeting scheduled for 28th January that included a chance to see this organisation's main communications processing facility. It was quite a straightforward journey down across Britain's southern motorway network and along the M5 to Cheltenham. But it turned out that he had an awful ulterior motive for undertaking this trip.

The meeting went along well enough and Phil was left with a strong feeling of business satisfaction. It looked like this could bode well for strong future relations with GCHQ. Phil drove off the campus and *appeared* to be leaving the area. However, he only drove a few hundred yards away where he parked in a street well within walking distance of the establishment. In his mind Phil was literally hell-bent on taking some form of revenge on GCHQ for all he considered they had done in an attempt to undermine him - especially that ill-fated London seminar the memory of which would remain stuck in his gut forever.

Now into the darkness of the evening Phil donned clothing that contrasted totally with the strict business suit and tie he wore for the earlier business meeting. He donned a simply-styled baseball cap, a neat green open-neck shirt, well-pressed blue jeans and trainers. And he walked steadily back towards the outer wall of GCHQ with a nondescript back-pack containing yellow and red paint cans plus a spray applicator. All this was readied for action well ahead of time (in fact back in Majorfield). Once directly outside the perimeter wall, in a relatively quiet area, he rapidly deployed his "paint-spray" kit and ensured plenty of paint was emptied into the areas on the other side. Reactions were first muted but soon intensified with: "Blimey - what's going on? Better sound the alarm and get the campus police onto this. What a dreadful and annoying thing to do. And all this paint will be very difficult and time-consuming to clear up."

Phil swiftly collected his equipment and calmly walked back to his vehicle - always unobtrusively checking that no one followed. As far as he could see no one did follow or even get sight of what he had done so he drove off confidently.

But some years later on he was practically sure that someone, some keen-eyed staff member of GCHQ or an external informer, *did* come to recognise that it was indeed Phil Kerridge who perpetrated the "paint-spray crime" on the evening of 28th January.

Chapter 11 A Decent Burial

On Wednesday the first of August, still around a year before the company's final demise, Phil made one of his now infrequent visits to Econometrics:

"It's Phil, haven't seen you for ages... How the devil are you and how did the Munich visit go?" Phil told Tony Cresswell about the trip, the genuinely interested responses to the seminar - and some flavour of the remainder of the "adventure". Tony listened very intently to the fibre optics news.

"This sounds fine Phil. So next let's mail out, carefully and thoughtfully, to some of the most interested people and follow-up as necessary to see what business we can generate from this."

Now Phil had become a little confused as to whom, Econometrics or Tekanalytics, should be beneficiaries here. But, for the moment at least, he kind of humoured Tony.

Then, once again, Tony popped the "time-dishonoured" question:

"Have you unloaded those Econometrics shares, yet?"

"No, of course I haven't Tony." Phil replied in his usual confident manner although inside he was now anything but confident. Concern gave way to downright worry. Did an Econometrics' business crisis loom? How could he "independently" verify this one way or the other? What could he realistically do about it anyway? Who, oh *who*, would now be remotely interested in buying his shares in this "dodgy" firm?

As usual in any busy office the telephone rang many times that late morning.

After one such incoming call Sandra, Econometrics' senior secretary, urgently phoned Phil and recommended that he journey back to Tekanalytics' offices because a highly promising phone message had been received there.

"Thanks Sandra, I'll get away now." Phil donned his cycling kit and pedalled his way through Majorfield's traffic, across the city to Tekanalytics. The incoming call came from a company previously unknown to him - Zantech. Someone in this firm, they didn't leave a name or even contacting data, was urgently attempting to talk with Phil Kerridge.

"Hello, is that Zantech?"

"Yes." Came the reply and Phil's hopes were raised. However, apparently it was *another* Zantech and not the one from which the previous call had come. Whatever Phil tried didn't work and however long he waited for the "original Zantech" to call again they didn't call. This "hot lead" just went completely cold.

Tekanalytics' first year would be completed within a couple of months and this very odd Zantech event would represent the beginning of a sequence of many other maddening occurrences.

The next eight years were to be liberally sprinkled with "strange events"……

"Ruth, in one week's time Tekanalytics will have its first birthday. We've not been doing too badly, have we?"

Ruth expressed enthusiasm for the venture, pointing out that the part-time teaching contract at Majorfield City University provided a reasonably regular monthly income that helped smooth out the considerable irregularities in consultancy revenue. It was by no means a reasonably large monthly amount, but my goodness it helped flatten-out the otherwise "roller coaster ride".

By the beginning of November that year they had indications from their accountant that Tekanalytics had actually made quite a reasonable profit - something almost unheard of for a small enterprise's first year of trading.

"Is this the president of the corporation himself I'm put directly through to? - The 'head honcho' so to speak?" It was unmistakably Matt Framlin's inimitable voice and humorous style both when on the phone and face-to-face.

"How would you feel about lecturing specialised seminars on electronics packaging, mainly for industrialists?"

"Well, as you know Matt it's something I've got a considerable background in……"

The upshot of this conversation was a meeting between Phil and a heck of a character known as: Colonel Roland Hoover-Amery.

Matt first introduced this guy's name to Phil over the phone:

"Hey, look Matt, are you having me on? That just can't be his real name, surely? I just don't believe that anyone would have a name like that. Come on, you're surely joking again."

"Oh no—I'm not joking this time and Colonel Roland Hoover-Amery most certainly is his real name." Matt was firm about this, so it must be right, Phil supposed.

"*Hello,* good morning to you. It's Philip Kerridge isn't it? It really is so jolly good of you to take the trouble of coming all this way down to Redhill for our meeting."

The Colonel was indeed a character. He was every bit the character Phil had imagined since that fascinating phone call from Matt.

Subsequent meetings would take place mainly in a small and cosy restaurant named "Tarries" just along the road. This charming hostelry is practically an adjunct of Hoover-Amery's company.

Roland was the epitome of classic old-fashioned English charm.

Ex-guards and Royal Marines, obviously a dyed-in-the-wool Tory party supporter and something of an "electronics industry" eccentric, Roland sat in his office that was full of silver trophies won for various pursuits. He always wore a smart, dark, three-piece business suit, a tightly knotted necktie and a brilliant white shirt with cuff-links (24 carat gold I'll bet, thought Phil…).

Another thing was that he had the agonizing

choice of which car to drive to work in the morning. Either it was the Roller (i.e. the Silver Rolls Royce) or, what a come-down, maybe this morning it should be the Jaguar. Phil never discovered what, if any, factors governed Roland's choice in this regard. Secretly Phil despised Roland in many ways, steadily growing in the belief that he really amounted to a greedy anachronism in today's business world.

Apparently, Roland was a multi-millionaire. He definitely owned something like eighty acres of prime Surrey country estate, embracing woods and even what amounted to a small farm. He employed two completely separate groups of people: one group looked after the house, grounds and farm; whilst the other made things like printed circuits, various electronics assemblies and administered both these and the seminars wing of the really small electronics company that was Roland's "professional hobby". His firm bore the name: "Home Counties Electronics".

Like most people who'd ever had business dealings with him, Roland thought a lot of Matt. Because Matt had recommended Phil for these lectures, it more or less followed that he would be expected to behave like any good Tory-voting guy with an electronics background should. Into the bargain, and of special importance as far as Roland was concerned, Phil's Birstington background and his impeccable professional qualifications rendered him practically ideal for the task of leading any "Home Counties Electronics" seminars.

There was a final exquisite touch. Phil now lived and worked in that "Home Counties city north of Watford", namely Majorfield.

Had Phil been located in almost any other "northern" city, worst of all, Rockford with its "dark satanic mills", this would have put an entirely different complexion on the matter.

Given this mutually supportive history Phil and Roland discovered rapid rapport together and their business liaison looked set for a virtually guaranteed lifetime.

On the eighth of January the following year Phil attended a seminar, run by Home Counties Electronics, held at the Forest Oaks Hotel near Redhill. The subject was naturally electronics packaging and Roland regarded this as preparatory to possibly organising a similar-styled event in "the frozen North", i.e. Majorfield later in the year.

Apart from "packaging", the year began with Telanalytics strongly researching what are known generically as "electronic displays".

Well known examples of these include modern TV screens, computer monitors, calculators, lap-top computers with their compact flat panels and also many car dashboard panels that are increasingly electronic.

Unlike advanced packaging, satellite communications etc., things like electronic displays are much less sensitive as far as international security is concerned. To some extent this meant that Telanalytics enjoyed an almost "interference free" year and business proceeded along steadily.

The first "Gulf Crisis", following immediately from Saddam Hussein's invasion of Kuwait five months' earlier, proceeded to fever pitch during the second week of January. Tekanalytics, like many businesses (especially international ones) experienced the effects of imminent war:

"Ruth: have you noticed – everything's exceptionally quiet?"

"Even by Tekanalytics' standards, do you mean Phil?"

"Look, it's not that bad," Phil was always naturally keen to stand up for Tekanalytics at all times, "There have been no mail deliveries and no incoming telephone calls for forty-eight hours now. And that *is* exceptional."

This situation continued right through the next few days until, overnight 16/17 January, tremendous activity occurred in the Middle East. The immense assemblage of weaponry that was positioned from the eastern Mediterranean to the Persian Gulf and Saudi Arabia exploded into belligerent life. The first Gulf War had begun. There were the cruise missiles, the sophisticated air power at both high and very low levels, and the Scud missiles, launched by Iraq, several of which landed on Israeli soil. Then it was on to the vast land offensive and the extensive taking of prisoners.

When the effects of war are relatively remote, like missiles killing people in foreign lands, many of us tend to become practically desensitised and incapable of really feeling for the people and those around them. However, surely no one will ever forget the carnage manifested on that highway out of Kuwait, the multitude of Iraqi soldiers attempting to flee only to be smashed down and blown to pieces by allied firepower. This is a typical legacy of most dictatorial tyrants. More recently another tyrant, Slobodan Milosovich, has been responsible for the most terrible inhuman acts in the Balkans. I wonder how many people are really sad this guy finally died at his own hands?

With the first Gulf War over and the allies obviously claiming victory, life began the process of returning to normal. This victory would remain Pyrrhic for many years because it could only have been maintained under strict United Nations resolutions. These required the removal of the Iraqis from Kuwait but not yet, most unfortunately, the ejection from power of the wicked Saddam Hussein and his henchmen. This process had to wait until 2003 and the second Gulf War with its aftermath.

At last we could say goodbye to that major hiccup in the lives of us all and the months ahead were full of positive progress. On Monday the fifteenth of April Phil and Ruth drove to London, where Ruth made her way by rail down to her sister in Kent. Phil continued on to Redhill where he visited Roland. After a brisk meeting the two retired to "Tarries" restaurant for lunch, which began with a dry sherry each - what else would two traditional English gentlemen sip before lunch? As a result of this meeting there now existed a plan for the "Majorfield Electronics Packaging" seminar campaign.

On the Tuesday Ruth and Phil enjoyed the best show either had ever experienced, namely Les Miserables at the Palace Theatre in the West End of London. To obtain tickets for this show in its prime location Ruth had to book many months in advance, but it was well worth waiting for because Les Miserables has everything. It tells a powerful story through great music and fun. This is an unconditional plug: make sure to experience this show at the first opportunity—wherever it may be on.

Whilst admittedly being a totally different subject Les Miserables was far better than Daisy Pulls it Off which Phil had seen with his first wife many years' earlier. Perhaps the absence of any agonizing pain after the Les Miserables show had something to do with it?

Following several phone calls, on the Wednesday afternoon Phil visited the US Embassy in Grosvenor Square to do some research. His research was quite successful and he innocently returned to rendezvous with Ruth and make the long haul back to Majorfield.

"Innocently" is the accurate word, because literally anyone visiting a place like the US Embassy is subject to the most intense security checks, whether they appreciate it or not. These have taken on a sophisticated electronic and optronic form for many years and the subjects will never be aware that they are being checked.

With Phil's history he would have been thoroughly checked, re-checked, and checked again. Now the authorities generated yet more details on his activities: his precise timings, his mode of dress and exactly what he ordered to read and scan, from the moment he even phoned the Embassy to the very second he left the building. With the aid of hidden "micro-cameras" high-definition video images of him would also have been recorded.

On a Thursday in the second week that June, Ruth and Phil set off for an address called "Patten House" which is located near Skipbridge. Sharon, Phil's first wife, worked there and they had an appointment to meet with her for the express purpose of obtaining her signature on an important and urgent document.

This was an extremely weird meeting. Sharon appeared dishevelled and looked ill. She also had a nasty disfiguring scar on her face.

Amazingly and disturbingly all the time she constantly referred to Phil as her current husband in spite of the fact they had already been divorced for some months. She even introduced him to her colleagues as her husband. And Ruth was not exactly pleased to observe this behaviour!

On the Monday following this extraordinary and disorientating event, Phil travelled to London again on contract to provide another seminar along the lines of the one he presented in Munich the previous year. The contractor had the complete responsibility for marketing this event, i.e. maximizing the numbers of delegates - generally termed "bums on seats". In different circumstances Phil would have added his energies to this marketing effort, but any such thoughts were entirely out of the question during the past six months.

Phil checked into his London hotel and slept a reasonably comfortable night. He always missed Ruth terribly when away on his own, but this is business and all one can do is "knuckle down to it".

Completing the short but very warm and humid walk from the hotel to "Howard's College", the venue for the seminar, Phil asked directions of several people he met. However, no one knew anything about the event and it took him almost one hour to locate the rooms in which this series of seminars were taking place. It would be well known to most of his friends and acquaintances that hardly anything annoys Phil more than this sort of "unbusinesslike" behaviour. For a start, prior to the event he had never been presented with any form of local map showing the location of the seminars. Then upon arrival at Howard's College there were no signs showing the way.

Perhaps the fact that *only three delegates* turned up explains something…..

During the summer the first electronics displays report was completed and mailed to the client, with a really good response. So at least something was moving in the right direction. Woven into his busy schedule Phil also had to find time for developing the electronics packaging seminar (remembering Roland).

Even this represented yet another strange experience. Roland's offices had only just about discovered the wonders of fax, and Roland insisted on using up old Home Counties' stationery. This had printed upon it the incorrect phone number and of course no fax number at all. Into the bargain the paper size must have been what used to be known as "quarto". It all seemed so extraordinary coming from a guy who owned a large estate in the county of Surrey, plus a "roller" and a Jaguar. - But then perhaps not…?

Came the day, October 30, and the seminar would be happening at the Victoria Regina Hotel. Around fifty delegates, excellent speakers and a small but well-focused exhibition ensured a highly successful event.

"Great stuff. Let's begin planning for the next one, starting Monday next week." Roland exuded his usual energetic business acumen.

Now of course, being an astute businessman, Roland had progressively and independently enquired about Phil's experience and general professional activities. By now the "international security machine" had very cleverly and deftly infiltrated misinformation into the system, including Phil's records. This had applied even when he was with the small Econometrics company.

One way and another Phil was effectively stopped from developing the seminars. This was through extremely subtle means such as extraordinary and otherwise inexplicable blocks when attempting to encourage people to attend the seminars. Obviously such an environment is extremely frustrating and it was several years before Phil caught on to what must be happening.

As the year drew towards an end and New Year approached, external events (especially the "global economy"), became less and less conducive to growing businesses of any kind. A global recession had already set in and intensified.

Another major event would unfold, as far as Phil and several others were concerned, with the news reaching Phil around three weeks before Christmas.

Now several significant things had changed over the previous few years. Firstly, he and Ruth were living some distance from Majorfield's city centre and neither of them had much reason to visit often. Secondly, since mid-year Econometrics hadn't offered any new contracts to Tekanalytics and for that matter there wasn't any need from Tekanalytics viewpoint because plenty happened.

As a direct result Phil had hardly contacted Econometrics for well over a year.

On Tuesday December 3 Phil phoned to make sure it would be acceptable for him to arrive and he entered Econometrics' offices, having driven from Shawbeck which was Ruth and Phil's new home village near Majorfield.

"Hello stranger, how are you then?" It was good

to see Econometrics' Sandra again and she certainly gave the outward impression of cheerfulness. The lady was always very good at disguising her inner feelings. But, under the surface, something was clearly wrong, terribly wrong....

"I'm fine, thanks. I've been so extremely busy for many, many months now and living outside Majorfield it's been practically impossible to come over. How is everything and everyone at Econometrics?"

Phil experienced that kind of awful sinking feeling even as he asked, because it suddenly occurred to him that these offices were nothing like as busy as when he last entered. Where were all the support staff? Why was everyone looking so gloomy, especially with Christmas less than three weeks away?

Tony Cresswell was still there, even sitting at the same desk. He said:

"I told you to sell those Econometrics shares long, long ago, didn't I?"

The forceful tone barely concealed within Tony's comments chilled Phil to his bones.

At last, albeit far too late, he now realised that Tony had been completely serious during the transitional years of the two decades.

All those occasions when he repeatedly urged Phil to make every effort to off-load those shares.

Swallowing awkwardly, Phil somehow managed to ask Tony:

"What do you reckon they are worth now?"

"Nothing - absolutely nothing," stated Tony flatly.

"I can't believe it," responded Phil. To him this dialogue was rapidly becoming almost surreal.

"Well, you'd better," continued Tony. "Want to chat about what's been happening here?"

"Yes, OK," said Phil weakly.

These two guys who had been close colleagues only eighteen months' ago left the offices and found a quiet pub in which to talk. Tony told Phil about the gathering storm, and the ensuing gloom, concerning Econometrics. It became apparent that the firm could not generate follow-on business from that large motor manufacturer with whom it had such an excellent contract during the previous year. No further worthwhile business was forthcoming and to cover even the fixed overheads like rent and basic salaries Econometrics desperately needed high-value contracts.

The advent of the global recession literally represented "the final straw that broke the camel's (i.e. Econometrics') back" and about two weeks earlier Jim had announced to all the staff the disastrous news: —he had no option but to place the firm into liquidation.

Tony would be taking up a European marketing position with the company who had been his major client anyway for the past four years. This meant taking the entire family to Italy - which of course would be exciting for some....

Tony had one final point about this dreadful saga: "There has been one other thing, Phil, and apparently it has something to do with international security and eavesdropping. Tony Brasher (you remember Tony, don't you?) first mentioned it at one of the management meetings around a year ago, and he should know because when he was at Telecable, before becoming a venture capitalist, this amounted to a serious part of his responsibilities."

"What Tony Brasher said is potentially extremely important for all of us Phil. Although many familiar influences bring small firms down in an increasingly large percentage of cases it is clear that truly sinister forces are also at work. I don't even know exactly whom we are talking about here, but I can say that international security agencies are involved and the backgrounds of both yourself and Jim Kidd, in particular, are vital aspects. You probably remember Jim used to be with the major defence supplier Krafton Aerospace? Come to think of it I now remember that when you worked at Birstington one of your projects was a contract with Krafton."

Tony continued: "I've spoken with Tony Brasher privately, Phil, and he actually mentioned one further thing that I must tell you about. Somehow Tony Brasher retains connections that provide him with credible knowledge concerning the activities of 'security'. Now never mind your background at Birstington, it's your marriage to Ruth, with her experiences in Israel, that is also apparently a serious factor. Tony Brasher is certain that these factors, not only the other better-known aspects, have been material and perhaps fatal in bringing down Econometrics."

This so stunned Phil he couldn't think of any sensible response.

Tony Cresswell was sympathetic and still very much a personal friend. Hopefully, when things calmed down a bit, they would meet again in more congenial circumstances.

Phil realised there would be hardly any hope of ever recovering any of the money "invested" in Econometrics – money that he had such difficulty raising in the first place six years back. So, no doubt this would be "goodbye to fifteen thousand pounds sterling". He paused for a moment and thought: "what with the awful divorce, and Ruth is by no means wealthy, and now this. It seems like God is trying to break me financially. The trouble is, the family are being effectively destroyed along with me."

Melodramatic or over-the-top? The more he thought about things the less he considered that he was being in the least bit melodramatic let alone over-the-top. There was one curious ray of light and it went something like this in Phil's mind: "I experienced two completely terrible Christmases way back and almost anything now would almost certainly still pale in comparison". However, although this news could hardly be construed any other way but highly negatively, this is *material* stuff. In reality it is not the mind-wrenching, soul-destroying, tear-jerking scenarios of impossible emotional circumstances, and then of impending divorce, etc.

Twelve days before Christmas, Phil very tentatively rang the front door bell of Jim and Mary Kidd's home. Admittedly Phil had phoned and arranged this get-together earlier that week, but all the same, things were understandably tense. How different, how very different, the atmosphere was compared with "the old days". Fair enough, everyone was friendly at least on a superficial level, but gone were the deep and ostensibly genuine relationships.

"Come in Phil, it's good to see you. Well, anyway I think it's good!" Jim opened the front door to him.

Mary, close to tears but admirably just about remaining in control, just said:

"Oh, Phil, this is absolutely the end of everything, isn't it?" The conversation was awkward and stilted and towards the end of the highly informal meeting Phil asked, nervously:

"Jim, do you consider there's any hope, even at this late stage, of saving Econometrics? After all, both of us know the effort and indeed the love, sweat and tears you've put into this enterprise over the years."

"No," The terseness of Jim's reply made Phil almost jump: "No, things have now reached a definitely irreversible stage, Philip. I think you know the basic financial problems that the firm has increasingly endured over the past year. We just couldn't overcome the appalling cash-flow situation and the bank finally found themselves forced into asking us to wind-up. For Tony Brasher at Multidimensional Investments (the venture capital company responsible for investing in Econometrics) it is also a terrible blow of course. Tony tried just about everything, as did we all, to rescue the firm from collapse. No, Phil. The only thing left to do is provide Econometrics with a decent burial."

This must have been tremendously ignominious for Jim who still is without a doubt a brilliant guy with a terrific talent for high-tech management. Perhaps indeed his expertise would be better deployed within a large, defence or aerospace orientated organisation?

The overall impact upon Philip Kerridge was decidedly mixed.

On the one hand his "sacred cow" amongst all conceivable company types, specifically Econometrics Limited, would be dead in the water, come the New Year. Not only fifteen thousand pounds (about $23K) would be lost forever, but confidence in such a robust organisation was also totally trashed. And Tony Brasher was *so* very positive about Econometrics' robustness only four years' ago?

On the other hand there was the distinct irony that Tekanalytics seemed to somehow power on with great new contracts. However, Phil's thinking was along the lines: "If this can happen to a growing, respected, incorporated and robust twelve-year old company like Econometrics – what chance Tekanalytics?"

And what about the points Tony Cresswell had been making regarding security?

All that applied equally to Tekanalytics because it involved both himself and also of course his lovely new wife Ruth.

Whatever sort of future could possibly lie ahead of them now?

Inside, Phil was frankly terrified. Outwardly he just did his best to remain calm. After all he and Ruth had a business to run…………

In spite of the recession the new electronics displays report continued selling well and, in the April, Phil responded to an enquiry from the major Japanese corporation known as Hynetsu:

"Am I through to Tekanalytics?"

"Yes, you are – who would you like to speak to?"

"Phil Kerridge, please."

"That's me. Can you please give me your name and then hopefully we can see how we could help you sir?"

From this simple beginning of a routine business conversation there followed a brief (all of thirty minutes) meeting at Hynetsu's European headquarters at Milton Keynes in England. Martin and Clive wanted to use the information-base Tekanalytics had developed for the displays research to perform some special work for Hynetsu.

"We've compared your data with information

provided by others, and it compares most favourably. In addition we also really like your report."

"Thank you very much," responded Phil enthusiastically.

"Right, what we'd like you to consider is…."

Martin and Clive went on to explain Hynetsu's requirements, which were complex at the same time as being wide-ranging.

Basically, they were driven by demands of the Tokyo world headquarters and the ultimate aim was to provide board level directors with the information needed to decide whether or not to invest in building a major factory in Europe.

There was around twenty-six thousand US dollars (approximately £13 thousand sterling) worth of consultancy work in this project.

"Now," thought Phil, "haven't I encountered a sum of money roughly similar to this somewhere else in recent years?" Of course one can never assume that such income will become entirely available because so much is disposed of by expenditure. But it was a nice if superficial idea anyway.

Tekanalytics staff worked extremely hard over the next four months, completing the Hynetsu project totally to their satisfaction. During this project such momentum was sustained and new research techniques developed that all Tekanalytics staff confidently believed they must now be "on a roll". It could only be a matter of time and marketing effort before vital new business came in.

Well, it didn't.

Whatever energetic attempts were made, however hard the teams tried, it seemed impossible to stir anyone else towards providing Tekanalytics with any more business. As Christmas approached (yes – yet another Christmas) it became clear that many staff would have to be "let go" and, remembering Econometrics' excessive overheads, the decision was also made to move back into much more modest premises.

One reason for the dearth of business was definitely the continuing global recession. Another reason could possibly be Tekanalytics relative newness on the scene, "and yet, we did excellent business with Hynetsu," thought Phil.

But – what about that more sinister underlying factor: the international security one about which Tony Cresswell spoke with such meaningful vigour? There wasn't a shadow of doubt in Phil's mind but that here was a true and really severe problem that was spreading like a 'flu virus and threatening to engulf us all.

Chapter 12 Stop Them!

"Ruth, have you looked at the incoming e-mails this morning?" Phil enquires in his usual frantically urgent manner.

"Yes," replied the tranquil Ruth.

"Well, is anything there, anything interesting?"

"Umm. Alright there's one saying 'gorgeous Moscow girlies', or thinly disguised words to that effect, and another telling us and thousands of others how to make at least £10,000 per month just by sending e-mails..."

"These sound really interesting - we'll have no problems advancing our business then if these enquiries keep coming!" Phil responds sarcastically.

One important aspect of e-mail is that whether its junk mail, business or "private domestic", your messages are being intercepted because they can be eavesdropped upon at any time and for many of us that's likely to be a major proportion of the time.

Mid-morning is fast approaching and Phil realises that he must place a phone call to a company based in Torquay, a coastal town in Devon, England. He picks up the phone and keys in the number:

"Good morning, this is Phil Kerridge here. Could I speak to Norman please?"

"Certainly Phil, I'll put you through now."

Phil needs to ask Norman for his views about a fairly sensitive issue for any company. He needs as much data as possible concerning Norman's company and its current operations. More than you could ever find from the Internet.

"Hello, Norman, how are you today?"

The conversation takes the usual courteous line and relations are reasonably friendly until the sensitive request for company details is broached.

"Are you still manufacturing millimetre-wave modules for communication links, and is this a growing part of the business Norman? Can you give me some idea of the price for a mid-range modem product?"

"Well Phil, the answer is yes to your question about our millimetre-wave modules but I'm afraid we must treat the answers to your other questions as company confidential. That is unless you have a specific application in mind and we get well advanced into negotiations."

This is typical of the usual situation and it prompts Dave, who has only been in this consultancy business a few months, to ask:

"How then do you find out the details on companies? Things like where their products sell, what prices are genuinely offered and some idea at least as to what their total sales might be?"

"You can get a certain amount of information

about most companies from public domain sources although you need to know exactly what you are looking for and a major irritation is that historical links are usually just left on the web servers. Additionally, incorporated firms - Limited, Incorporated, etc. - are legally required to annually lodge, in national facilities, details of their company's structure and financial performance. This information is then obtainable from central government operated sources and, in the USA for example, it can be accessed on publicly available computer databases in major libraries. Indeed, you can access annual and often even quarterly reports from the companies' web sites."

"So, even quite small firms have to do the public lodgment if they are incorporated?"

"Yes, and naturally companies tend to regard this as quite a pain. They would rather not have to do it at all, in the same mould as having to pay one's taxes. Worse still of course when companies are advised that various people are indeed accessing the national databases and obtaining details about them they do tend to become suspicious and at the extreme will 'blacklist' such people. When the companies concerned are in the high-tech sector, anything to do with satellite systems for example, their suspicions are intensified and 'security' agencies of the appropriate national governments can often become involved."

"But for goodness sake the key question surely is how can anyone or any company, determine that it's you who is trying to access information on them? Fair enough, when you communicate with them by telephone, e-mail or fax then obviously a link has been established and they know it's you. But what about when you access information from these central sources?"

"This is indeed the most serious issue Dave because they can find out by contacting an appropriate agency. It's all to do with what is sometimes euphemistically called 'security' and this 'security' thing comes in various guises, some of which are downright insidious. Whilst everyone, from individuals to international corporations, needs protection and some reasonable level of security the crunch comes in deciding just where 'security' ceases to be just that and degenerates into eavesdropping and worse. Where do you draw the line between the legitimate provision of security and the violation of civil liberty?"

"You see, the fact is there exists an international network which has a more or less hidden agenda. This really amounts to a global conspiracy and the agencies involved already possess a highly sophisticated capability for global electronic eavesdropping and message analysis. Our telephone, e-mail and fax communications are frequently intercepted and analysed on a selected basis. It's just as easy when any of us visits a central source for accessing a database, whether we do this by physically going there or 'going there' electronically e.g. by 'surfing the Web, the Internet'. This can be monitored in much the same way." "Repeatedly the agencies claim a foul i.e. they want to suggest they don't do this. But then they would, wouldn't they? And in any event how can anyone check because by definition the activities are secret?!"

Ruth and Dave interjected almost simultaneously and Ruth just won out by exclaiming:

"Hey, wait a moment, surely you don't mean *everyone's* conversations are intercepted from time to time?

It must be stretching credulity to believe that dear old Peggy Jones at number 21 actually has her phone conversations intercepted, analysed and recorded by some security agency in a foreign land."

"Oh yes," continued Phil, "I'm afraid that even dear old Peggy will be monitored at least occasionally. She probably won't be monitored to anything like the same extent as someone who is involved in the high-tech sphere of things. Also - and this is extremely important so please listen carefully - the security agencies use search techniques including software that searches for key words and phrases, like 'security agency'... These systems also learn automatically with time and experience so that anyone, via any telecom links, that's tending to use these key phrases frequently becomes fair game."

"Our organisation, indeed myself particularly, are special targets for several reasons which I think are quite clear. By the way, did you know we could be accused of treasonable activities if anyone in 'authority' came to hear about these conversations?"

Now, there is of course absolutely nothing new about small businesses as such. From time immemorial many innocent people have occupied themselves and obtained their livings by running small businesses. Indeed in early times, well before the industrial revolution of the 18th and 19th centuries, sole traders and small firms were *the only enterprises*. This applied to everything from grocers' shops to cabinet makers.

The prime example from two millennia past was Jesus Christ who worked as a carpenter in his father's joinery business in Nazareth during his early years including his teens.

The 21st century business environment is however absolutely different, with big business in the ascendancy and large, often international corporations having the power and making most of the running. This "information age" is principally driven by hundreds of these enormous corporations, each often having tens of billions of dollars in annual sales, as well as hundreds of thousands of relatively small firms - many being sole traders or not much larger. The domination of global software markets by Microsoft is well known and both IBM ("Big Blue") and Hewlett-Packard enjoy annual sales that currently push relentlessly towards and through the hundred billion dollar level, i.e. $100,000 million.

What a contrast with the tiny companies many of whom consider themselves to be doing well if their annual sales enter the "dizzy heights" of perhaps $200,000. The arithmetic's rather easy, isn't it, with these smaller brethren selling in the region of *one-millionth* the trade value of the large international corporations. Several of the smaller and medium-sized fry are frequently bought-up by the predatory "big guys" and this picture applies to business on the world scale.

A real contrast exists if your small firm is not such a large-scale business, and not a sales outlet (an agent) for manufacturers, but instead makes its living by selling information. And that's true of a consultancy.

"Our small and specialised consultancy firm is headed by a guy whose background is in the security-critical areas of radio-frequency and microwave engineering. The trouble is that he keeps 'suspiciously' enquiring about the financial and other operational aspects of technology companies right across the globe ranging from 'minnows' to giants. Ideally, if our firm could come to know all there is about every technology-based company in the world, and store this information for processing towards our studies, then business life would be fine—except for the fact it's necessary to keep up-to-date almost on a continuous basis. No wonder that before long corporations become suspicious and essentially 'blacklist' us".

Phil is now in full swing.

"What is more we have even sold reports to customers as far apart, geographically and politically, as California and the Russian city of

St. Petersburg. Also remember that we have sold both 'off the shelf' reports and conducted custom consultancy business with departments of the British Government."

"Another interesting factor must be the fact that my wife, Ruth, has that history of working with the Arabs in Israel and the security risk that has flowed from that. Again, Ruth could be in terrible trouble eventually - flowing from this past involvement and her subsequent marriage to me."

"One more thing, as if these features alone were not enough, your founder did indeed teach British military staff electronics and telecommunications back in the early 1980s and for several years before. All this means that we just have to be on the active files of several national and international security agencies. So, you can now see the potential danger we're in."

"Should I consider that my job here is safe?" Dave is now noticeably worried about the entire situation. "But in any case we surely cannot consider that all or most of our 'lost business' can be placed fairly and squarely with subtle blocking tactics by these security agencies?"

"Are any of our jobs safe, Dave? Maybe the best idea would to seriously consider writing a book on this entire background and our experiences to date. However, you are absolutely right to point out that this security situation is almost certainly not the only reason why, in certain instances, we lose business which we thought we stood an excellent chance of obtaining."

"Whilst I am convinced that security agency tactics are a major threat to us, there are also other influences which almost any trading company would encounter. These include the simple fact that organisations develop away from any need for consultancy services from time to time. They also enter periods of such massive preoccupation with other important on-going corporate matters that consultancy is the last thing on their minds, and finance available for desired consultancy is just unavailable. Over time we must have unwittingly encountered all these factors and usually, in such circumstances, customers won't be exactly forthcoming with describing their problems or pre-occupations - especially with an outfit like us."

"Our small size can also be a problem. Often during a presentation it's when I'm forced to admit that we are only a 'ma and pop' show that things become awfully quiet. Lots of organisations just don't like dealing with small firms. Well, not *this* small anyway."

"Also we do have a specific example of a large corporate client with whom we enjoyed excellent repeat business stretching over several years. Later, on attempting to develop further business we learnt through our senior contact there that their particular division was virtually broke and therefore under the severest financial pressure. Such honesty and openness is unusual. Remember, we did check the likely validity of our contact's comments and they stacked up almost perfectly with other information available to us at the time."

Dave said, "We've all noticed that customers do 'clam up' on us from time to time, and you are saying this is not always because they've been nobbled by whoever it may be in some security organisation? And about this small size aspect? Doesn't it lead to a classic chicken and egg situation: we can't get work because we're small, but we can't grow because we can't get work?"

"Yes," said Phil: "but none of us should become paranoid about the security thing. Although we all realise this to be a risk, let me state categorically now, that I am actively resisting paranoia about this wretched problem. And you're completely right about the small size paradox. Although Dave, isn't the term 'nobbled' a bit strong?"

Dave: "No. I don't think the term 'nobbled' is unduly strong at all. It means 'tampering with' and that's just what would be happening if your theory is right at all. Also, while we're about it, who are these outfits and where do we reckon they're located?"

Phil: "This does get us into the nitty gritty, doesn't it? In the UK where we are based there are obviously the well known 'MI's', namely MI5 and MI6. There's also the shadowy Government Communications Headquarters (GCHQ). All of these will be aware of our backgrounds with Ruth and the Arabs and myself teaching British military staff electronics and telecommunications. I reckon that they will also be knowledgeable of practically all our business activities."

"Flipping heck, Phil," Dave is getting increasingly nervous by the minute, "How could this possibly be? How on earth can you support that kind of statement? This sounds way off beam to me?"

Phil again: "Well look, for a moment let's consider some examples of client situations where we either did what we can realistically consider good quality work (do we ever do anything else?). And yet the entire process stopped for no apparent reason. Also there are some other interesting scenarios where 'non-security' 'normal' reasons for a full stop to any business seem unlikely. Let us be absolutely clear: there are two directions in which this thing can work. Either a corporation can enlist the assistance of an agency on a perceived security threat, or an agency itself can alert corporations to individuals and organisations thought likely to present security threats."

"Before going over examples let me complete my answer to your previous question about the likely identities and locations of agencies. I've just mentioned the British 'MI's' and GCHQ. Now in the States, apart from the well-known FBI, there's something which I understand is termed the National Security Agency (NSA), or similar and there's evidence that this outfit extends internationally. For a start it would be amazing if this NSA didn't have bases in the UK given that 'special relationship' that is talked about in government circles both here and in America."

"Don't you think it would be equally surprising if there weren't formal link-ups between British and US agencies, given the tools available in this advanced computer and communications age?"

"There's one more thing, which I think would be of importance in certain areas of our business—and that's the 'Israeli connection'."

Now Ruth, who had been hearing most of this conversation, came in abruptly with: "Do you mean because some of the corporations have bases in Israel, or at least sell into the country?"

"Frankly, yes. Several of our client contacts have Israeli bases and many have customers in that country," retorted Phil.

"For a start look at Global Radio Systems, who have facilities in both New York and Tel Aviv. This is the corporation I first contacted back in the early 1990s and then met senior board members at that trade show in Los Angeles in 1994. We had an especially hot off-the-shelf report newly published and absolutely in their sector of interest, in fact they were even one of the companies covered in that study. Much time was spent including taking them through the study. But there was never a subsequent sniff of any real business and we never did get even slightly close to closing a deal with them."

"At the same show an Israeli electronics corporation, Islectron Limited, showcased its products and Islectron actually became a hot prospect because their president was keen to purchase a copy of the study at the time. We were verbally promised an order but as we all know nothing further happened. Since we had no previous dealings with this concern whatsoever I am prepared to state almost categorically that this must have become 'security blocked'."

The scene now is the National Security Agency, based in Maryland, USA:

"You are most strongly advised not to have anything further to do with this guy, or his consultancy organisation, - right." The demand is being put on the line in no uncertain terms by one John Goldinberg who is a senior business advisor with this Agency.

Gary Lindsee (a board-level executive with Islectron) replies: "But, we have already been specifically recommended to Phil Kerridge by an executive of ours who operates in another division. Jeff Finn knows him well, trusts him, and what's more Tekanalytics did an excellent job for that division recently. In turn, we also thoroughly trust the opinion of our executive. Look, we need the product of this consultancy contract..."

"Never mind that. We are instructing you, on grounds of national security, to cease all active contact with this guy and the related consultancy firm immediately. You absolutely must not have any further communications with Kerridge. If you desist - if you were to decide to ignore our instruction - then I'm afraid we should have no option but to shut down on all our business with your company and indeed further restrictions are likely to follow such as a possible cessation of all business between yourselves and the national government."

This type of "big brother blackmailing" tactic may sound overbearing and even horrific—but it happens frequently. Most of these types of strong and sensitive dialogues would only take place in relatively secure environments, such as "quiet" corners of pubs and bars. Also it will have been ensured that both parties are extensively debriefed and debugged, including tables, chairs and any remaining local bar fittings, before the meeting and this "discussion".

Over the years the world has become increasingly sensitive, increasingly worried about security for a variety of reasons ranging from commercial concerns to deeper concerns surrounding the expanding activities of terrorists and despotic national leaders of one-party states. It's all highly understandable and everyone is affected.

"Obviously we are not in the least involved in any way with terrorist activities of any sort, let alone anyone remotely connected with Al'Qaeda or the 'Continuity IRA'. It's the possible unknown and subtle connections with the industrial ramifications that have got the security people worried about us." Philip is particularly keen to make this point clear to all those present.

"There are many other examples of problems we've encountered, that strongly imply a 'security dimension', and I just want to run over a couple of these."

"A year or two back I was contacted by a senior guy in the Israeli offices of a large international industrial research and publishing company. As a result of various telephone discussions and fax exchanges we agreed formats and sent them two 'solid' well-honed proposals for consultancy. It's worth mentioning that they were effectively driven by an already existing customer requirement. They seemed to receive our proposals well and expressed a desire to meet at a mutually convenient time and location."

"As it happened, I had to visit Rome for just one day whilst en route to Southern Italy and this fitted in well with my contact. We agreed to rendezvous for breakfast - isn't it funny how it's 'always breakfast', in the foyer of the Hotel Roma Ritz de Luxe which is near the city centre and this arrangement went to plan, with no major problems."

"Now even at the time I thought there was something strange about the whole affair. This applied not only to the meeting itself but also its immediate aftermath. We settled down to the meeting and appeared to get on perfectly well. Relevant experiences were related and my host informed me that an unusually high proportion of their company's proposals led to final consultancy contracts. Towards the end of the meeting he requested yet another proposal, in the field of fibre optic systems, adding that back at the Israeli offices they were this moment primed to await the arrival of this as soon as possible."

Apparently a fax from the Israeli offices was due to be with Tekanalytics in Majorfield that very morning.

Phil said: "I'll inform our office immediately following this meeting and get on with preparing the proposal as soon as I'm back in the UK."

"We initially parted outside in the street, right in front of the Hotel Roma Ritz de Luxe but, as previously mentioned to my host, we both planned to visit a local trade show and I suggested sharing a cab for making our way to this. The strange thing was that he suddenly, for no apparent reason, refused to share any cab. We did eventually both visit the trade show but, although I saw him briefly there the atmosphere was distinctly cold and we didn't speak. On contacting Majorfield it was clear there was, of course: *no fax*."

Within a few days Phil was at his desk again in Majorfield and, in spite of not having received the promised fax, the new Tekanalytics proposal was duly faxed to Tel Aviv.

"The whole episode was extraordinarily strange and in fact this was the last we ever heard from that organisation. Our new faxed proposal was not even acknowledged and all follow-ups were likewise ignored."

"This was in all probability a good example of combined personal and photographic surveillance. It would have been relatively straightforward to install a digital micro-camera in an unobtrusive location in the dining room and/or the foyer of the Hotel Roma Ritz de Luxe and arrange for this to focus on yours truly.

Then the stored images would be transmitted back "real time", i.e. there and then probably by satellite, to Israeli HQ for immediate study, analysis and comparison."

At Mossad HQ in Tel-Aviv: "Yes, this is the same guy whom we followed and interviewed, including his wife, a few years ago in Israel. This is definitely the same guy on whom we have a file and he is a suspected security risk. We can tell you that, on grounds of national security, you must cease all active contact with this man and the related consultancy firm immediately. You absolutely must not have any further communications with this guy."

Dave: "Haven't we heard something rather like this before? Didn't the NSA in Maryland, North America come up with a commentary not dissimilar to this Israeli security one?"

"Well, there is one distinction well worth making here. In this instance there would be no quibbles, no one would argue even for a moment. In fact it is even possible that my host may not even be a direct executive employee of the industrial research and publishing company at all. He could be an agent with the security organisation itself."

"Here's another example, with the difference that in this case not only did we supply two high-quality consultancy reports for the corporation involved but the entire venture was initiated by a personal friend of mine. In a way this further drives home the point about quality because there's no way we would come short on quality bearing in mind the personal friend involvement. Quite the contrary."

"Phil, is this the one where we both did so much intensive research on antenna companies which was a real sweat, back last summer?"

Ruth understandably wanted a part of the action here so she broke in with:

"Yes, you're quite right. We first provided rapidly an available study we have on markets for them to look at. This seemed fine and so I met their guy when he was in the UK, because they wanted to proceed with that large analysis we had proposed. If you remember it was on a Saturday and meant that I had to drive quite a distance to the meeting."

Now, in business today no one in their right senses complains about the need to travel, sometimes substantially, to meet contacts and clients. Especially irritating, however, are those occasions when all this leads to is either low-value work or - worse still - nothing.

"Do you recollect the main locations of that corporation?"

"Was their headquarters in the UK and didn't they have a fairly large outfit in Israel, again?"

"Well, you *almost* have them sorted out accurately, Ruth, the only thing is that their ultimate HQ is in the USA."

"Our dealings were entirely with the USA

and our friend here in the UK. But isn't the Israel connection interesting once more?"

"We did *all* the right things, with our usual high quality input, providing that initial report rapidly as requested and then completing the large analytical task in depth. We frequently exchanged various aspects of the work with the company to ensure that the final product was precisely what they wanted. The final well presented study, almost entirely tabular you probably remember, was faxed to them and we even made sure to include carefully thought out and listed ideas for further much-needed consultancy effort by them and indeed by us."

"During follow-ups later on our friend in the corporation told us that their president would like to meet me and, perhaps a tad naively, we were encouraged by this response. Maybe he really did want to meet in an effort to find out about our so-called security 'misdemeanors'!"

"That's many, many, months ago now," said Ruth, "Can you remind me about what's happened since on this one?"

"That's easy: nothing, completely 'bottom-barrel nothing'. I know we shouldn't ever get annoyed, still less let it show and especially in business, but in this event I must admit that I have sent them e-mails that must come across as evidence of considerable irritation. Looking back on that 'the president would like to meet me' comment I now reckon that he was probably hoping to retrieve anything he possibly could, rendered dreadfully difficult for them by the security situation."

"You see, these people are in an even more sensitive situation than most others to whom we have supplied services, because their products have to do with things like satellite and other wireless communications. Into the bargain, we know they also have the Israel connection. Given the undoubted quality of our last study for them specifically, in terms of its excellent match to their needs, the ensuing dialogue must have been remarkably similar to the one I was talking about earlier regarding Global Radio Systems."

By this time Dave is busy working on another new report. He'd heard more than enough about all the firm's problems and decided to "get his head well and truly down"... So discussions now continue mainly between Ruth and Phil, with Ruth exclaiming:

"All the examples you have just been describing and reminding us about have this common feature of an Israel element. Are *all* our 'problem clients' likely to be in this category, then?"

"No. And I think it's important for all of us to get the Israel element into proper focus."

"I guess you're referring to the fact that this nation continues to experience major threats to its sovereignty from all sorts of quarters, ranging from various Arab states through terrorist groups to factions outside the Middle East. What with the appalling tragedy at the Munich Olympics, the ongoing and not-infrequent car bombs in Israel itself, the terrorist hostage-taking, explosions on board El-Al aircraft and the general history of persecution. No one considering all this can or should be surprised at the stance regarding security that Israel now takes."

"That's right and then as we have already noted you and I are 'special cases' because of our various backgrounds. In your case with Israel itself, and in mine because of my military-oriented electronics experience."

"Put the general scenario and our special situation together and you have the underlying rationale for much of the problem."

"It's ironic, because we know and most of our friends are well aware that we both love the country and its people. We respect Israel's heritage and also we have an abiding love for both Arab and Jew regardless of race. You and I are just about the last sort of people on God's earth to be prejudiced one way or the other."

All Tekanalytics staff are aware of other clear examples of client problems where security issues are certainly significant, if not paramount, but there is no discernible Israel connection.

Take, for example, the affair regarding that UK government research department. The firm had enjoyed good repeat business with this department over a period of several years and a senior executive dropped by the firm's stand at an international exhibition. He (the senior executive) spent about two hours in discussion with Phil and clearly considered that Tekanalytics could provide them with support they considered they were going to need.

Fully two years and many meetings and discussions later, almost precisely to the day, an initial meeting had been fixed at the department's stand at another exhibition:

"Hello, it's good to meet you Peter." The stand manager was alone, which is never recommended, but he seemed a nice guy.

"Good to meet up with you as well. I guess Clive has told you about me and this idea of our meeting here to discuss various matters relating to possible consultancy business?"

It turned out that Clive was anything but prepared for this meeting but since hardly any other people were now around and still fewer were coming on to the stand they enjoyed a useful, pleasant and wide-ranging discussion. They agreed to wait until the division's relatively new Business Manager, Andy Traksby, returned to the stand from conference attendance duties so that everybody could then share in more detail. Eventually Andy did return and again an apparently useful discussion ensued, albeit truncated due to yet another conference session that Andy needed to attend.

"Well, Andy, following all this can we set a time for us to meet again on Thursday, when Clive has indicated he will be present here? I know he wants this meeting."

In something of a rush everyone agreed that 10:45 a.m. was a mutually convenient time for all to meet on the Thursday since it happened that it was coffee time at the vital conference. Everything, literally everything it seemed came a long second to this practically revered conference. Admittedly this was slightly risky, because Phil appeared to be the only one who actually entered this meeting arrangement in his Blackberry. At this time Phil considered these people to be true professionals who would automatically set this information in place almost immediately. He also reasonably assumed that they would naturally inform Clive at their HQ just to ensure that he would know what to expect on the Thursday.

Ahead of that Thursday morning Phil planned his journey to the exhibition venue, and arrived there at 10:30 which was good timing… There was a comfortable fifteen minutes to spare that provided enough time to tidy up and enjoy a brief comfort break just ahead of this meeting. Then it was along the concourse and up to the client's stand that was now clearly in sight and he could already recognise Clive standing there. Both guys stated, almost simultaneously:

"Good morning. It's great to meet you again." – It had been well over a year since they last met.

Clive responded with: "Did you have a good trip?" and then Phil briefly described the efficiency of the various train journeys, since considering that he was staying in this city for several days, local public transport was the preferred method of travelling. Admittedly Clive seemed rather surprised:

"Oh, you've not come from your offices this morning or last night, then?"

This was hugely unsettling. How could Clive possibly make the mistake of thinking he had only just arrived at the exhibition for the first time, when only two days ago, at this very location, he had arranged this meeting specifically to include him as well as Andrew Traksby? There was something spooky about all this, but Phil sort of brushed his uncertainties aside and pressed on in a friendly technical/business discussion with Clive.

After *about twenty minutes* into this one-on-one discussion Phil suddenly became agitated and rapidly looked at his wristwatch. He observed that the time was well past 11:00 and yet there was still no sign of Andy. Obviously Clive was alerted to Phil's sudden actions and Phil felt obliged to explain:

"Andy's late. I suppose he's held up with someone he's met at the conference?"

"Yes, probably - why - is this a problem?" Clive queried.

"Well," Phil replied (still believing that Clive understood about the pre-arranged meeting): "We won't get much time together for our meeting unless he gets here soon because I know that time for him, indeed for all of us, is at a premium."

This completely "threw" Clive who obviously had no idea about any meeting and this episode was not exactly a good portent towards advancing business. In a few minutes however Andy turned up and a meeting of sorts was started. Now at least Clive could be deeply involved, and it was he who was, after all, the guy who approached Philip all of two years ago and was still sharply keen about developing a consultancy relationship. The meeting was interesting but all the time Phil was uneasy about Andy's body language and other quite negative indications. The meeting began to draw to a close.

Clive: "Well, don't you think that it would be a good and positive idea anyway for Phil to come over to us and spend a few days immersing himself in the technologies and the people? Generally getting up to speed regarding what we do and where we think we're heading?"

This seemed fair enough and a most positive and progressive suggestion, based upon experience and a good knowledge of the capabilities of your opposite number. Bearing this in mind, Andy's response was especially interesting:

"No, I don't…." said Andy, "I can't see what benefit could possibly come to us from any such exercise."

This was such a bland, yet from Phil's viewpoint ignorant response that it drew the following somewhat dramatic final retort from him:

Phil said, whilst rising out of his chair:

"Well, I just have to say that I am extremely disappointed, *extremely disappointed.* And I should like it to go on record that I mean this in the most pragmatic business sense. After all the time, two entire years, that has flowed by since Clive and I first met and the unprofessional attitudes displayed regarding this meeting arrangement for example it would appear most reasonable for me to expect better than this. I repeat that I am, I think most understandably, *extremely disappointed*."

That "plonker" Andy returned to his much-cherished conference without further comment, whilst Phil attempted the difficult task of settling down. Clive remained on the stand with Phil and, whilst also not commenting on the debacle just witnessed, acted surprisingly positively about various technological developments in which they would probably require support. Phil couldn't understand how he (Clive) could now possibly imagine that Phil would ever want to develop any form of business relationship with them again - ever.

For little more than the sake of common courtesy, after all this was a "public" stand, Phil pretended to look excited and went so far, later on that week, as to supply them (i.e. Clive) with some brief material gained from a little research effort.

"That's rather like another story we discussed just a few moments ago. And once again many, many, months have elapsed haven't they?" said Ruth:

"Can you bring us up to speed regarding what's happened since on this one?"

It is Phil's turn for near-repetition, "Oh yes, as you'll probably guess, nothing from them and therefore nothing from us either. This sort of thing is great for business, just great!"

"Particularly when they originally approached

us and when the prospects appeared so genuinely excellent. But I think I know what probably happened. You see, the mature and experienced Clive would probably not be made somehow aware of our 'security problem', whereas Andy could be so aware. In any case it could well have been that Andy was made so aware (or ensured this on his own initiative) in those precious two days between 'arranging' that meeting and the meeting time itself..."

"All of this was in the UK – at 'home' so to speak. But we've also experienced yet another bizarre episode that began life in the UK and ended in California..."

Like so many of Tekanalytics' experiences, this started with selling its off the shelf industry reports. The firm received an e-mail from a big player in California, who requested further details on two of its studies. Obviously the details required were supplied and to cut a long negotiating story short they purchased the reports. Some problems were experienced with software versions but these relatively minor difficulties were soon overcome. In all practical respects the customer appeared more than happy with the reports and that, for the moment at least, was that.

It was at Stansted airport in the UK that Phil first met Rod Sterman. Phil found his way to the correct queue for check-in applying to the one-hour flight to Paris and simply began talking with the smart and alert American standing beside him. Could it be an extraordinary coincidence that he was also in the same line of business as Phil operated? Also he was working for the same big player to whom Tekanalytics had earlier sold those copies of its reports. Although to be precise his division was not the same one.

Rod worked for the government systems division on the corporation's software side. The manner of this meeting meant that Rod and Phil had adjoining boarding passes and therefore sat together on the plane.

That was, for Phil at least, a pleasant, interesting and constructive conversation, an enjoyable flight, and the two businessmen parted after some highly useful new directions from Rod regarding Phil's journeys in Paris.

Later that same year Phil was committed to a business trip in California. This trip was centred on San Jose and took in firms as far north as the San Francisco environs. It was summer time and the weather was hot – it was even unusually hot for California. He rented a car and began the journey north out of San Jose. As anyone knows when they've done it, the journey takes you through the rolling foothills, which are dry and parched at this time of the year, up through Palo Alto and Stanford and on towards the Golden Gate Bridge of "San Fran". It was to be Phil's first sight ever of the Golden Gate and on this northerly run you get glimpses of this beautiful structure from several miles south. Then, quite suddenly, the imposing and famous bridge is only a short distance away and you are on it in a trice. The experience, for that's what it is to the newcomer, is hard to describe and really is awesome. It is also hard to imagine the fact that regular commuters etc. just accept this as part of their normal surroundings.

To visit his client he had to take a hotel room that night and had been fortunate enough to find, and book, a suitable room in the beautiful Hotel San Bernardino. There were gorgeous carvings of horses in the foyer area and "comfort" was an understatement. He even managed a short swim in the hotel's pool. It felt a little like Birstington, this. For some strange reason almost like Birstington in the sun!

The following morning he drove along to the client's facility and stopped at the usual security gate. The guard looked at him and asked the same question he must ask hundreds of times each day:

"Good morning, sir." There is a slight pause, then:

"May I see your ID please?"

Now this raised a slight problem because time is now short for the meeting, there being about ten minutes to go, and Phil had left all his ID back in the hotel, where he is staying for one more night. This is very naughty since in the States you are supposed by law, as a minimum, to have your driving licence with you at all times when in charge of a vehicle.

"Sorry, the best I have is this official letter from Mrs. Dwightham, which verifies that I have been invited here for a meeting."

"Sorry, sir, but I must insist upon something including a recognisable photograph of you."

"Oh, heck, I'm afraid that I have inadvertently left my passport back in the hotel safe. Do you want me to return and get it - although the meeting's due to begin in ten minutes?"

There ensued a phone conversation between the security guard and Mrs. Dwightham. Things were finally sorted out and Phil was allowed through. Approximately ten people were present for the meeting, which was all about the corporation's current activities at this facility as well as Tekanalytics' activities and offerings, those that could benefit the corporation.

"Could you perform for us, if we commissioned you, a study on the industry - the players, products, and competition - in the area of multi-mode radio modems?"

Phil knew about the corporation's products of this type and had a good grasp of the industry, so he was able to answer with confidence and credibility that Tekanalytics could indeed perform this work. Mrs. Dwightham is kind enough to take time in showing him around the local area of the facility, which he finds extremely interesting. She knows Rod Sterman but unfortunately he is out that day visiting a customer in another State. However, Phil is able to leave a friendly message on Rod's voice mail that morning and obviously looked forward to hearing back from him. Phil's message included "local" contacting information and also a reminder of his UK co-ordinates. He also asked Mrs. Dwightham to remember him to Rod. Without a doubt he can expect, on normal human past experience, to hear from Rod in the fairly near future at least.

Can you guess the real outcome? That's right, you guessed correctly, there never has been any response from the guy from that "San Fran" day to this—and Phil was not in the least surprised.

Remember how Phil and Rod had met in that small UK airport check-in queue? The normal friendly conversation they easily struck up, the generally congenial atmosphere? No doubt about it, and it can't be paranoia of any form, Rod had been "got at" or maybe had taken what for him were standard security precautions. He had been decisively told or at least guided not to have any further contact with Phil. On thinking seriously about it there can be no other answer that makes any sense whatsoever.

At the time Phil had considered that airport meeting to be sheer coincidence, and not so much of a coincidence at that because there are many organisations around that require microwave expertise and products. This included his geographical region and also of course the fact of the Paris event.

However these subsequent happenings (or non-happenings) strongly suggested that the airport meeting itself could even well have been deliberately engineered by people acting on behalf of security agencies, so that the face-to-face rendezvous would be highly likely to occur.

Effective facial and body language, from a well-trained person, could indeed ensure that it would definitely occur (disregarding extremes such as emergencies).

Once the face-to-face meeting is established then information "mining" of the most immediate and active kind is taking place. In today's world superficially attractive meetings can be subtly engineered without raising suspicion, instead stimulating the belief (however fleetingly) that all's well and "this is a marvellous potential business opportunity".

The real reason, however, is of course *industrial surveillance and concerted official efforts at high level to stop trade in several situations – particularly anything involving individuals whom they consider in any way suspect.*

Chapter 13 Searching

It all began with the supposedly chance discovery of an extremely interesting feature about the security agencies, which appeared in the supplement on computer connectivity attached to "News Daily Digest", a national paper. Two Tekanalytics staff experts, Derek Rawlings and Frank Goodley, were working together on a wide range of security matters that could affect Tekanalytics' business.

"Frank, have you seen this?"

"Let's read it through together Derek. Look, I think this could well be highly relevant to us."

Derek and Frank scanned the feature article, and then read it carefully in detail. Frank exclaimed:

"Take a look at those large white balls and the dish antennas. Also, note what they say about intercepting microwave link beams and even underground cables. We should be concerned with this. Let's be clear about it, our expertise is deep within most of the technologies themselves. As responsible executives in Tekanalytics you and I are literally up at the sharp end in terms of interest from these people. OK, so they monitor most transmissions as a matter of course anyway - but, boy wouldn't they just be vitally interested in what we're all about?"

"You know we must, we just have to, find out much more about these 'comedians'. It's obviously in our interests and we could also assist others in the process by at least making them aware as to what's happening."

The feature article provided just enough information for Derek and Frank to get started and their first "port of call" would be Harry Blackwall, who was a Euro MP with interests in this entire security thing.

"Have you e-mailed Harry Blackwall, at the European Union?"

Derek is keen to ensure that no stone is left unturned in this quest for information on all avenues concerning international security issues.

"Yes," replied Frank, "I did that three days ago but there's still no reply at all."

One week later an interesting looking package arrived in the normal Tekanalytics mail. This, it turned out, contained a complete report provided by the European Parliament on several subjects concerned with political control technologies. Included within these subjects is indeed the issue of the shadowy security agencies and the threat they posed to free international trade.

There were further extraordinary developments. For instance, fully two months after Tekanalytics had obtained the report by normal mail, they suddenly received an e-mail from the European Parliament. This mail item was an apology for the delay in replying, telling them that unfortunately they didn't hold a copy and suggesting they try the European Information Centre - contacting information was provided....

Although the amount of material on this subject, in the report on political control technologies, is relatively brief it is very useful in itself and there are several references to published books and reports.

Frank reacted. "Look at all those references to research work which various people have completed in this area. It's been rather like walking through a region where you're imperilled by land mines. Back in the 1970s there was that key UK-based team, led by Duncan Campbell, the original discoverers of the National Security Agency's global capabilities for eavesdropping on anyone. These people were actually arrested under Britain's Official Secrets legislation, being accused of literally 'plotting against the state'. Yet all they had done was to uncover material available from open sources, i.e. literally anyone could have done this from material directly available."

"The trial was effectively thrown out of court and this represented a major shift in official attitudes towards such research."

"Duncan Campbell wrote a tongue-in-cheek book about all this:

'The Unsinkable Aircraft Carrier', was published by Michael Joseph (that's London) in 1984. Meanwhile a guy named James Bamford performed research on global signals intelligence operations and reported upon what he termed 'The Puzzle Palace'. He wrote a book with just that title, published by Sidgwick & Guildford, London, way back in 1983. Bamford assessed the total investment involved in the worldwide security apparatus as being around one billion US dollars at that time. And investment has continued apace right up to the present, so there's almost certainly over ten billion dollars in it right now."

"Well," remarked Derek who is listening intently to all this: "Isn't there anything more up-to-date and still detailed?"

During the 1980s and 1990s many people made further discoveries about the security networks and wrote articles and papers that were published in various journals and magazines. One of the most diligent researchers (probably *the* most diligent) is a Kiwi called Nicky Hager who reminded everybody in graphic detail that this security thing is far from being confined to the northern hemisphere. The Antipodes had also been hijacked by these insidious security people and Hager's New Zealand was very much in the forefront. Nicky Hager wrote: "Secret Power: New Zealand's Role in the International Spy Network" which was published by Craig Potten Publishing, New Zealand in 1996.

Now with this book Craig Potten has bravely published an excellent treatise by Nicky Hager, although the publisher is barely known outside its home country and this fact made it quite a challenge for Derek and Frank to try obtaining a copy. Notably, it proved virtually impossible to obtain contacting details for Craig Potten (telephone or fax - no e-mails in those days) via the usual sources.

Derek reported: "Frank, I've just received a fax by return from those people we tried in Wellington and they've never heard of Nicky Hager. They did, however, provide co-ordinates for Craig Potten, for which we should forever be in their debt."

Craig Potten responded most helpfully to Derek's fax, supplying full details with ISBN number, price and availability for the book.

Whilst planning on purchasing the book for Tekanalytics in the future, to suit present purposes, Derek explored traditional library loan possibilities.

"Do you stock a copy of 'Secret Power: New Zealand's Role in the International Spy Network' amongst your reference or loan items?" Derek always gave full details of the book including the vital ISBN number.

"No—sorry—we've checked carefully and this is one that we just don't appear to have."

This story was repeated many times as Derek phoned a range of likely large city libraries. Suddenly he had one of those vital, if unexpected, brain waves. Surely there would be a much better chance of a library having a copy of a book like this where it is associated with a research group concentrating on international governments and defence-orientated studies? And Derek not only knew of such a research group, he also had a personal friend who worked at the appropriate institution - the University of Rockford.

"Bingo! Frank - we've located a copy of that mercurial book by Nicky Hager and we can arrange for borrowing it. What do ya know?"

"Derek, isn't there a problem here? Since this book was written mainly about the New Zealand situation does this not mean that we have lots on the Kiwis but hardly anything on any other country?"

"No. Although obviously written with a strong Kiwi—i.e. New Zealand—emphasis, Secret Power provides an excellent and deep coverage of the subject in an overall sense. There are getting on for 250 pages to the main part of the book and with the appendices included the total length is nearer 300 pages. Yes, there are obviously lots of New Zealand details but when we remember that here we are dealing with a truly global network it's necessary to include much of great interest regarding other countries (especially the UK and the USA). Nicky Hager weaves this story together very well."

For about five minutes Frank scanned through "Secret Power", put it down on the table, and then said in a loud voice: "Flipping heck, it's almost unreadable... Open it at practically any page randomly and you find loads of acronyms and a text that's almost impossible for a layperson to read. Most of the diagrams and many of the pictures are however really well presented but some are a bit naff I reckon."

"I don't dispute what you say, Derek. I'm sure that it amounts essentially to a condensed thesis and by the way I'm afraid acronyms and technical terms are pervasive in defence and telecoms discourses. Nicky Hager prepared that text for people who are professional in the field or in related government departments or indeed academics. There was never the intention of reaching out to the ordinary person or the uninitiated for that matter."

Nicky Hager's book is about what is known as the UKUSA System, the global network known as ECHELON, the effects of the Cold War, much on New Zealand-based security installations (also much on others elsewhere—globally), electronic eavesdropping and military intelligence missions. He discusses security indoctrination, GCHQ and Charteridge in the UK as well as Fort Meade in the USA, the ubiquitous security buildings without any windows, the importance of satellite communications systems -and much else besides.

Extraordinary as it must seem, given the relatively small size of the islands in terms of both geography and population, there was yet another brilliant Kiwi named Barry Smith who provided everyone with the fundamental reasons behind all this. Behind most of what humanity gets up to these days and exactly how it fits is foretold in the Holy Bible. Many years before Tekanalytics was born, way back in Phil Kerridge's Birstington days, a guy named Harvey Stockbridge had talked enthusiastically about Barry Smith.

Now, back to the "Derek and Frank show":

"Derek, an hour or two ago you asked a pertinent

question, which was along the lines of 'were there any further up-to-date books that were relevant to our deliberations'. Well, it's not just the 'high profile' books and articles with a clear emphasis on security that we need to look at. This 'other Kiwi', going by the name Barry Smith, uncovers some highly significant and fundamental stuff that underlies much of the security paranoia."

"Barry, sadly recently deceased, is mainly remembered for the uncompromising talks which he gave in most countries. Over the two-year period 1987 to 1989 he turned the main themes of his talks into a book bearing the title: 'Final Notice'. This was published by 'Barry Smith Family Evangelism' back in '89. In his book, as in his talks, Barry develops the background to the present-day world political, sociological, spiritual and economic scene. He clearly shows that many of the political ills of today go way back at least several centuries, to the times of the Illuminati and then, later, the Jesuits. Apparently a noble-sounding guy with the name Ignatius de Loyola started the Illuminati and he used a range of behavioural techniques to very effectively influence people, amongst them logic, metaphysics and telepathy."

"I guess that, two centuries ago, there weren't many computers or telecoms around so things like metaphysics and telepathy had to be resorted to!" joked Derek.

More or less ignoring that comment, Frank continued. "There are many other links, but you have to read Barry Smith's book to gain a real understanding. Barry also blends in much concerning personal and corporate security and he comments on satellite systems together with the Australian intelligence gathering facility known as 'Pine Gap'. This is located right in the middle of the continent - near Alice Springs."

Derek is eager to interrupt (otherwise he had that disconcerting feeling that Frank could possibly continue forever) "What about the Internet?"

"What are you getting at by asking 'what about the Internet'? Do you mean how does it fit in with all this security stuff?" questioned Frank.

"No - well that's important too, of course, but I was thinking that surely we could obtain some useful information by surfing the Net?"

By the mid-1990s the concept of "Internet Cafés" had spread to many regions of the world. The idea is simple enough and quite entrepreneurial. An interested trader, usually a partnership or small firm, decides to set up a facility which must be open to the public and which is fitted out with an array of computer terminals. Each of these terminals is capable of connecting to the Internet. Either the trader will already own or rent suitable premises, or he or she will identify and obtain something that would suit this type of operation. Particularly good locations are around reasonably large towns or cities providing access to business people, academics or students who would make up most of the potential customers. Most public libraries and many hotels have Internet café facilities comprising arrays of computer terminals.

Frank responded to Derek by suggesting: "Let's explore to see whether there's anything like an 'Internet Café' located fairly locally and then book time for some intensive 'Web Surfing'. This way we can avoid any 'eyes that are most likely spying on our internal systems'"

Although their local town has a population of some 100,000-plus people Derek and Frank failed to identify any Internet Café or similar establishment there. However, checking further afield yielded positive results and two such cafés were identified.

"There's this one in Fairhead, Derek, and I've arranged to go over there on Thursday afternoon."

Frank duly arrived at this café at 2 o'clock in the afternoon that Thursday.

It's a surprisingly scruffy place in a questionable neighbourhood - the sort of location where you wonder if there will be any of your car left when you return to the parking lot. Everything is in a ground floor area with around fifteen PCs on tables set against the walls. None-too-comfortable stools are available for you to sit upon whilst booting-up the PC that is to be yours for the next couple of hours or so.

When you plan visiting this kind of facility it is recommended that you bring along your own means of saving material you come across and this is usually in the form of a USB Drive. It's also a good idea to have a pad of paper for making brief notes on web sites, search names and a summary of your progress. This is serious business and progress is usually something of a struggle.

What might appear perfectly logical names and approaches when planning ahead of the visit, frequently turn out to be blind alleys.

Although something of a mess, the Fairhead Internet Café is close to centres of business and also two major universities, being within a large city. On this basis it might be expected to be reasonably successful even if it did tend to attract mainly the "anorak computer freak" brigade. And this is not an unreasonable description of most clientele whilst Frank performed his web surfing that Thursday afternoon (except Frank, of course …). To be fair the guy who is there to help clients this afternoon is extremely helpful when needed. This café enjoys the benefit of having a guy there who'd obtained a PhD at a university elsewhere, and, whilst it certainly overqualified him for this (temporary) job, he really is a tower of strength in this business.

This first visit is a *qualified* success and Frank gains much useful information, mainly on global organisations, from the various web sites he visits.

On returning to base, Frank tells Derek. "Good quality information from that scruffy little Internet Café. But let's check the files by attempting to load them into one of our PCs."

Derek did the loading attempt, beginning with plugging the USB Drive into a compatible port on the PC, clicking the mouse on "My Computer" and then opening and selecting the file names. A selection of files is displayed on the screen, and clearly most are those that had been "downloaded" from the Web at Fairhead. Two or three of the files themselves are successfully viewed and transferred into an appropriate folder on the PC's hard drive. On this basis they all appeared kosher and all the information looked good quality.

"Frank, I've noticed there are several further files and items generally that you discovered and jotted down during your Fairhead 'mission', but didn't have the time to pursue further. What are you planning doing about these?"

"Fed up with the scruffy Fairhead place, really Derek, so in about a week or so I plan checking out the other one. You know – that one located in Stutlow."

Now, Stutlow's a classy city, full of character and with a history going back literally thousands of years. It blends this with also being a thoroughly modern city by virtue of having an active, broad-spectrum population, a strong business district and, like the city close to Fairhead, its own university. Unlike Fairhead, which Frank had found just by searching local yellow pages, the Stutlow Internet Café came recommended to him by a good friend who lived in that city.

Although it took a little finding, being practically hidden away in an ancient courtyard, the Stutlow Internet Café is different again. It could hardly be a more complete contrast to the one in Fairhead. It combines the advantages of a traditional café as well as those of an Internet one, there being coffee and snacks available in addition to the computer terminal "fare". It definitely expresses an ambience, is well appointed and appeared relatively clean. Its immediate environs are also smart and classy - reflecting the city in which it is located.

"Good afternoon, I'm Frank Goodley. Don't know if you'll remember, but I phoned yesterday and booked two hours on the Internet here. I trust this is still OK? Please tell me: what's the score here? How do I start? I've brought along two USB Drives for saving files."

It is impossible to ignore the fact that this place is "staffed" by two girls: one rather "hippy-ish", with rings in her nose and goodness knows where else, whilst the other, wearing "normal" earrings, is a very pretty Irish girl.

"Yes, we have been expecting you. Please take a seat. Would you like a coffee?"

"Take a seat - would I like a coffee?" Gosh, at Fairhead all you get is: "Coffee or tea, mate?" And this was then provided in a plastic cup, whilst you twisted somewhat uncomfortably on a high stool and surreptitiously blew dust off the nearest terminal and of course into one's coffee....

The downside to all this plushness rapidly dawned on Frank. All the computer terminals in this café are of the *Macintosh* variety and these are generally not compatible with (IBM-like) PCs. This usually means that any files downloaded on to one's saving medium (in this case the USB Drive) from a Macintosh system WILL NOT be immediately retrievable by one's PC... You will possibly have heard of Apple computers. Well Apple bought what was previously Macintosh back in the 1980s and the most recent Apple machines provide for conversion of files between IBM-type (i.e. PC) and Apple-Mac. The terminals at this Stutlow Café are NOT of the latest variety...

Frank is absolutely amazed, totally gob-smacked, to find any business open to the public and yet equipped only with Macintosh-type computers. Given that the vast majority of people have PCs this could only turn away many potential clients. By the 1990s publishers represented almost the last preserve of Apple-Mac installations, because these systems supported software that is practically ideal for type-setting purposes. And publishers could only provide a tiny fraction of much-needed "punters" for the Internet Cafés.

"Well, I'm here now and I might as well make what will hopefully be productive use of my time," said Frank, somewhat disconsolately.

"Well, I just suggest you save all you can onto one of your USB Drives, check it out when you're back at your office and see what can be done," said "Ms. Body-Rings", trying to be helpful.

Again, like the experience at Fairhead, Frank downloaded many useful files onto his diskette that afternoon. However, unsurprisingly he is always subconsciously worried that all his work might be in vain this time because of this amazing Macintosh incompatibility problem.

"Derek," Frank has now returned to the offices

of Tekanalytics and is faced with explaining somewhat sheepishly to Derek what had transpired. "Derek, I *think* that once again I got some useful information - some most useful files - as a result of my Stutlow trip yesterday i.e. my latest foray into the Internet Café scene."

"What do you mean, you *think* you got some useful information? How can you seem so diffident about the results of spending a whole afternoon surfing that Web and downloading selected files of data? Come on, Frank, I can read you easily after all these years working together so tell me what went wrong?"

"Well," Frank is doing his none-too-successful best to appear positive in the aftermath of an annoyingly questionable exercise:

"Well, Derek, on this USB Drive I'm sure we have another set of highly useful files. But the trouble is they're in Macintosh format…"

This is how Frank went on to tell Derek the basic story about the Stutlow Café.

Derek is incredulous, "…Macintosh format, that's ridiculous, we don't stand a cat in hell's chance of doing anything with them I reckon. How could you be so stupid as to stay at that crazy place knowing that you could well be wasting your time, obtaining files that we in all probability couldn't ever use?"

There followed an awfully pregnant pause, then a sigh. "Well, the girls there are pretty—let's see if anything even lists as being on that USB Drive." Derek is prepared to test and see whether

Tekanalytics' PCs would even display the files presumably saved on the "Macintosh" Drive.

Once again it's down to Derek who attempted loading the files which are purportedly on that offending USB Drive, beginning as usual with plugging the USB Drive into a compatible port on one of Tekanalytics' PCs, clicking the mouse on "My Computer" and then attempting to open and select the file names.

But on this occasion it was as Derek predicted and as both of them feared. No data whatsoever appeared on the screen and they knew that none of Tekanalytics' PCs would be able to open any of those wretched files.

Both Derek and Frank knew several experts, computer consultants, in the area and one in particular who was generally considered to be au fait with Apple Mac types of files, including conversion to PC format. He tried and, although he could see the files listed, even he couldn't manage to open any of them.... Further attempts with different people all failed and ultimately Derek and Frank considered there is nothing for it but to tell the Stutlow Café outfit the position and see whether they could help.

Fortunately the "Stutlow Café" people were owned by an "umbrella" company which included computer experts who, hopefully, would be able to convert files of this type that had been saved on what amounted to one of their own machines. At last this did work out, although it cost Tekanalytics another $40 (about £25) for the trouble. Worse, much worse than the $40, was all the wasted time.

At this point, whilst Derek and Frank are ending this Internet Café discussion, their Managing Director Phil Kerridge swept into the area.

Phil rapidly spotted their topic of discussion and said, "First of all – and don't get all disgruntled and mad about this – both myself and Matt Framlin (remember Matt?) knew quite a lot about the NSA, Charteridge, etc. previously. But in fact you two have managed to 'prise out' much more extremely useful data. However, you guys also need to take a lesson from this experience of Internet Cafés."

Frank is clearly apologetic over this entire affair. "The clear moral of this story can be summed-up something like: 'scruffy place, effective computers; fancy place (and staff) but: rotten computers…'"

Tekanalytics had inadvertently encountered just about the extremes of Internet Cafés. On the one hand you had a quite miserable-looking (and feeling) establishment that's seemingly dirty but sensibly equipped with PCs so that your downloaded files are immediately accessible. On the other hand you find yourself in nice surroundings, pleasant staff and fine coffee, but incredibly old Macintosh machines so that your downloaded files are completely inaccessible (except by going to considerable trouble).

There is one thing however that is common to most Internet Cafés:

You can pay with old-fashioned cash (at present) and you are using someone else's terminals and networks. This means that you are truly anonymous. It means that your presence cannot be electronically traced and you are essentially immune to eavesdroppers and interceptors.

Not even the Café proprietors need to know who you really are. For the moment you're "safe" because it cannot be determined that it was you who visited that specific Web site on Wednesday May 7, 2008.

But for how long? How long will it be before, in an entirely cashless society, you will not be able to pay by cash and then the very fact that you've paid with your credit card or some other more sophisticated system will expose who you are and where you are located. They will know for certain that it was you who visited this or that Web site and it is therefore you who are on their blacklist because it was you who deigned to show such an interest in this or that security agency.

And of course it would not be beyond reasonable expectations if security officers were to infiltrate, undercover, many Internet cafés with the express mission of checking precisely who visits and uses these facilities even today. How dare anyone even attempt to search and gather such sensitive information?

Chapter 14 The Global Influence

The planet earth, viewed from space, is a now familiar sight to most of us. As many have correctly remarked it looks beautiful and is probably the most glorious planetary body in the entire cosmos.

Now imagine this singular planet virtually covered with the entwining tentacles of a horrible family of gigantic octopus. The view is now appallingly tainted and nothing is able to function anything like so effectively as when the octopus were absent.

Although, thank goodness, observations do not in reality show the earth with giant live octopus surrounding and throttling it, there does now exist the electronic equivalent of precisely this. The "giant octopussies" of the international security organisations are, at all times, tapping into the telecom networks - including, of course, the world wide web, or Internet.

"How interesting. Many in the media have been writing about this outfit called the National Security Agency, with headquarters in the USA, and I've just found their web site address, it's: www.nsa.gov/home_html.cfm." As one of Tekanalytics' senior researchers Serena had been researching on various aspects of telecommunications and security considerations for about two months now, and this is another major breakthrough.

"A web site – the National Security Agency? That is hardly believable. Why on earth would that dreadfully secretive bunch of spies go to the trouble of having a web site?" Phil is understandably sceptical, but Serena suggested, "Well, I guess they reckon that by having a web site, like most other people in business and government these days makes them seem almost respectable."

The National Security Agency (the NSA) was gradually developed by the USA during the years of the Cold War, the 42-year stand-off between what were perceived by most to be the world's two super powers i.e. the USA and the USSR. With electronic intelligence gathering (ELINT) being widely recognised to be critical in modern warfare (both cold and hot) it was completely understandable to find the protagonists evolving sophisticated global eavesdropping facilities.

By the late-1980s the NSA had grown to become America's most secret, largest and almost certainly most costly security organisation.

The NSA is the main "giant octopus" and it is continually tapping into most of the world's telecoms and other means of communication. It has access to land-based, ship-borne and air-based facilities and uses satellites together with other communications to channel information back to its intelligence bases. Linked security systems are on board ships, submarines, aircraft and spacecraft located globally. And the NSA's interests are most definitely not in any way restricted to defence - not nowadays.

Importantly, the NSA has built up intelligence links with four notably close allies: Australia, Canada, New Zealand and the UK.

The resulting secret agreement has the acronym UKUSA (pronounced "youkuu-za") and all five flags of these nations are frequently displayed at each UKUSA location, most notably and definitely on days of special VIP visits.

Derek: "So things really are formally linked-up - I mean those 'special relations' and so on have been put into practice with this international security set-up then?"

"Yes," Phil stated categorically. He is now profoundly interested in the operations and effects of this "security apparatus" because many people now appreciated that the effects this must all be having on the business of Tekanalytics could only be substantially negative.

"I first encountered UKUSA way back in my old Econometrics days and of course Nicky Hager had much to say about it. So, yes, we are in here for the long haul and it's going to be a tough fight. Serena, what sort of information does the Web provide about the NSA?"

"Easy, it's apparently a perfectly 'standard' sort of web site. Although I've been careful to hit it from a remote location so they don't have any chance of finding it's us searching. There are several pages and the first one starts with a colour picture of the NSA 'campus' and is titled 'About NSA'.... I thought that, for a start, the term 'campus' was pretty quaint considering the term is usually reserved for academic outfits. Actually it's a huge multi-storey structure."

"Apparently it all began at the height of the Korean War in 1952."

"For many years following its inception Fort G. Meade was a genuinely legitimate and highly useful defence intelligence outfit. In fact, as recently as 1986, it became designated a 'combat support unit of the US DoD' – whatever that may be construed to mean. The information on their web site confirms much about their primary role, i.e. *military* intelligence gathering, but of course we know there's very much more to it than that bland exterior would suggest."

"The NSA at Fort G. Meade is Anne Arundel County's largest employer although I can't see any data on the actual numbers of employees. It's also one of the largest employers in the entire State of Maryland. There's much on the web site concerning human health, the environment, recycling, their blood donor programme, bone marrow donors, disability support, teaching, coaching, etc. You can't take it from them, and it's not much use being cynical about all this, the fact is they do a considerable amount of good within the local community."

Derek is the first to comment on the information presented on the web, as uncovered by Serena:

"Look at that 'additional mission' with such an innocent-appearing title. This is the one set up in 1984 with the title: 'information systems for national security missions', phew, that has turned out to be a cover for many activities - mostly highly valuable and legitimate - but certainly not all."

"Oh yes, and what a year to have chosen. Of course 1984 has all those connotations with George Orwell whose famous book carried that very title," said Serena, "and at that time Ronald Reagan was President and the Cold War was running strongly. Relations between the White House and Moscow were hardly even lukewarm then, with Breznev apparently firmly in power and the U.S. starting up their Strategic Defense Initiative or 'Star Wars' programme."

"It occurs to me that President Reagan would almost certainly have intended this to be a genuine Defence commitment as such, targeted against the Soviets and supporting that Star Wars effort. With his strong beliefs in free markets and the market economy I'll bet he never for one moment thought that this very directive for the NSA would in fact be used in a role that would undermine - and still today continues to undermine - those same market economy dynamics. Obviously I could be wrong, I could be providing excuses for the President of the day, but at the very least he would surely have been highly unlikely to have foreseen the potential misuse of the NSA's original brief?"

"I don't like the sound of that earlier 'Central Security Service' (CSS) thing either," said Phil. "It might seem pretty innocent again taken on its own. But guess who was in power at that time and actually in his heyday? Why, none other than President Richard Milhouse Nixon, and look what happened between that guy, the CSS and the CIA only a year later…"

Serena: "There are some unusual terms used in the descriptions here. I'm picking out: 'cryptologic', 'SIGNIT' and 'INFOSEC'. Does anyone know what these mean, please?"

Phil is quite expert on most of this sort of thing, so he piped up:

"OK Serena, everyone, 'cryptologic' is USA-techie-speak for cryptographic systems which is encryption and all that. 'SIGNIT' just means SIGnals INTelligence, performed electronically. It's a term that's been used chiefly by the military traditionally, and 'INFOSEC' is to be regarded as another bit of techie-speak for INFOrmation SECurity."

"As far as the last two are concerned, the old jokes are: you don't have to be particularly intelligent to progress with signal intelligence and yet you do have to be extremely secure when it comes to information security!"

Derek is the next to 'stake his claim' to observations on this interesting NSA web site information: "Another thing I don't like at all is those CIA connections. That really does come across as pretty sinister to me, especially the references to 'covert' and 'counter-intelligence' that are explicitly there for all to see. And the CIA also operates internationally."

All four gathered at the meeting to discuss

the NSA's information, Ruth, Serena, Derek and Phil, agreed that at first sight the reference to the Agency's "ground-breaking developments in semiconductor technology"' appeared inappropriate. After all, what on earth were they doing with this kind of thing? When all is said and done this "semiconductor technology" is the stuff of microchips and almost exclusively the preserve of the mainstream semiconductor houses, like AMD and Intel, and the universities for research (also the vitally important Lucent Bell Labs). Upon discussion all they could think was that high level of secrecy extended, for the NSA, even to details such as microchips.

Another mystery is just why Fort George Meade would want to behave in such a high profile manner as to have an open contribution to a paper read at a technical conference. Anyway, at such a conference in Baltimore in 1997, an agency staff expert known as Mark Brearley was listed amongst the researchers responsible for a paper on advanced microelectronics (an additional seven contributors work elsewhere in the States). This was in all probability a public relations exercise. They're wanting to say: "..hey, look, we are really kosher, we do real electronics research too…".

Serena now wanted to add two further observations of her own to this discussion. The first is:

"Huh, did you notice the location, between Baltimore and Washington DC? As they say that's certainly 'centrally located' and if all else fails an

NSA employee could presumably bike-it to the White House with vital information affecting national 'security'."

"Another thing is those 'extra mural' programmes. They make much mention of their educational (indoctrinating?) programmes, their blood and also bone-marrow donor programmes, disability support etc. What a benevolent outfit indeed – how could anyone possibly criticise such a much-needed and supportive organisation?"

Serena is not in any way looking to "pour cold water" on these "extra mural" activities as such, she stressed that all she wanted to point out was the apparent irony of such a secretive and controversial organisation offering good works and making the statements about them in its website.

Phil mused about the funding of the entire NSA global operation:

"In order to cover its tracks and appear 'truly' global, which is highly popular these days, it wouldn't surprise me in the least if the NSA didn't have sources of funds quite apart from the US Government. In fact, I would have thought that the World Bank (supported by the UN) could well be involved here given this apparent electronic policing of almost all that portion of the world we call 'western'."

Derek wondered whether there was any further information on the NSA's web site: "All this is highly impersonal stuff. Is there anything about individuals, real human beings, on the staff of the organisation? I guess that's a question directed at you, Ruth."

"Well, the answer's a qualified 'yes' because only the director and his deputy are listed. However, this is in considerable detail because virtually their full resumés are given. You wouldn't expect other staff to be cited, would you? After all, even small public or private corporations don't usually provide details of staff with the exceptions of the Boards of Directors, the CEO and so on. This is the basic information as given. I'll summarise the background because the whole lengthy thing hardly makes interesting reading." Serena clicked the mouse on the "Leadership" item and displayed the NSA's director's resumé on the 42-inch computer screen which made everything large enough for them all to see.

Now it was clear the current Director of the entire operation was one Lt. General Andy Plumore. There's quite a detailed description of Andy P's background and his position is backed-up by a deep and extensive experience in the US Military. He also possesses university degrees in security matters and military concerns. Anyone - literally anyone - can visit this web site and read all the information. Please bear in mind however the NSA itself will be monitoring your every mouse-click and absolutely everything you type in...

It is definitely best to do this in a public domain such as an Internet café or library where you can either surf for free or pay cash—like Frank Goodley did some while back. Even then the "authorities" could possibly trace it was you but it's much more difficult and can hardly be accomplished electronically.

Ruth remarked: "Andy Plumore would appear to have planned his career carefully and taken opportunities for advancement as these became available. He's hard to fault on this basis and in many ways he's a role model for anyone interested in following a military or political career within the bureaucracy of a modern state's structure."

"He's been around widely - both from an establishment and also from a geographical viewpoint. His biography tells us that he's held increasingly high-level jobs in various defence outfits both within the USA and also prime positions overseas. Now all this would fit him well to direct an organisation that is without a doubt very international - like the NSA."

"Here, then we have the quintessential professional man for the job - a truly impeccable background in every sense."

"And then", Serena continued: "there's the current Deputy Director Ms. Jill Borston. Again, Jill has an excellent resumé for the job and - just look at this - she was based at MI5 in London from 2003 to 2006. So this means she has recent strong London connections which must be invaluable considering UKUSA and hence the doubtless frequent dialogue with Charteridge. Isn't it interesting she's a 'Ms' - not an ex-military person and indeed a lady? Looks like they're going for some form of 'balance' again."

Phil also thought: "How superficially like Birstington this all seemed, with the senior people changing on three or four-year tours of duty."

"Indeed the top echelons of the NSA appear relatively harmless. So, what's the problem? What is it that's of such great underlying significance and definitely tells us that, for all its fine web site information, the NSA, as it operates these days, is truly shady and literally potentially dangerous?" Phil wanted to set the record straight and to be seen as being balanced in this judgement. At this point Serena and Derek spoke out almost in unison:

"That's just it, without realising you've stated it just then."

"What on earth are you on about?" Phil exclaimed.

"You used the word 'echelons' and, although I don't think you knew this, but it's indeed 'echelon'. That's just what they call it—only in capitals because it's yet another composite word: ECHELON."

Now, if the NSA had stuck to its original rationale and concentrated entirely upon defence as such, particularly had it desisted from overseas, let alone practically global eavesdropping, then practically none of these troubles would ever have occurred. The outfit would almost certainly have simply remained a vital organ for genuine defence surveillance. However, it was mainly during the 1980s that the NSA outgrew its original boots and a horrible spying development code-named project ECHELON came into being.

Serena again: "The ECHELON project is

global, is entirely NSA operated and is beyond any government's control. But it's well protected by various national security outfits like the MI5 in the UK and the CIA more widely. ECHELON is aimed at the interception of literally any types of messages, originating anywhere, anytime, and the decoding of the most confidential information.

This very much includes messages to and from people who, with or without justification, the NSA regards as potentially 'hostile' or just bad 'security risks'. It also includes messages to and from people who simply happen to work in *competing* companies...."

Derek is almost speechless now which is pretty unusual for him:

"....but... this is truly terrible. Without any shadow of a doubt it's treacherous... Do you really mean to say that the NSA spies on competitors within industry sectors? I shudder to think what they could do with the information. They could even sell it."

"Sell it? Do you really mean perhaps they could sell it to outside customers?" Serena is doing her level best to remain cool and succeeding to a large degree.

"Well, how does one say this 'sensitively': *yes* in several instances that's just it – they *sell* the critical and sensitive information on to competitors. This hardly squares with today's emphasis on 'free' market economics, does it? And if you don't want to believe me then ask yourself why the NSA openly boasts about its marketing operations? Who, oh who, else could they possibly be marketing to but these competitors?"

Phil tried to summarise the situation by saying: "Although it remains an ostensibly innocent operation that in many ways does a magnificent job maintaining international security, by its more insidious actions the NSA and quite possibly therefore other security agencies has effectively tended to undermine its own credibility."

Chapter 15 The Bases

International security is precisely that. It is international and it is truly global in reach.

As far as project ECHELON is concerned, if the Internet is the generally understood "LIGHT" world wide web, then you could regard ECHELON as being the DARK "companion" to the web.

This is a reasonable contrast because the Internet functions by using the existing national and international telecoms, with its service providers (the ISPs) having their own subsidiary networks and computers. It's on those computers and similar machines (usually called "servers") that they store your web site (and the NSA's web site) and also where they transfer your e-mails around the system until these reach their intended recipients' e-mail "boxes".

The NSA's ECHELON also operates with well-known international communications systems. In this case they're mainly satellite but also microwave and fibre-optics and it uses powerfully computerised encoding techniques. ECHELON's main function is to intercept as many messages as possible and then pass these on to a highly sophisticated sorting system.

ECHELON staff, working in any of the 'UKUSA' countries (also countries such as Japan and South Korea) are trained to decipher messages in a wide range of languages. Hence there's a need for good linguists and mathematicians. In fact, the computers used throughout the ECHELON system are themselves known as the ECHELON Dictionaries. The term "Dictionary" is used because each computer holds huge databases, containing a vast amount of vital information on people and companies.

Derek came up with: "So much for the freedom of information acts, then?"

"Yes," said Frank, "And remember all this gets progressively worse as time goes by. And this is simply because everything's got continuous momentum. You've so much happening here with the rapid and dynamic advances in technology, the global paranoia about security and the voracious appetite for competitive strategic information no matter how it's obtained."

"Another thing is: how do these NSA people minimise the chance of information leaking out of the system? I mean, surely there's always a fair chance of the occasional slip or even yielding under pressure?" queried Serena.

"This is mainly achieved by means of indoctrination," said Frank.

"When anyone new joins an NSA 'cell' their very first experience is security indoctrination and apparently this is precisely the word explicitly used. The indoctrination is carried out by a senior officer who gives a strict lecture during which attendees are forbidden to ever talk about anything connected with their jobs to anyone except other indoctrinated colleagues. Not even their nearest and dearest, their wives or husbands (or other partner), must know anything. Not their families or friends and indeed nobody outside the indoctrinated clique. The process is always concluded with each attendee signing a two-page indoctrination form that usually refers to Criminal Legislation providing for punishment in the country concerned. This originates in the UKUSA regulations."

"In fact is also true that this Criminal Legislation includes a provision for lengthy jail sentences to be applied in what are deemed severe cases."

"There must be masses of material, forever increasing, that the NSA needs to intercept, scan and explore. How on earth do they manage to perform effective scans?"

Although the question was mainly directed toward Frank, Derek kind of asked this of everybody. Frank responded with:

"This is down to the powerful software which is now generally available on a commercial basis to anyone who wants it and can use it. These are the sorting, searching and database handling software packages, two of which are frequently used by various NSA stations and are termed 'BRS Search' and MEMEX. BRS is employed, for example, in New Zealand and MEMEX is implemented at the giant Charteridge station in England."

"Incidentally, the NSA also has tremendously powerful computers they call 'Oratory' that are used in 'listening' in to telephone conversations that have been intercepted by the system. Oratory recognises when certain key words are spoken and covers practically all the various intonations and accents likely to ever be used. Oratory also learns, for example, new words and accents as time proceeds and interceptions become more widespread. Typical key words doubtless include: NSA, SIGINT, 'bomb', Charteridge, Meade (within Fort George G. Meade) as well as 'interesting' combinations such as: microwave signals, electronic interception. In fact this includes most if not all the terms used quite extensively by specialist engineers, consultants and other professionals in much of modern high-tech industry and academe..."

"It then depends critically upon the person who is initiating such a conversation. If they work in a 'legitimate' organisation, like a substantial company or at least one 'known to be above suspicion' then so far as these people are concerned, or on the 'approved' academic staff in a university, then the chances of their becoming targeted are small. If on the other hand they are in the slightest way under suspicion, even if this is actually unwarranted, then they will be targeted. And anyone setting-up and working as a 'consultant' in high-tech, especially anything to do with advanced radios or microwave stuff will be treated as a *major* target."

"So," concluded Derek. "When you think about it, virtually everyone in the world with access to just a telephone (never mind fax or e-mail) is from time to time subject to this sort of surveillance.

And anyone who is in high-tech may be subjected to more intense surveillance, grading up to almost continuous interceptions for many sad radio buffs..."

Derek's remarks essentially wrapped up this discussion in a highly pertinent manner. It really did seem that global surveillance and the single world government could not be so far off because the potential power was becoming available to a "chosen indoctrinated few". So that redoubtable Kiwi known as Barry Smith was going to be proven right after all.

Meanwhile things continue developing all over the world, including of course in New Zealand. In 1989 a lady named Fiona Sudborn took a position as a senior intelligence officer at the NSA's station there and this turned out to be highly significant. Although not a university graduate, Fiona was without doubt "the right stuff" as far as the intelligence agencies were concerned. She was previously with the British Army and had been on special army officer courses in several UK locations - including, yes, Birstington(!) Indeed Philip Kerridge had encountered her around ten years before her NSA involvement. Could this fact represent yet another link in a complex and entwined chain? In New Zealand Fiona became the Dictionary Manager and it was her job for the next few years to receive requests through the local system and also from other UKUSA agency locations and to enter appropriate key words and numbers into the computers.

"How can we be so confident about the structure and activities of UKUSA and 'affiliated' agencies? Are our sources reliable? Surely there will be plenty of 'sour grapes' around with plenty of old scores waiting to be settled and getting at the security people in subtle ways would be one very effective way of achieving just that." Serena wanted more detailed information to bolster her confidence, although by now everyone was practically sold on this one.

"There were several instances during the late-1980s and early-1990s when various individuals provided incriminating open Press statements about security scandals. As we all well know it's one thing going to the 'Press' but quite another to be able to fully and convincingly support your story. In my view most of these people did just that. They indeed had highly convincing supporting evidence and rational connecting descriptions in support of their stories. The first event worthy of mention is the 1991 Granada Television expose on GCHQ."

"In that year a former official of GCHQ in the UK gave an anonymous interview to Granada Television's *World in Action* programme. The guy was particularly concerned about abuses of power at GCHQ and what he had to say rang true. He also mentioned an unnamed red brick building bearing the address: 8 Palmer Street, London, which is where GCHQ carries out secret interceptions of every call that is transmitted into or out of Britain's capital city. The intercepted telexes are then fed into powerful computers, using a program known as 'Dictionary', he said. Staffed by carefully vetted (probably indoctrinated) British Telecom employees, 8 Palmer Street has nothing to do with national security but instead it has everything to do with this insidious personal surveillance. All business deals, all private notes, all embassy communications - everything is fed through this system and into the Dictionary."

"This *World in Action* programme missed out just one vital aspect: the Dictionary is not just a UK element - it is truly global."

"For a public reference to the *ECHELON* system we need to go back to 1988 when a statement was made explicitly mentioning the Charteridge station in England. A newspaper known as the Ohio Weekly Chronicle (US) published a feature concerning the electronic monitoring of phone calls allegedly made by a Republican senator known as Dave Critchet. And guess where this alleged monitoring took place: why, at that major installation known as Charteridge of course."

Also during 1988 it turned out that a congressional hearing had been taking place following allegations of corruption and misspending at that major spy base. These allegations had been made by Marion Musford who was for a period an employee of the Lockheed Space and Missiles Corporation working under contract at Charteridge. During this period she said that she was, whilst wearing earphones, able to listen in to phone calls that were being monitored.

Her responsibilities included software manager for around fourteen VAX mainframe computers that functioned as part of the ECHELON system at that time. And there you have it: a specific mention of that so-secret word: ECHELON....

During the course of this hearing it became evident that no formal controls existed over who could access the ECHELON! Even junior staff could regularly feed in target names and other information about individuals that would then be automatically searched. There never was then, and almost certainly isn't today, any checking concerning the authority of staff. Furthermore, the complete lack of democratic control or accountability for ECHELON (or the entire UKUSA for that matter) makes it almost certain that insidious espionage must occur and this will increasingly provide financial gain for the NSA, being paid by its clients. After all, we are all living in a global market economy now, aren't we?

And today the ECHELON system is much, much more powerful now than it ever was in the 1980s. Needless to say, the entire system almost became over-stretched during the terrible events of 11th September 2001 and in the months and weeks that followed. As the "War against Terror" gathered pace in Afghanistan the system settled down somewhat, but remained on "Orange Alert" throughout. In periods of genuinely severe national/international emergency ECHELON has little time for or interest in its civilian insidious espionage side.

"Is this all?" Serena was not really asking a question so much as making a dry and somewhat sarcastically rhetorical statement. But Frank was going to answer as if this was a question anyway:

"No. In the 1980s GCHQ staff anonymously passed on to their contacts the information that international arms dealers and potential buyers of weapons were definitely being targeted by this electronic eavesdropping centre. Whilst most of us feel nothing but revulsion towards arms dealing, this approach is hardly the most honest way of handling the matter."

"Another important development came around 1989-1990 when a former GCHQ intelligence staff member revealed that Mrs Margaret Thatcher, then the all-powerful Prime Minister heading-up the Tory government, personally ordered the interception of communications with the Lonrho Company who owned the UK-based *Observer* newspaper."

"According to a series of articles published by the *Observer* there had been highly suspect and underhand activities involving Mrs Thatcher's son Mark, during the negotiations towards a UK/Saudi Arabia arms deal worth several billion dollars. Mark Thatcher was reputedly paid a sum of about $20 million as commission on the signing of this deal."

"Several other people, in at least two cases openly named and, breaking their indoctrination oaths, have provided detailed information about the abuse of the enormous power vested in the

ECHELON system. Again, the UK's *Observer* newspaper has been particularly forthcoming and in June 1993 some active 'high level intelligence officers' at GCHQ spoke to this newspaper. Their great concern was the fact, as they alleged, that this eavesdropping centre regularly intercepted communications to and from at least three charitable organisations that included Amnesty International and Christian Aid. Phone tapping took place using a system known as 'Mantis' and telex interception employing something termed 'Mayfly'."

"This is all highly sensitive information you are coming up with here, Frank," said Serena, "Can anyone check the sources that you must have used? Or is that secret too?"

"Easy, all anyone needs to do is look at the book with the title *Secret Power*, by Nicky Hager, which was published by Craig Potten in 1996. There's also the neatly titled *The Unsinkable Aircraft Carrier*, by Duncan Campbell, that was published by Michael Joseph in 1984 and James Bamford's classic *The Puzzle Palace* which is a 1984 Sidgwick & Guildford book."

"On top of all this there are the magazines such as *Spyworld* (yes, this really is the title) and many other references. Again, Nicky Hager's book provides a wealth of material."

Now, everyone who was present during these conversations had to conclude that to all intents and purposes the project ECHELON must exist and regrettably must have been (and doubtless still is) carrying out insidious eavesdropping. Interestingly, many of the intelligence staff recruited into NSA cells located in British Commonwealth countries had careers that included experience in the British Army – or occasionally within the USA system. Both Mervyn Howe and Cliff Merrion had the appropriate background and both entered service in Antipodean NSA cells. Mervyn Howe's family was steeped in the intelligence side of army life, his father having been a senior agent in this field.

Cliff is a Russian linguist who had sharpened his expertise during his career with the British Royal Signals regiment. He also had met a guy named Philip Kerridge briefly during a spell of duty at Birstington in 1975. So now ECHELON had people functioning within its tentacles who knew "some highly interesting outsiders".

Derek was the last team member to ask a final question: "I'll bet the various stations, following almost standard practice, use some form of abbreviations so they can be rapidly and unambiguously identified?"

"Right again," said Frank, "Nicky Hager provides a list of what they previously thought (before Nicky Hager, that is) would remain secret designators. These all start with a three-letter sequence followed by a two, three or occasionally four digit number sequence."

"For example, one of New Zealand's five bases is labelled NZC-333 and this is located at Tangimoana. Charteridge is ECH-55 and ECH-28 refers to the NSA special liaison officer at GCHQ in Cheltenham. There are several others - for example at various UK military bases around the world and also in Germany and Japan. Until China (the P R C) re-acquired Hong Kong in mid-1997 there had been a cell there also, which was run by UK civilian staff and had the 'secret' designation UKC-201. This was, understandably, gradually dismantled during the run-up to the Chinese re-appropriation."

"By the way, there is the Palmer Street telex interception facility in London and this might seem anachronistic these days: 'who uses telexes in the fax and e-mail era?' Well, telex is still used by organisations that need to communicate efficiently with several East European and Third World countries. And these types of organisations include the likes of Amnesty International and Christian Aid."

"Finally, let us all take note of the fact that Charteridge is the largest of them all - it is the largest US spy base in the world and is essentially continually expanding."

Chapter 16 Listening Spheres

"All passengers are now requested to fasten their safety belts and ensure that their seats are in the upright position. Within thirty minutes we shall be landing at Seattle-Tacoma International."

Phil was flying into Seattle, Washington State in the USA and then, thirteen hours later, after the stopover and onward flight, above an area close to Alice Springs in Central Australia. Along with several of his fellow passengers he noticed, near both Seattle and Alice Springs, some similar-looking strange and mysterious installations down there on the ground. What at first sight appeared as giant golf balls were distributed across the terrain, interspersed with bland, yet sinister-looking, building blocks.

After driving around ten miles along the easterly-directed highway near the city of Majorfield, located 100 miles or so north of London, England, it's a similar picture - only more extensive, because **this is Charteridge**.

Jack Tozer had driven along this stretch of road many times and was well used to noticing "growth by stages" at that base. He guessed it was the same kind of story for most of the other spy bases around the world, but what he didn't know was that Charteridge is far and away the largest of all the installations. Anyone who frequently or even occasionally uses this stretch of highway would know that it has continued growing over a period of many years. Jack had been back home in the UK for a while now and he wanted to find out more about these developments, at the very least to satisfy his personal curiosity. He first asked his close friend Phil Kerridge who was considered an expert in antennas and related "high tech" things, having recently worked for the UK government's MoD as well as some major firms in this sector. After many weeks away Phil has just now returned from Alice Springs.

"Phil, I've observed these unusual structures - ground-based installations - in several locations literally distributed across the globe. There are usually groups of strange-looking buildings and often highly visible white spheres of various diametres. They are mostly located well away from major conurbations, easily visible from the air and most passengers would notice them from time to time. Have you ever seen any of these installations and do you have ideas as to what they may be for?"

Phil responded in a somewhat sarcastic mode with: "Look, Jack, you'll be amazed to hear that in the course of my travels I have noticed these also. In spite of many nasty rumours to the contrary, I actually don't spend most of my time as an airline passenger in a drunken and disorderly state! Apparently there are people who would be surprised to hear that I do in fact occasionally observe the odd thing and, on looking out of the windows from time to time, yes I've seen the kinds of structures you've just described."

"I'm not an expert on the organisations involved and it's my guess there are few if any experts on these installations outside of the people who are directly involved anyway - and they will doubtless be subject to heavy indoctrination - virtually brainwashed concerning their jobs and activities. You will never find out by asking any staff, or ex-staff, anything about what is really going on in these places. However, some fairly detailed information has trickled through from various reports and from people who have made something of a study of these outfits. Good examples are people like James Bamford, Duncan Campbell and Nicky Hager. It must be frustrating for these security outfits to realise physics ensures that it's impossible to make radio receivers that can adequately receive weak signals from ground links and satellites, *without* having large antennas with even larger radomes. And this begins to speak volumes concerning what has to be going on there."

Jack exclaimed: "*Radomes*? - What on earth are 'radomes' for goodness sake Phil? You are already getting me lost amongst the jargon and I've heard that in the communications technology game jargon, unfortunately, does tend to rule. Please enlighten me at least a little about radomes."

So Phil set out to tell Jack some relevant basics regarding these science-fiction-looking white coverings. "I like the bit there Jack where you said 'what on earth' - no pun intended I'm sure... But it's true that most radomes are found on the surface of our planet and there's a good reason for that. The word 'radome' derives from RAdar DOME and you have to picture a radar or communications dish covered with a dome made of a material that's transparent to the radio waves. Most forms of expanded plastic will do the job and then it's down to structural strength and weatherproofing. Expanded polystyrene, that white and very lightweight packing stuff, makes an excellent basic radome material and this can be covered with a tough, thin weather-resistant coating."

"Look at your satellite TV receiving antenna Jack. The standard dish fixed onto an outside wall of your home. These are never covered, there's no radome, your satellite TV dish is fully exposed to the weather and within reason most people are not in the least bit concerned about its appearance. If you ever did place a radome over your dish then almost certainly within a few days or weeks some kid would vandalise it and probably destroy it easily."

"It's relatively straightforward to ensure that good quality satellite TV signals are obtained with modest antennas. However, when you are looking for relatively weak signals and the quality must be excellent because its accurate data you want to receive, then you can't get away with small exposed dishes like your satellite TV one. In these situations quite large dishes with radomes are essential."

"The radomes protect from the worst effects of bad weather, help keep the important parts of the dish clean and they also stop any onlooker from seeing the direction in which the antenna is pointing. This is particularly critical where security is paramount."

Jack: "OK Phil, I think I've got a really good concept about radomes now. These are what we mainly see when looking at these 'antenna farms'. What we are looking at are the external white spheres. The antennas proper - the dishes or whatever are located inside these radomes. By the way may I ask if there's any special reason why they're almost always white?"

"Indeed there is, Jack. White reflects the sun's rays and limits the amount by which the antenna heats up. As a rule of thumb the hotter the satellite receiver gets the worse the reception quality becomes. Otherwise I guess the security people would prefer them kind of 'mid-green', camouflaged to merge with the natural surroundings."

"Organisations that are highly active in the satellite communications business include Intelsat (*the* major international concern), Eutelsat (the European carrier) and Inmarsat - then there are more local regional operators such as Arabsat, Indosat, etc. Mobile and highly broadband satellite services are now available that enable users to access the Internet with bandwidths similar to those normally requiring fibre-optic connections.

Examples of satellites include ViaSat1, several Inmarsat satellites, Jupiter 1, MegaSat and Hylas2. Major corporations such as Astrium, Boeing and Space-Systems Loral are building the spacecraft.

When looking from the point of view of highly localised areas, such as a particular country and its immediate neighbours, satellite signals are indeed spread out across this region. But on a global scale these areas appear anything but localised and as a result of this, all round the world, practically all satellite systems have their signals (your telephone conversation, fax or Internet connection) intercepted by allocated UKUSA stations.

The original station in Hong Kong with its mass of satellite dishes (before the re-acquisition by China) had this notice at its entrance:

"No photographs whatever from this point". The story goes that an Indian guard there, having been asked why this notice was in place, replied in a sombre manner: "This is communications facility and it's velly, velly, secret"…. Sometimes a rather endearing and yet enthusiastic colonial innocence can be highly revealing…..

The Hong Kong station was almost ideally located to monitor Pacific as well as Indian Ocean Intelsats and it also embodied a special dish pointed towards a United States Defense Satellite Communications System spacecraft - enabling communications to proceed "back to base" (Fort G. Meade) in the USA. Presumably all these facilities, and many more, are now available via the Misawa station.

Interestingly, Morwenstow, Sugar Grove and Yakima are all located about 100 km from international satellite earth stations, and this makes it easier to intercept signals intended for these legitimate stations.

Jack asked, "Phil, look, I know that satellites are now a major ingredient in the world's communications, and it's also very interesting to hear you say it's so easy for satellite beams to be intercepted. But we all know there are other communications media and that some of these compete with satellite or are at least complementary to a certain extent. The principal example must surely be optical fibre communications. As we all know these types of cables, running underneath most oceans and criss-crossing the continents, carry most of today's communications traffic. Then there's terrestrial microwave links - and what about mobile phones? Doesn't the NSA have an interest in these types of communications also?"

"It's easiest to deal with the fibre first off Jack. This one *hasn't* got the security lot beaten completely. But the fact is that it's very hard to eavesdrop on the light signals running through fibre. In a way the situation's completely the opposite from satellites: in fibres the light is extremely constrained and it all passes down a central core of glass that's only a few microns or thousandths of a millimetre in diametre. This is in complete contrast to the miles of spreading beams of microwave radio with satellites."

"Also the fibre scenario involves a cable as such

and this has to be physically tampered with in some way in order to be tapped. There are non-invasive techniques but even the existence of these can be detected and the fact that tapping is taking place thereby revealed."

"The NSA is of course well up with this technology and, for example, most people are now aware of the Charteridge-to-Stutlow fibre link that was installed way back in the 1980s.

"The vast majority of present day communications are digital and special methods of signalling have been developed to enable data (fax and Internet) as well as voice (telephone) signals to be handled in the same exchanges using precisely the same electronic switches. One feature that is not generally known is the fact that these special methods of signaling also enable phones to be taken 'off hook' so that unauthorised listeners can easily listen in to private conversations without either party having the faintest idea that they are being eavesdropped upon. This is without doubt a serious operational drawback with digital communications - and please bear in mind that the appropriate types of telephone exchanges have been exported to both Russia and China!"

"The digital technology within mobile phone systems, necessarily providing the approximate location of the user, means they amount to tracking devices and automatically give away your location—even merely where you are receiving an incoming call e.g. a text message. This information is typically stored in the mobile service company's computers for up to two years. Linked with the electronic exchange switches I've just referred to, this all essentially provides an efficient custom built track, tail and tap system."

"Terrestrial microwave links raise rather different issues. For a start they involve radio beams once again and, as I mentioned earlier for satellites, radio beams can easily be intercepted."

"An excellent example of the microwave radio link situation is provided by looking at that Charteridge station again. Duncan Campbell has shown us how this type of station can directly tap into the existing British Telecom (BT) microwave network. It turns out that BT's local microwave network has been deliberately designed so that several of its major microwave links converge on an isolated tower that has direct underground connections into the stations..."

Jack said, "I suppose that with such an enormous operation they would by now have thought of almost everything. So it's not surprising to hear that practically anything involving radio systems is taken care of in the security sense. But surely there's another dimension to all this? Isn't it the case that radio signals will pass through glass plates such as windows, and other materials that are transparent to radio? Rather like your radomes? In this way it's surely possible for reasonably competent engineers to play them to some extent at their own game and eavesdrop on the eavesdroppers, so to speak. And, by no means incidentally, aren't you in this up to your neck so to speak – I mean all this detailed knowledge about the NSA and so on?"

Phil: "I'll deal with your questions in turn Jack. On the first one, well, they've thought about that too. Most of their buildings, certainly the top security installations and the most recent ones, are two-storey, made of steel-reinforced concrete and windowless. This of course must be *great* for the staff who have to endure no knowledge of the outside world until they reach the reception areas en route home. And there's another basic reason for 'going windowless', which is the fact that remote detection of the information appearing on the computer screens is then avoided."

"Going windowless also removes any chance of long-range photographs from outside the complexes."

"There's the Joint Telecommunications Unit Melbourne (known as JTUM) building near St Kilda Road in Melbourne, Australia which is obviously windowless, although the adjacent Department of Defence buildings do have windows."

"The Yakima, Sugar Grove and also the previous Hong Kong Stations all include or included large, windowless, reinforced concrete buildings. The extensive use of reinforced concrete helps to keep emissions from computer equipment down to extremely low levels outside the buildings."

"Inside the complexes computers are regularly tested for emissions and are shielded by covering with two-layer metallic screens. Service technicians from organisations outside the remit of the NSA are carefully vetted before being allowed to enter the sensitive areas and are only allowed to see stripped down components associated with computers. Discarded computer monitors are completely destroyed by literally smashing them into small fragments. So there are no opportunities for purchasing used monitors from NSA facilities. The reason for this is found in an effect due to the phosphor coating on the inside of the screen. This coating retains information formed when the raster scans the screen and such information can be retrieved. Clearly such a situation could compromise security in the event that monitors were allowed out of any station."

"Your second question Jack – the one concerning my personal vulnerability – is easier to answer, but doesn't really bear thinking about too much. The fact is that both Ruth and I are potentially in an extremely difficult situation. The security outfits in all the countries concerned are very powerful and intertwined. Without a shadow of a doubt they'll know practically everything we've been up to and involved with – including all our contacts of course. These security organisations have authority beyond national government jurisdictions and, in the event either of us gets 'interviewed' at this stage, there's little doubt but a very strong case would be presented and most probably won against us. I'm afraid that long-term imprisonment would be almost certain. You see, although in fact what we've been doing is supporting the free economies, as far as they are concerned they have files on us both that strongly imply we are serious security risks. Their files include my background beginning with teaching the British armed forces and Ruth's experiences whilst nursing the Arabs in Israel. In their eyes together we make a highly suspect couple and either or both of us could go down for potentially state-damaging activities - no less."

"Remember Gary McKinnon who spent a solid year hacking into Pentagon and other US military computer networks from a small bedroom in that North London apartment belonging to an aunt of his girl-friend? Apparently the UFO-obsessed Gary M spent about £3,000 *($5,000) in dial-up charges* in successfully attempting to hack into the Pentagon and other US Military systems as well as NASA."

"Well, after a British court case followed by some strong appeals Gary M was forcibly extradited to the US where essentially he was tried for: 'activities likely to cause damage to the security of the State'. As a result he was imprisoned for many years."

Jack is now very alarmed: "Phil, I'm just desperately hoping that you're greatly over-pessimistic on that last frightening aspect. But we're all interested in this Charteridge place. Could you tell me what you know about the external features of Charteridge. I'm talking about the appearance and the locality, what surrounds it and something about *the people*?"

"Sure Jack, be glad to. After all, now we've both got a considerable insight as to how all this works across the globe. So, let's go highly focused locally...."

"Let me take you on an 'imaginary' journey out of Majorfield, travelling by car in a more or less easterly direction. You are now on the main eastern highway, making your way towards Skipbridge. "On leaving Majorfield's built-up areas about one mile out of the city, just past the Berrywell turn (on the right) you drive straight across a roundabout and get your first glimpse of Charteridge on any reasonably clear day. Over to the right there's that multitude of glistening white spheres, looking like menacingly giant golf balls or, perhaps, more appropriately, resembling massive white round fungi. A few miles further along the same road takes you to the entrance of the world's largest high-tech spy station."

"A few weeks ago I actually made this short journey for the express purpose of studying and reporting on the overall picture. Just before the entrance to Charteridge you encounter a women's peace camp on the opposite side of the road. This comprised eight caravans, three or four egg-laying hens and a windmill driving an electric turbine for power. At least one door was unlatched and I looked in to that particular van but there was absolutely no sign of anyone around. – Could it be that trouble had somehow visited these women in their exposed camp? Had police even taken them away? They had been 'high profile' for several years, with banners on vans encouraging us to go in, share, watch videos about the spy bases etc., so they were not exactly friends of the Americans and others operating or staffing the base."

"About one mile after the women's peace camp you come across a well marked crossroads, just as this major highway is beginning to slope down a hill. To the right the sign blandly reads: 'RAF Charteridge'. Now it seems that the British Royal Air Force (the RAF) may effectively 'own' that land, or part of it, and also has an historical claim to operations there. But given the now undisputed UKUSA (NSA) ownership of current activities at Charteridge it is certainly quite a misnomer to call it 'RAF Charteridge'... Obviously, 'NSA Charteridge' is accurate, but this would bring too much attention to the role of the NSA here."

"I took this right turn, which takes one along to Savorley village some distance further on down another hill. Now, around 500 metres from the main gates of the station itself and therefore well away from the principal area of operations there are prominent red signs warning: 'danger, dog patrols'. High fencing topped with curled barbed wire is in place all around the perimetre and the place is fairly bristling with police jeep patrols. These patrols are evident both inside and also outside the area and this was something I hadn't noticed in the past. At the time I made this reconnoiter something like 22 radomes were installed at the base."

"If you examine the appropriate Ordnance Survey maps you will soon see that the entire region encompassing Charteridge and further afield is called "Tetley Moor", which is a beautiful rural area of the English countryside covering many square miles i.e. thousands of hectares. In any given year, particularly in the summer, the surrounding countryside attracts many visitors who will be on vacation or just out for the day or evening. Pubs such as the wonderfully atmospheric Queen's Head in Potley Bottom, or the equally friendly Smith's Arms in Shawbeck play host to a large number of such visitors who enjoy the food and the convivial environment. Watch out, however, because *Charteridge* people also frequent these establishments!"

"Many of the visitors come from places as far away as Japan and North America and naturally a good many of the Americans, as well as local British, work on the staff of Charteridge. Again, it's no good asking them what they do at their place of work because understandably they shut up like a clam."

"Another thing about Charteridge is that, like many large organisations, the base has its own travel company on site. In spite of, or perhaps because of this, I know for a fact that at least one *private* travel company in Majorfield is frequently used by Charteridge staff. The University of Maryland (remember Fort G. Meade?) also operates a campus on this site - but the fees paid to part-time external lecturing staff are frankly abysmal. This seems especially bad given the security pass level demanded of them. They also have their own school on the complex and from time to time they advertise for new teachers. Here's an example of one such ad that appeared on page 16 of the 'Majorfield Advertiser', dated Thursday 5th June 2008:"

Department of Defense
Dependents' Schools, DODDS,
at RAF Charteridge requires a
HALF-TIME MATH
and
SCIEGCHQ TEACHER
for school year 2008-2009. The applicant
must be fully qualified and hold a United
States State Certificate to teach Algebra,
8th and 9th Grade Science.
For further information call:
Dr. Smith, Principal, on 08774 240 250
Ref: ECH5-99 MA 241 2000

Phil now made some observations about this advertisement:

"Notice some interesting features about this? Well, for a start look how it begins. 'Defense' is spelled with an 's' i.e. the North American way, and then we have that ridiculously misleading 'RAF' ahead of 'Charteridge'. The term 'math' rather than 'maths' or more precisely mathematics is also characteristically American. But particularly notice that the applicant must hold a 'United States State Certificate to teach...' and that really narrows the field a bit 'cos not many non-Americans will meet this criterion. - And this is surely the intention. They want people who they can readily get to sign the official secrets acts and whom they can indoctrinate. These will ideally, and far preferably, be *Americans*. So it's 'Brits beware.'"

Jack came in with: "Phil: There's a lot of extremely interesting information you've been divulging here, and we can see how most of it fits in with the insidious nature of this security 'scam'. Is the entire Charteridge complex occupied by NSA staff and supporting people, like the teacher who'll presumably be appointed following that ad?" He pauses, "What I mean is: are there any employees of private corporations active on the base? Oh, and did you notice the 'ECH' in the reference—first three letters of 'ECHELON'!?"

Phil replied with:

"Regarding employees of private corporations the honest answer at this precise time is that I don't know, Jack. But there certainly have been - and in recent years."

"Until US Space Technology acquired most of the original Spartom Corporation in 1996 the satellite operations part of Spartom, known as Spartom Aerospace, had a facility within the Charteridge complex. Their telephone number was even conveniently provided in the local public phone directory... Rather mischievously I personally attempted a telephone call to this number but this resulted in an American answering with a 'systems division' message. He was most insistent in wanting to know what I wanted and confirmed that the number used was indeed to be Spartom

Aerospace. He also threatened to put a trace on the call..."

"Such a deep and universal indoctrination of staff easily leads to difficulties, misunderstandings—and upsetting reactions. The only reason anyone would need to place this telephone call at all was an entirely innocent interest in electronics, a cursory scan through the local public classified directory under 'electronics' and having noticed the well known Spartom to just phone to find out whether they were still there and what sort of subsidiary this was. But one then ends up with what amounts to discourteous and aggressive behaviour."

Frank has now joined this little discussion and he asks, in feigned innocence: "Is this 'RAF Charteridge' place the only base of any kind in the area? Is it isolated to the extent that no other defence-related establishments at all are in the vicinity?"

Phil, "To answer your question let me take you a little further on my journey along that local road towards Savorley. Having passed the main entrance to the NSA spy base, in around one mile you can take a sharp right turn and this leads you past another type of base. This one has the name: 'RN Radio Station, Tetley Moor' and appears to be an 'innocent' British Royal Navy (RN) installation. Interestingly enough this place looks, if anything, even more like a fortress than Charteridge, being very heavily guarded. In the past I've even seen armed guards carrying machine guns marching to and fro across this RN Radio Station's entrance."

"RN Radio Station Tetley Moor is surrounded by multiple high barbed wire fences. Its function is, however, totally unlike that of Charteridge and you can easily determine this just by looking at the antennas within the base. These comprise long wires supported by high masts and this tells us that HF radio signals are the order of the day here (HF used to be called 'short wave' - referring to radio signals lying between your medium wave and your VHF radio). The frequencies are very much lower than the microwaves used for satellite communications and the wire arrays transmit and receive signals on a worldwide basis which is most useful especially for ships in this instance."

"On leaving Tetley Moor Lane, to the north of this Naval station, I turned left and then sharp left again to get back onto the main trunk road east but travelling west towards Majorfield now. In the distance, to the right (south side), the tower of a base station for mobile communications (cell phones) can clearly be seen. This is around one mile south of Charteridge. There's also a large BT microwave communications tower a few miles further south - and isn't all this really just so convenient?"

"Up the hill to that crossroads, keeping 'RAF Charteridge' now to my left, I turned right towards Battleby. Then in about half a mile it's turn left again on to Pound Road. Several miles along here one finds another fine example of Britain's military heritage: 15th Signals Regiment."

At this point Phil and Frank's stomachs inform them it's lunch time. They are practically exhausted with the discussions of the morning and feel they need a good break. Meanwhile it is worth while looking at some local features in the area because these features reflect how Charteridge influences the environs.

Driving straight across the next crossroads, along a straight stretch of road and then down a steep hill over a beck, one is soon back into Devon Drive on the outskirts of Majorfield. In this elegant centrally-located English city with its classic Victorian heritage live many of the 1,370 American staff working at the Charteridge base. Ronnie Kaylie and his family, of Durham Avenue, is amongst these and naturally they do tend to keep themselves noticeably private. Most of the spacious homes occupied by the most senior staff are in the £500K ($800K) bracket and located in the better areas of the city. It is entirely possible that their presence helps keep Majorfield real estate prices unusually high for this part of England. However, this is by any standards a prestigious and lovely city in which to live, and the bustling business city of Stutlow is only about thirty minutes away by car or rail. So there are other factors leading to the notably high property prices. Whilst the Americans may be especially private at their residences, they are anything but when it comes to their vehicles around the city. It will come as no surprise when I tell you that relatively large cars are the norm and many of these are left hand drive (remember: Brits mainly use right hand drive vehicles). Four-wheel-drive roadsters, often gaudily coloured jeep types, preferably equipped with chrome-plated "style bars", are also quite common.

Between eight and nine in the morning, and again around three o'clock or so in the afternoon, during term time, one regularly encounters American mothers driving around in these types of vehicles - fetching and carrying their children to and from school.

Just a few of these Charteridge staff manage to afford to send their older children to the highly-regarded private Majorfield Sixth Form College, which happens to be on the best side of the city for 'Charteridge types'. However, this college has seen its oriental population grow more than any others over recent years.

Jack and Phil have now returned to the office after their lunch break during which Phil has mentioned to Jack a few aspects of "the Charteridge environs and people".

Phil attempts to summarise the situation:

"In a way here you have it in a nutshell: historically the three basic defence services for any nation are all represented in this small area. In this case the UK Army, Navy and Air Force all have a presence in the beautiful Tetley Moor region. Except that now it is seriously marred by that cancerous outgrowth that has evolved in the name of - *security - security....*"

"It may be thousands of miles around the world from Seattle and even further from Alice Springs - but it's *effectively* very close indeed."

"Although most are not at all aware of the

fact, all of us in the 'western world' are essentially extremely close to the NSA at Fort George G. Meade in Maryland, by virtue of the up-to-date files on all, or most, of members of the population."

Chapter 17 Consequences

The New Year began peacefully enough for the Kerridges and at first they had absolutely no inkling as to the terribly dramatic events that were soon to unfold. Surveying both the business and personal scenes, Ruth said to Phil:

"I suppose, if you've got a background like mine, and especially if you go and marry an ex-Defence Ministry guy who's into sensitive stuff like radio and satellite technology, then maybe, just maybe, you'd better watch out."

"After all, I befriended Arabs in Israel and this brought me into contact with the military police. With this history it's small wonder that, on a return trip to the Holy Land with my high-tech husband we (mainly me really) became subject to a Mossad interrogation. *And* we were supposed to be on honeymoon for goodness' sake..."

"I also guess it doesn't help if you've mistakenly driven into the police academy training unit. Also the fact that you, Phil, took photographs galore almost everywhere, including the Western Wall area..."

"And, Phil, do you remember the ultra-strict security check at Heathrow, followed by what was effectively the confiscation of our return tickets and car hire voucher on the plane?"

"Certainly do," said Phil. "How could I possibly forget?"

Ruth: "Well, at least the two hitch-hikers - one 'down' and one 'up' - to whom we gave lifts whilst in Israel, must have been genuine - absolutely no chance of 'plants' there - complete coincidence of course...."

Under the distinct impression that Ruth might just possibly be kidding on this point, Phil moved to a different tack - feeling the urge to remind Ruth about intriguing day-to-day issues and future prospects.

He said: "In a large organisation practically anything can happen these days. Even if you do become 'contractorised', as happened to Birstington where I was then you can still 'progress' on to become completely privatised..."

"Now here's a thing: either way, whether you remain working within a large outfit or not, the 'eavesdropping supercomputers' will get you. The security people, those vast transnational organisations we now know so very much more about, have bases all around the world and they routinely intercept our every telephone conversation, fax and e-mail transmissions."

"Their main headquarters is in the eastern US and their largest base is only a few miles from this precise location. We could easily walk to it from where we are talking right now. Also Ruth, as we both know so well, you can't always even believe what you think you've just heard. For example, there's good reason to believe that senior government communications executives were actually ordered to 'gatecrash' a certain seminar that I was just in the act of preparing. This was a concerted effort to 'kill-off' the professional future of the seminar leader."

"In fact the probable outcome was not so much the 'death' of the seminar leader as the contributory effects towards the eventual 'death' of the small high-tech consultancy for whom I once worked. In the end that died for mainly different reasons, which is ironic, isn't it?"

Ruth chipped in with: "I wonder how many people *really* know who their neighbours are: where they work, what they do, the constraints upon them and where they come from in most major respects? For example, we always liked Sandra and Ronnie when they were living next door to us in Durham Avenue, didn't we?"

Phil had to agree with this: "Well, we still like them pretty well as people, don't we Ruth? It's *only* the implications of Ronnie's place of work that increasingly bothers us. And that brings us right back to those terrible 'international security' people."

Another interesting little episode had occurred at the building in which Ruth and Phil's flat was located. A quiet, middle-aged American had taken a one-year letting of the flat immediately beneath theirs. "Remember", Ruth said, "sounds mainly travel downwards – so he can hear more of us than we ever could of him."

Lucille and Tim, neighbours of Ruth and Phil's,

coolly commented that after he'd been in residence for a few weeks they believed he must be "an American spy"!

Is it remotely possible that someone might just be steadily moving in on this couple?

In any event, Phil continued on the occupational theme: "It either takes some courage, or downright foolishness, or most probably an overheated mixture of both, to set-up your own small firm - whatever you plan doing, from a corner shop to a software house."

"If it's anything remotely to do with radio or satellite electronics and you've previously been associated with anything defence-oriented, then you are in for massive problems."

"Wherever you are - provided it's in the vicinity of planet earth or even in near-space - they will be there tracking you down. You might be enjoying a highly progressive breakfast meeting in Rome, joining with business contacts in Hamburg, attending a meeting in Santa Rosa - or talking amiably with a friendly fellow professional on a plane bound for Paris - they'll get at you eventually."

"And the greatest frustration of all is that this 'hunting down' ultimately has absolutely nothing whatsoever to do with your performance in your work, in your company. You could be anything from the very best to the very worst at what you do as a profession. No, it has everything to do with their perception of your past history and, *most important,* whether your beloved has a history of any connections with 'security' - anywhere."

"When, as with us Ruth, both husband and wife manifestly have what to them are 'dubious' backgrounds then they'll do everything within their expanding and not-inconsiderable power to 'stop the perpetrators'."

Ruth said: "I suppose the obvious question is: what do we do from now onwards, knowing what we are into and up against? Should we give up this kind of consultancy operation? Perhaps we should move as rapidly as possible out of this business and into, gradually, running something like a nursing home - something medically related? Or perhaps some other line of business that's nothing to do with high-tech?"—At this point Ruth was relating to her extensive nursing background.

Phil: "Oh, no—certainly not yet at least—no, no—we're not going to let these beggars beat us into the ground. No, we are going to act in a very determined manner. The first thing one needs to have regarding any enemy, and any form of challenge for that matter, is absolutely the maximum amount of detailed information about them. Anything else is out of the question because you must have this maximum information. Only when armed with the largest amount of high quality information can you hope to succeed."

Ruth interjected: "Well we've been running this business for over ten years and, whilst it's been easy to ascribe several disappointments to 'normal' business difficulties, there have clearly been a large number of occasions when extraordinary things were taking place – things we just could not fathom. What we have now discovered brings practically everything together and really serves to explain those otherwise inexplicable events. It's like a giant jigsaw puzzle that becomes rapidly solved when a particular code is applied to the positions of the pieces. I tend, somewhat reluctantly, to agree with you Phil. We must face this challenge head on."

"For the moment we have the cushioning effect of preparing and marketing both technical books and reports. This almost certainly won't turn us into millionaires ever, but it should provide a viable living. Beyond this we can continue to see just how far, and for how long, they are prepared to continue applying pressure on us. By this I mean we shall maintain close contacts and send corporations frequent proposals as we have always done."

"How about the medium and longer term – both for the security operations and consequently for us? How do you visualise the future scenario Phil?"

Phil: "Remember early in 2000, when we were all anticipating at least some pivotal effects worldwide because of the much-heralded Millennium Bug? Then, midnight on January 1st when all the traffic lights sequenced correctly and the electric remained on, for increasing numbers of people the reality began to sink in. It became obvious that most aspects of the 'Bug' were the product of one of the most effective and insidious international scams ever. *What* a scam indeed - designed by and kept top secret by all those Y2K IT consultants who made a lot of money out of it. I wouldn't be at all surprised if we encountered a rumour to the effect that the NSA was to some extent behind that scam. In fact we both know at least one NSA employee who actively promoted Y2K 'bad news' throughout 1999 - don't we?"

"About the *only* examples of actual Y2K problems that surfaced during the first week of 2000 were the two-day computer shutdown at the Pentagon and several electronic cameras failing. The late and much-missed Alastair Cook told us about these incidents in his radio programme on Sunday January 9th and these were not exactly world-shattering effects, were they?"

"I also believe that the NSA will always be enjoying massive support from the United States government as well as probably internationally derived funds. Essentially, the security outfits - the entire ECHELON network - will literally become a world-within-a-world, and a highly sinister one at that. And they are currently well on the way. Picture a scenario rather like an advanced form of George Orwell's 1984 - but mainly confined to this secretive global network."

"Further, in this situation I have no doubt that internal policing will flourish and grow. Ultimately these transnational police extend to the remainder of the now-rebelling populations and all hell is almost certain to break loose under those circumstances. Nation-by-nation, region-by-region, armed police units - with no national government controls - are going to take charge of the world's populations in support of the inevitable world government."

Ruth came in with, "Phil, it is this prospect as much as anything that must drive us on and provide the driving force to maintain our freedom which is, for us, enshrined in our business."

Meanwhile, at the same time that Ruth and Phil were surveying the overall scene and discussing their possible futures together, Nigel Penley at GCHQ in Cheltenham was building a strong case against them and submitting this to the relevant "MI's". During this period the highly-secure information flow regarding these targets, via both satellite and fibre cable, was globally intense.

Files on each of the targets were assessed and re-assessed in detail, ranging from Ruth in Israel again (Mossad) to Phil in Birstington, Boston, California, Italy, Melbourne and, of course, Majorfield. His activities whilst in Boston, California, Italy and Melbourne were handled directly by the relevant NSA command bases whilst those in the UK were processed by GCHQ itself.

GCHQ was also acting as the active collation centre for all this. The "MI's" reviewed the case closely because it represented one of the most complex cases ever built against a British subject. And GCHQ owned certain specific information regarding Phil, regarding that paint-spraying activity that he thought and hoped had remained anonymous. Having spotted Phil returning to his car on that fateful January evening a local GCHQ contact had tipped this organisation off regarding the vehicle's ID plate number.

At the end of all this both targets were to be charged with what really amounted to quite high levels of offences, notably activities likely to endanger the security of the state.

The doorbell rang and, simultaneously, insistent hands banged on the Kerridge's front door. It was four o'clock in the morning and a very weary couple slowly awaked from their shortened slumbers.

Further ringing and banging. Now both Ruth and Phil were obviously alarmed at the noise for their neighbours sakes as well as their own. Was there a local emergency? Is there a fire or has some crime been committed in the vicinity of their home? Maybe someone dear to them is ill - even dying....

Each crawled out of his and her respective sides of the bed and threw on dressing gowns and slippers. Phil took the precaution of grabbing an all-metal hand mirror and keeping this under his gown - in case this may just possibly be needed as an elementary weapon with which to surprise an unwelcome stranger.

Now there were also shuffling and mumbling noises at the rear end of the property, and this caused Phil and Ruth's alarm to turn to naked fear.

Very tentatively, keeping all the lights off and maintaining a discreet distance, Phil peeped through the front window. And there they were... three men standing outside and looking distinctly official. Two sported what appeared to be senior police uniforms and the third was dressed in a good quality civilian suit.

"Ruth, what do you suggest we do in these circumstances - and who do you reckon these guys are anyway?" Phil whispered this to his wife in very low trembling tones.

They both agreed that there was little to do but check as best they could from within the front vestibule and then decide whether or not to let these people in....

"Who are you and what do want at four o'clock in the morning?"

Phil's voice remained unsteady and he only slightly raised the volume.

One of their "guests" responded simply and firmly with: "Ruth and Philip Kerridge?"

"Yes."

"We are the police so may we step inside please sir? We need to ask both of you some urgent questions."

"Can't it wait until daybreak, at least? - It's just after four in the morning and everyone's really tired."

"Afraid not sir. We really must come in now please."

This is how the three "front door officials" gained a "polite" entry into Ruth and Phil Kerridge's home.

Within twenty seconds these three are standing in the Kerridge's private entrance hall.

"Could you please be kind enough to also let our colleagues in – from your rear yard area sir?"

It occurred to Phil: How ironic again. This guarded courtesy in such mind-wrenching circumstances too. It all reminded him of the atmosphere at the hotel in Jerusalem.

Now a total of five people stood before Ruth and Phil: the three from the front plus two equally smartly dressed, a man and a woman, from the rear door.

The civilian suited guy, originally seen by Phil at the front door, is the first to tell them what's happening. And he certainly didn't mince his words:

"We are arresting you, Philip Kerridge, under the Official Secrets Act, section five, 1967. We have reasons to believe that you are in breach of your signed commitment under that act, sir. It is also understood by us that you, Ruth Kerridge, have been actively involved with your husband in terms of his security breach as I've just defined. Therefore we are taking both of you into custody for questioning on this matter."

"As usual I have to remind you that you are at liberty to make any comments you wish, but anything you say may be taken down and used as evidence against you at any subsequent trial."

The Kerridges naturally protested their innocence, but to no avail.

They were allowed to collect together a selection

of basic clothing and other necessary personal items. Then they locked their home and were taken to a local police station, by their uninvited early-morning visitors.

It's always interesting at times like these to observe those items that one fails to bring. For example, Phil forgot his electric shaver and Ruth omitted to bring her wristwatch. Thus one could not readily tell the time whilst the other began growing an involuntary beard! The "questioning" of each captive steadily grew into full-blown interrogations. This started at 08:30 that same day and continued right through until twenty-hundred hours. Each had been allowed a solicitor of their choice, as standard practice, but even their legal representatives became weary by the end of the day.

Ruth fidgeted in the area of her wrist, where her watch would normally be, and Phil's stubble made him look increasingly like an international terrorist. For some unknown reason these authorities refused him the use of any alternative shaver (perhaps they believed he would use his electronics knowledge to turn it into a secret weapon….)

Both were now angry and felt inhibited from answering any of the questions regardless of how forcefully these were being put to them.

"Look, we know that both of you have been involved in a conspiracy to endanger at least three states - Great Britain, Israel and the United States. We know about all your movements over the past two decades or so, in detail. For ***** sake let's get going here and please do answer all our questions - now if that's alright with you sir?"

The interviewing officer thumped the desk hard. Phil decided that this could well be mainly for effect and maybe this officer had hurt his hand in the action. But he didn't dare say anything that could be construed as being really cheeky and could make matters even worse than they already were.

Oh, no –he didn't dare…. Things were bad enough now without adding to the misery.

"OK. If you are so determined to play hardball then we'll just let you sweat it out and we ***will*** get something sensible out of you two tomorrow morning, you'll see. It might cause you to respond if we tell you that some months' ago the CIA requested extradition to the States so you would face a trial over there. They only decided not to proceed when we convinced them we had a 100% watertight case against you here in Britain."

It is now eleven p.m. the legal reps have gone home (and how Ruth and Phil would dearly love to be tucking into bed at home). Instead they are faced with the prospect of a fitful night in the police cells for the first time ever…. - At least the police allowed them to share a cell.

'Brrring, ing, brrring'. Achingly, both Ruth and Phil turn over after an awful night of intermittent dozing. 'Brrring, ing, brrring'.

The station clock showed six a.m. and this is

clearly the regular time for the morning alarm to ring.

"What's this?" Phil mumbles to himself as he half-wakes after a very fitful sleep. Slowly the realisation of the dreadful predicament sinks in. "Oh, heck, this is a terrible situation for both of us. What is going to happen and what on earth can we do?"

Without really knowing themselves precisely what's being required of them Ruth and Phil were at a serious disadvantage.

There now occurred a minor improvement in the circumstances in that both suspects were provided with basic bathroom materials like toothpaste, talc and so on. Also, Phil was loaned a wet shaver and soap - which was very awkward because he always dry-shaved. The couple were separated and sent to cells situated in different wings. Both were kept under 24-hour surveillance.

"Philip Kerridge." Phil's now being shouted-at by a guy who is entirely new to him. This "new man" strutted rapidly into the interview room, wearing a somewhat scuffed light grey "fifties-looking" three-piece suit.

"Mr. Kerridge, you worked at Birstington in the 1970s and 1980s. In fact until January 1987 full time."

Nigel Penley of Britain's GCHQ made this sound as though it was just a statement, stopping abruptly when he ended what he had to say. Receiving no response whatever from Phil, he became clearly angered:

"Did you hear me? I asked for your confirmation regarding your employment at Birstington during the 1970s and 1980s. Do you concur Mr. Kerridge?"

"Yes, I do sir. Indeed I did work at Birstington as you state."

"I *asked* you. I didn't *'state'*." Penley's anger rose and this could not be a good sign.

"And did you sign official documents?"

The questioning seemed almost endless. Indeed, although Phil couldn't imagine what the outcome of all this might be he would very soon find out.

By Friday morning, fully four days after their arrest at that dreadful early hour on the Tuesday, the couple are ushered into one of the interview rooms - together in the same room for the first time since being arrested.

"I am the Chief Superintendent of Police responsible for national and international security matters and you are both being committed to stand trial for activities likely to endanger the security of the state. In Mr. Kerridge's case it is the UK whereas in Mrs' Kerridges we would be talking about the State of Israel."

"What? - What are saying to us? How on earth can this be? Surely this is an enormous mistake, a terrible error." Ruth became distraught, but the guarding officers would not allow Phil near to her and this made him feel even worse.

"We have a mass of evidence indicating in the clearest possible terms that you have worked for many years against the state. The evidence takes the form of computer files, CCTV, paper documents and taped phone calls - acquired by several agencies in this country, the USA, Israel and Australia. In one instance we also have an eye-witness account. Both of us know that you are also the actual author of a best-selling book - crafted to bring maximum embarrassment to security agencies globally. Most of these agencies are friendly to the UK. In fact this is all so solid that there can be no escape - there's no way out of this one my friends."

Isn't it irritating when an "enemy" refers to one as a "friend"?

Ruth asked, "Where are you taking us?"

"You are going on the 12:30 flight to Tel-Aviv, whilst your husband stays here in England."

"*What*? - You're not splitting us up so completely and severely as that surely? This is utterly inhumane and heinous because we are a completely innocent married couple." It is Ruth who's naturally the most openly upset of the two.

"I'm afraid that the Israelis have evidence to show that you, Ruth Kerridge, are in contravention of several national security laws. As far as your husband is concerned we've enough here in England to have him 'banged up' for at least 15 years."

They were almost accurate in their predictions regarding Phil's initial fate. His trial was set to begin in just three days' time and would be held in camera. No jury was present and no members of the press or other media were allowed in. This special High Court trial proceeded rapidly:

"Your name, sir?" the court superintendent asked and of course Phil duly obliged.

"And your current address?" once more Phil was almost tempted to say it was the local police station but fortunately he decided against such a cheeky response.

The charge was formally read out:

"Mr. Philip Kerridge you are charged with indulging in activities likely to endanger the security of the State of the United Kingdom. How do you plead?"

"Innocent." Stated Phil blandly.

"Do you have any barrister to support you in your defence?"

"No, I do not Sir – I propose acting in my own defence."

But poor Phil effectively had no chance of putting his case before this bench. Instead the prosecution just described in detail all the charges and presented the damning evidence.

As a result he was convicted of activities likely to endanger the security of the State of the United Kingdom (which was enough!) and was sentenced to 18 years' detention, the first five months of which must be in solitary confinement. He committed suicide by self-hanging after just ten months in Pentonville Prison's special high security wing.

As for poor Ruth. Until recently the last anyone had heard about her she had also been tried, found guilty of activities likely to endanger the security of the state of Israel and sentenced to 12 years in a Jerusalem prison. The ultimate irony indeed - *Jerusalem.*

Chapter 18 Ruth

During her twelve hard years in Jerusalem Ruth Kerridge had aged enormously and she now presented a deeply lined and haggard face beneath a head of almost completely white thinning hair. But deep within she's as tough as ever. She was released on 1st April 2007 – All Fool's Day – but Ruth is certainly far from being one's fool. The feel and smell of the fresh air stimulated and strengthened the sense of her new-found freedom and her hope for the future.

Absolutely no money, not even 165 Shekels (she still remembered when she was with Phil in Israel several years' back), was provided for Ruth on her release from that prison at the age of 52. She was, however, totally committed to somehow returning to her home country of England - and this required, money!

After much prayer and hunting-down by pleading with the local cleansing department she found a job as a street-cleaner and, in just over one year, she scraped together enough cash to travel over sea and land that should eventually lead her back to England. In fact she managed to accumulate a total of 6,000 Shekels out of which she converted 5,400 into Euros. This she calculated would roughly be enough to get her across Europe and back to her home country.

The initial leg of that journey comprised taking the first local bus of the day to the port of - The bus left Jerusalem bus terminus at 6 a.m. and arrived in Jaffa two hours' later. Ruth's heart almost stopped as she approached the town into which, many years back, she and Phil had driven via the outskirts of the Gaza Strip! In some ways Jaffa had changed in the usual respects of housing and business development - but the old port was almost exactly as she remembered it. Being spring the rich colours of wild flowers covering many areas, including road borders were beautifully inspiring.

After alighting from the bus she set off for the old port with the express aim of getting on a ship bound for the Island of Cyprus.

"Do you have a seat left to take me to Cyprus - better still a bunk?"

"Yes, in fact we still have several bunk facilities available." the booking clerk responded to Ruth's relief. "Would you like a one way or a return ticket madam?"

"One-way please. Once I arrive on Cyprus I will not be returning to Israel."

"Oh, we're not that bad you know!"

A few moments later it was:

"Welcome aboard madam - we expect to dock in Larnaca early this evening."

The Israeli authorities had retained (in a special secure locker) Ruth's passport. After the twelve years and as she was being "processed" coming out of the prison they returned her passport to her as well as providing her with a document stating she was now free to travel virtually anywhere - on this 17-year-old British passport! It was almost as if they wanted to get rid of Ruth Kerridge well away from Israel and indeed the entire region!

Ruth enjoyed a calm and relaxing sea journey that afternoon and her ship arrived in Larnaca on time. Following a modest meal at a local café she found an inexpensive hotel and settled down for a good night's sleep - easily the best she had experienced for over 12 years.

Ah, the wonderful Mediterranean island of Cyprus where the Apostle Paul was shipwrecked as described in the Book of Acts within the Holy Bible. Also the island where she and Phil had enjoyed just one memorable holiday many years' back. Just like Israel so also in Cyprus seas of multi-coloured wild flowers—including blues, reds and purples—radiated spring now and all that follows on from this magnificent season.

Still at Larnaca, the main port of Cyprus, Ruth was left wondering how she could travel to the European mainland and she tried several possibilities around the quayside. On this occasion it was the possibility of journeying on a fishing boat that attracted her. Upon noticing a boat registered in Taranto, a port tucked up at the inside top of Italy's heel, she found its owner tidying the decks and so she asked him loudly:

"Excuse me - but are you by any chance planning a trip to Taranto some time soon?"

"Actually I do plan just such a journey starting tomorrow ma'am - who wants to know - and why?

"My name is Mrs Ruth Kerridge and I want to reach Italy as soon as reasonably possible. Do you have a separate cabin, better still one with a bunk, and if so could I please travel on your boat - the 'Taranto Prince'?"

"Well, this is extremely unusual but I might just possibly be able and willing to help you - Ruth." the boat owner was understandably rather diffident. "Before anything further I need to check your papers if you don't mind, ma'am?"

It turned out the fisherman's name was Boris (some Russian background here, Ruth thought) and after checking her papers he was quite content to let her come as the only passenger on this small vessel. Ruth checked in to her previous hotel for the one extra night and joined Boris on his fishing boat early the next morning.

This was obviously quite a risk - this Boris guy could be anyone including possibly a drug smuggler or some other criminal. However, following much prayer again, it turned out well and these two got on famously. Around the half-way point it became clear that Boris was a fellow-Christian so of course Ruth felt she could relax completely and share many past experiences. This "courteous boatman" was appalled when he learned about Phil and Ruth's treatment by the "security" authorities although they both fully understood just how the suspicions and dreadful misunderstandings developed.

After a full three days' sailing they had docked at Taranto harbour and these two new friends must part because Ruth has to decide upon her mode of transport up through Italy, etc. Just before parting Ruth paid her "courteous boatman" the balance of what they agreed would be a reasonable fare following which she and Boris exchanged contacting information and shared a nice hug.

It was: "Farewell, Boris, farewell. I hope very much we might meet again sometime."

Although gruelling and very tiring Ruth reckoned the remaining journeys would have to comprise a combination of buses and maybe just one train so she first obtained a ticket on the bus travelling from Taranto to Bari - on the Adriatic coast. This was a fairly straightforward journey during which our "heroine" was naturally surrounded by local mainly rural Italians. A few even had much local produce and one, memorable for sight, sound and *smell,* entered the bus carrying a large box containing - chickens!

Bari was especially interesting because Phil and Ruth used to have a good friend who was born nearby, name of Carlo Stakiti who ultimately settled in England. Ruth wondered what had become of Carlo and his family over these past twelve years. Would they be remotely interested in her and Phil once she was back home?

At the main Bari bus station Ruth lost no time

in purchasing a ticket - destination Napoli. This rather more varied journey took twice the time of the Taranto-to-Bari one and she was very tired when this bus drew into the Eastern Napoli station. So at this point she opted to stay in what turned out to be a run-down Napolitan guest house for just one (smelly and noisy) night.

But at least she was refreshed to some extent and very early the next morning she travelled across the city aiming for the Central Napoli national bus terminus where she got another one-way ticket for: Genoa on the Italian Riviera. Being long-distance - travelling north-east up through Italy from south to north - this journey experience was totally different from all earlier trips. Ruth found herself on an express bus and most of this journey was via the country's autostradas. Even with these high-speed drives it was late evening when the bus finally rolled into the principal Genoa terminus and by then she was very tired indeed.

Once again she checked into a local hotel - although this time, being on the Italian Riviera, it was more expensive and Ruth had to be very careful about spending her dwindling Euros. After an unintended sleep-in followed by a "scratch" breakfast she caught a short-range bus which travelled over the Franco-Italian border to the famous town of Nice in the south of France.

This was where Ruth decided to change over from buses - after all she had experienced several bus journeys - and instead she purchased a ticket for the TGV to Paris. These are magnificent trains which are maintained in excellent mechanical and interior order. And yet the fares are most reasonable. The journey across France was easily the most comfortable she had experienced - again for well over twelve years, so naturally Ruth easily fell asleep and remained in this condition for most of the time! During the relatively short spells when she was awake yet more memories flooded into Ruth's mind because many years' before she and Phil had driven through some of this terrain. She remembered occasions when they went wonderfully wrong and that man on his little cycle in Dijon - complete with sidecar in which a little pet dog was passenger who dutifully crossed from side-to-side enjoying the scenery!

In Paris she found she still had plenty of money for the Eurostar train which would take her through the Channel Tunnel and, at long last, back into England.

Once through the Channel Tunnel she struck out west across the south of England. At this time she had absolutely *no plans* for journeying north of a line roughly through Oxford. All along the way England's version of the wonderful spring season was marvelously in evidence. "Oh to be in England now that April's there..." so penned Robert Browning famously getting on for two centuries' back. Primroses were in abundance and classic carpets of bluebells could occasionally be glimpsed in some of the woods. Sometimes Ruth could just make out the rather cheeky sound of the cuckoo bird.

But she was by no means yet ready for any really active life back in her home country and for several years Ruth lived the miserable life of a recluse in a village known as Tingallen, which is in the eastern part of Cornwall, England, about twenty minutes' drive from the Devon border.

No one who had previously known her could recognise her at all and earlier friends and acquaintances would easily inadvertently pass her in the street. This even included people whom she had known for many years. Eventually she managed to pick-up again with many past friends but she broke down dreadfully when Megan told her, as gently as possible what had happened to Phil.

Recently she moved back to Stutlow to live with her sister Mary. Ruth has now learned much about the "security people" and she has progressed from being initially almost computer-illiterate to operating an advanced and specially built "security protected" machine. By adapting truly leading-edge opto-radionic technology she has managed to penetrate, without their initial knowledge, Charteridge's computer networks. Ruth has also borrowed detailed ideas from the NSA's own heavily-shielded hardware approaches.

She has been seen shopping extensively at several local supermarkets - mainly the Stutlow Morrisons. And this is not only for food and other essentials but also for a total of 500 packs of "Baco-

Foil" i.e. rolls of aluminium foil normally intended for kitchen use.

Morrisons' customers expressed total amazement as they watched this lady approach the checkout with a large trolley loaded to the brim with all these Baco-Foil packs!

"Excuse my saying..." - one white-haired lady asked - "but are you planning an absolutely *huge* dinner party for which you are doing all the cooking?!"

Ruth's stock answer was always "You are largely correct but you know these rolls of aluminium foil do have other uses too." Fortunately no one ever pursued the matter further!

Special components for connecting into her computer systems have also been purchased, mainly using paper-based catalogue shopping. Ruth has used the "Baco-Foil" to double-line the floor, walls and ceiling of her office and she properly installs the special components around her computer. As a result she ends up with just about the most impenetrable working room conceivable as far as radio wave transmissions are concerned. It is in all probability one of the world's best.

Her software "firewalls" combine the most advanced commercially available versions with clever proprietary approaches that she has developed herself. Through a sequence of visits to a mathematician friend (Pete, who was previously a close friend of Phil's), always held at "neutral" remote places, she is able to install extremely powerful encryption. This means that the chance of anyone actually penetrating Ruth's total shield, however advanced and powerful the perpetrator may be, is in the region of one in a googolplex. A googolplex is an extremely large number which is related to the googol—and the concept of a googol originates from a nine-year-old kid in 1938.

The name "googol" apparently goes back to American mathematician Edward Kasner's nine-year-old nephew Milton Sirotta who coined this name in 1938.

A googolplex is 10 to the power of a googol i.e. 1 followed by a googol of zeroes!

See, for example: http://en.wikipedia.org/wiki/Googolplex

In the documentary Cosmos, physicist and broadcasting personality Carl Sagan (who sadly died several years' ago) estimated that writing a googolplex in numerals (i.e., "1,000,000,000...") would be physically impossible, since doing so would require more volume than the known universe occupies!

Ruth also ensures that her office is soundproofed and regularly "swept" for any possible eavesdropping "bugs".

Using her "intelligent worm-tunnelling" software she cunningly plants a unique form of virus there which rapidly spreads through the systems—repeatedly ruining all of GCHQ's and the National Security Agency's software concerned with civilian (i.e. "commercial") espionage.

Ruth's intelligent worm-tunnelling software automatically and continually adapts itself so that all the "standard" systems are left intact and fully operational. These vital systems include those concerned in any way with the fight against terror, the campaigns in Afghanistan, Iraq and indeed all 21st century efforts on the part of the free world.

To date none of the security agencies have been able to overcome Ruth's extremely effective approach. There is no way any of them can do anything further actively against Ruth because, by the very nature of her background with Phil and the widespread public sympathy she now enjoys, she is completely assured of her international safety and security.

On this issue at least it looks as though the highly deserving winner really is a truly brilliant widow.

One piece of information attracted Ruth's attention – as she scanned-through the latest obituary list in Britain's "Daily Telegraph" national newspaper. There it was: "Penley, Nigel M. died 9th March 2009 following a long struggle with intestinal cancer."

In no way, of course, did Ruth gloat about this news. Whatever else he may have been Nigel Penley was another human being with a family who would now doubtless be mourning his departure. On the other hand however almost certainly no one who had ever encountered Mr. Penley on a "professional" or related level would be particularly sad to know he would no longer be around……..